Original Son

By Bernie Lincicome

Dedication

To all of us who were not flushed down the toilet.

About the Author

The credentials of the author of this book include his boyhood recollections, some of which are true and some of which should have been.

Chapter 1

The Great Bus Ride

It did not bother the boys that Mrs. Elsie Mears had a chest full of scabs. They did not wonder why she always wore a blouse cut low that presented the scabs like little red and brown flags on a battlefield map. Sonny Tolliver knew his history and he thought of The Battle of Bull Run. Maybe San Juan Hill. Each day one side lost, usually the brown side because Mrs. Elsie Mears would pick the brown ones until they turned red.

"Harold Ryan. Spell 'Recognition.'"

Pick. Pick.

Poor Ink Ear Ryan. Only teachers called him Harry, and only Mrs. Mears called him Harold. Even his mother Dixie called him Ink Ear.

His small brown eyes seemed to be even with his forehead, recessed hardly at all under his brow. The overall effect was that someone had hit Ink Ear in the face with a skillet, pushing in everything at the top and causing it to stick out at the bottom. His ears were rather ordinary, two of his better features.

A few years earlier than the day he was called upon to spell "recognition," in Mrs. Mears' sixth grade class, a blue ballpoint pen had leaked onto Harry's fingers. Harry as usual had been daydreaming and did not notice the mess the ink was making even after he had bored his forefinger into this ear hole, scratching at something inside. By the time Harry had satisfied the itch, his ear was smeared with blue ink. The smearing of an ear with blue ink might not have been enough to get him the name Ink Ear, a name he carried ever after if he had immediately or even eventually washed the ink away.

But Harry did not take eagerly to bathing, and there the blue stain remained for days. Finally, after a weekend had passed with no reduction in the blueness of the ear, Principal Worthington pulled Harry off the playground by his un-blue ear and tugged him all the way to the boys' bathroom.

No witnesses were there to recount what happened but the yelps and howls were loud enough to give everyone a good idea. Harry's ear was scrubbed and scrubbed, and Harry called the principal several blue names that he should not have known. The ink had been there so long that it felt at home in Harry's ear and it much preferred where it was to being washed away in a basin of the boys' bathroom of Perry Elementary.

Some traces of blue remained in Harry's ear throughout the rest of the school year. Duck and Sonny knew that Harry retouched the ear with a pen every now and again just to be stubborn. Sonny saw Harry once dig into the off ear with a ballpoint, staining both ears without favor.

Forever after Harry Ryan was Ink Ear to his friends and to his family.

"Harold. Spell 'recognition,' please." Pick. Pick.

"Recognition," said Ink Ear. "R-a-k..."

Mrs. Elsie Mears's class knew that four syllables were much too far to go for Ink Ear, but they thought he could get past at least one. The class groaned and Duck Stadler threw a wad of gum at Ink Ear's ear.

"Donald Stadler!" Mrs. Mears pointed her ruler at Duck. "Are you chewing gum?"

Duck opened his mouth so Mrs. Mears could see inside. He wagged his tongue around and stuck it out. Visible were several dark cavities, but no gum. Duck was a handsome boy, his fair hair cropped in a crew cut. Blue eyes and clear skin made him the most wholesome looking boy in the class. He had a natural grace and easy way about him. Mrs. Mears liked Duck and never punished him for anything. Ink Ear picked up Duck's gum from where it had come to rest, between Ink Ear's collar and his neck, and stuck it into his mouth.

Pick. Pick. The brown flags on the teacher's chest were losing again.

Sonny Tolliver knew how to spell

6

"recognition." Sonny knew how to spell all the words. He was never called upon in class because Mrs. Mears knew that Sonny knew. Everybody knew that Sonny knew. When Sonny used to raise his hand without being called upon, he felt slighted. Now he felt superior and he much liked to feel that way. He was darker than either Ink Ear or Duck with straight brown hair and brown eyes set back above high cheekbones. Sonny was able to give off an air of mystery, as if he had some special, secret knowledge. Without any real effort, Sonny learned the spelling words each week and watched helplessly as his friends flailed and failed.

The special privilege that went with being the smartest kid in class was being the one who got to buy the Neccos.

Invariably, Sonny was chosen by Mrs. Mears to go across the street from Perry Elementary to Young's Market and buy the class a roll of Neccos, the sweet pastel candy wafers that came in eight flavors and with enough wafers for each child with some left over for Mrs. Mears.

A Necco was the reward for spelling words correctly and by the time Ink Ear came close enough to spelling a word correctly, all the licorice was long gone and the chocolate, too. Ink Ear consistently was stuck with either the pink wintergreen or the purple clove.

"I don't like licorice, anyhow," said Ink Ear, but he did. All kids like licorice.

It is easy to understand how Donald became

Duck and how Harry became Ink Ear but Sonny became Sonny for the same reason most boys named Sonny become Sonny. He was a boy and he was a son. He agreed with both facts but sometimes wished he knew who his father was.

And he much preferred Sonny to either Theodore or George, his given names. Only Mrs. Mears ever called him what she now called him.

"Theodore."

She wanted Sonny to spell the word that Ink Ear could not. She had neither the patience nor enough scabs for the protracted war that waited between Ink Ear Ryan and Merrill's Rational Speller, Book Two.

Sonny ripped off the spelling of r-e-c-o-g-n-i-t-i-o-n with just enough sympathy to please Ink Ear and just enough ease to reassure Mrs. Mears that whenever she needed the right answer, she knew where to go.

Being the brains of the boys gave Sonny a special responsibility. It was he who had to think of things to do. They had to be good things, too, or Duck and Ink Ear would shrug and say, "Naw," and not do them. The other two would rarely think of things themselves but left it up to Sonny to think and think until he thought of the right thing.

Had Sonny never done anything more than think up what became known ever after as "The Great Bus Ride," he would have remained a legend in his time. And there are those who still believe that smart, studious Sonny Tolliver was too reliable and conscientious to have done it, but he did it and never denied that he did it to anyone but Principal Worthington and Sheriff John Brown.

The lone school bus of Perry Exempted School District collected students each morning for school, starting very early for some and gathering others at a more reasonable time of day.

The route began where the bus was parked at night, behind Neff's Standard Oil station just beyond the town line. Students who lived near there had to get up and get ready a full half hour before those at the end of the line, or rather, the single student at the end of the line.

Carl "Butchie" Booker lived at the last stop, at the very top of Summit Hill, the highest point in Perry. Butchie had not lived in Perry long, had not gone through school with the rest of them. He was naturally suspected of being strange, which he was. Butchie sucked something into his lungs from a contraption he put into his mouth. It had a plunger that Butchie would press down. The plunger and his slurp of medication into his lungs made a noise that sounded very much like a wet fart.

"Sshhurrrp-ftttt."

The sound was funny at first but over time it became annoying. Butchie had taken the fun out of farts and he could not be forgiven for that.

Butchie said that his inhaler helped his cough

and the boys automatically resented that, too. Almost everyone they knew in Perry coughed. They coughed and they spit and when they needed to, they coughed and spit again. They didn't need gadgets with plungers in order to cough.

Butchie also wore glasses, with round pinkish plastic frames that were always sliding down his nose. But none of this was the worst of it.

The worst of it was that even though Butchie could sleep in, he was always late for the school bus and Harold Ethel, the bus driver and town clerk, always had to honk and honk until Butchie ran out of his house yawning and gasping and farting. The worst of it for Sonny and Duck and Ink Ear was that Butchie did not appreciate his good fortune at being at the end of the line, and Butchie did not show proper respect for their inconvenience.

The climb up Summit Hill strained the engine and the gears of the old yellow Chevrolet. The school bus had been around longer than the children that it carried. But the ride down Summit Hill could be a thrill and the highlight of the daily ride to school.

If Mr. Ethel was feeling playful and he only felt playful on those mornings when his wife, whose name was Ethel Ethel, remained in bed instead of getting out early to plan the club menu or attend to some other duty. On those mornings he would put the bus in neutral on the way down, the children would chant, "Go, go, go," and the bus would swing around the sharp curve at the bottom of Summit Hill, never putting any child in real danger, but with enough force to cause the children on the left side to press against the windows and cause the ones on the right side to hold onto the back of the seats in front of them, both sides squealing with the pleasure of imagined peril.

The occasional carnival ride down Summit Hill almost made the bother of collecting Butchie worthwhile. But as the boys got older, and Ethel Ethel tended to get up earlier, the rides were fewer and the thrill was not what it once was. They were now nearly 12, much too old to be screeching with third graders.

"I know how we can teach that asshole to be on time," said Sonny to Duck and Ink Ear.

"How's that?" asked Duck.

"Meet me down at Neff's tonight. After midnight. And bring your dad's tool box."

The only light at Neff's Standard Oil shone out towards the twin pumps on the fuel island, leaving the school bus mostly in shadow. But there was enough light reflected through the bus's windshield for the three of them to put Sonny's plan into action.

"Give me the socket wrench," Sonny said to Duck.

"What size?"

"Looks like half-inch."

"What are you doing?" asked Ink Ear.

"You're in my light," said Sonny.

"What are you going to do?" asked Ink Ear, moving slightly so Sonny could see the floor of the aisle leading back from the driver's seat.

"Just a tiny adjustment," Sonny said.

He began loosening the nuts on the bolts that held down the first seat on the right side of the bus, the seat that was always saved for Butchie Booker. Mr. Ethel would hold the door open and Butchie would slam into the seat and the bus would be off.

"We'll see what we shall see," said Sonny, removing the last nut. He shook the seat slightly. Rust and the grime of time kept the seat in place. Sonny shook it harder. He felt the legs give slightly. He twisted the seat sideways, pushed it, tugged until it finally broke free. He put the seat back in its original position.

"Our work is done here," Sonny said.

The plan, as Sonny imagined it, was that Butchie Booker would come running out of his house, pushing his glasses up his nose, leap onto the bus, flop onto the seat and the seat would go sliding sideways, Butchie would fall and everyone would laugh.

"Why don't we do 'em all?" asked Duck.

"All? Every seat?" asked Ink Ear. "Why?"

"For the hell of it," said Duck.

For the next 20 minutes the three worked steadily, but the novelty of the task lost out to the actual amount of work required. By the time they decided enough had been done, only the two seats on the right side of the bus directly behind Butchie's seat had been unbolted. And the seats were not jostled loose from the grime holding them fast to the floor as Butchie's had been.

Sonny, Duck and Ink Ear made sure to sit on the left side of the bus the next morning, and far enough back to be out of the way of any sliding seats. The bus filled at the usual pace and with the usual bodies, leaving the very front seat empty for the always tardy Butchie Booker.

Sonny noticed as the bus climbed up Summit Hill that Butchie's seat was teetering a bit in place. But no one else seemed to be aware of it. As Mr. Ethel slowed at the very top and prepared to lean on the horn for Butchie, to his surprise and to the disappointment of Sonny, Duck and Ink Ear, there Butchie stood at the end of his driveway, on time and waiting.

"Shit," said Duck as Butchie stepped calmly onto the steps leading up to his seat. He placed his books neatly on the space next to the window, pushed his glasses up his nose and sat quietly down.

"Go, go, go," said Butchie. And the chant began.

The children's voices grew louder and more insistent as Mr. Ethel started back down Summit Hill. Maybe because Butchie on time or maybe because Ethel Ethel had lingered under the covers that morning, Mr. Ethel was feeling playful.

He put the bus in neutral and gave over to the law of gravity.

"Go, go, go."

And down the bus went, full of laughing, happy children, approaching the curve at the bottom with more enthusiasm than usual. Mr. Ethel hit the brakes just a little harder than needed to slow for the curve. Just as Mr. Ethel began to turn the wheel to make the curve, he felt something bang into his shoulder. Butchie's seat had begun to slide sideways. Behind Butchie the seats that had been firmly held by years of grunge began also to move.

Two seats behind Butchie, the one holding the Frash twins, a boy and girl in the fourth grade, began to slide. The seat right in front of them, with Martha McLaughlin and Jenny Rolle, jerked forward.

Butchie Booker was already down in the door well and Freddie Frash had dragged Sally Frash on top of Martha and Jenny. Mr. Ethel had Butchie's seat half in his lap, half up on the dashboard and the bus was not making the curve at the bottom of Summit Hill. The bus was careening straight off into the field that held Walter Gorby's livestock, in particular his award winning Holstein, Cammy Lynn, who gave enough milk to feed the whole of Perry Exempted School District, and she had the ribbons to prove it.

"Ohhhh, shit!" shouted Ink Ear, watching his schoolmates tumble towards the front of the bus, feeling the bus leave the roadway and knowing soon that if something did not get in the way the bus was going to crash into Cammy Lynn and her full udder. The bell around the cow's neck dinged and clinked as Cammy Lynn calmly chewed her cud. Her big wet eyes stared straight at Harold Ethel.

Duck had the best view of what happened next and whenever he told the story he would finish the same way. "She was like a deer in the headlights, only fatter."

Duck would then pause to get to his punch line.

"She just wouldn't Moooooove," Duck would always add, giving the word his best Holstein accent.

Chapter 2

Why Did the Moron Help?

Ink Ear Ryan loved to tell moron jokes. He was not sure what a moron was but he figured it was someone dumber than himself. In every moron joke was the reassurance to Ink Ear Ryan that he would never do anything so stupid.

"Why did the moron throw the clock out the window?" Ink Ear asked Sonny.

"I give up," said Sonny.

"He wanted to see time fly. Ha, ha, ha, ha. Get it? Time fly."

Sonny and Duck always got it. They laughed along with Ink Ear and contributed their own moron jokes to Ink Ear's repertoire.

"Why can't the moron see the sun at night?" Duck asked Ink Ear.

"I give up," said Ink Ear.

"Because it's too dark."

"I don't get it," said Ink Ear.

16

It was not that Ink Ear Ryan was stupid. Or maybe it was. He did have his own way of seeing things. He was asked by Mr. Snyder in geography class to name the capitol of Ohio.

"Oh, that's easy," said Ink Ear. "It's the letter 'O'."

Little injury resulted from The Great Bus Ride other than to poor Cammy Lynn, the unfortunate Holstein. The damage to the bus was minimal. A cracked windshield, a broken headlamp, and a few new dents that were indistinguishable from the old dents.

Butchie Booker's glasses were broken and Martha McLaughlin's lunch of two mayonnaise sandwiches, a half eaten Mallomar and a small jar of home canned peaches was smashed and scattered. These were the main casualties.

The bus was already in need of an overhaul. Butchie learned that he really did not need glasses and Martha and Jenny shared Jenny's lunch, a single package of Neccos, under the schoolyard slide and wouldn't let anyone else have any, especially the licorice.

Only Sid Frash, the father of the twins, raised any stink at all. He owned one of the four remaining potteries in town, making a profitable line of stoneware. He was listened to when he talked. He talked the town council into firing Harold Ethel, from both his town clerk's job and as driver of the school bus.

Ethel Ethel was humiliated and did not join Harold when he moved to Coshocton to become a bookkeeper for CEMEX, a hydraulic cement company.

It was not that the other parents were unconcerned about the safety of their children. But most of them had faced danger themselves at one time or another. They adhered to the no-harm, no-foul rule of living. A mine cave-in or a kiln explosion, either would be of concern, but a harmless ride down Summit Hill did not seem to be a big deal.

Ron Miller, Sonny's stepfather, carried the scars on his back from a saggar of soup bowls that had fallen off the conveyer belt at Perry Pottery. Ron was fishing through his pockets for small change to pay for snack crackers at the employee's honor bar at the time. Had he not been fishing by feel for a nickel to pay for a pimento cheese sandwich that cost a quarter, Ron might have noticed the fireclay container wobbling down the conveyer belt.

The conveyer belt was elevated above the floor at that point, coming out of Kiln 3, just beginning to head down to the production line. Ron himself had complained that the change in direction of the belt was too abrupt.

"Someone's going to get hurt one of these days," Ron told foreman Jeff Wilkins.

"I'll bring it up with the committee," said Wilkins, but he never did.

18

A saggar is a crude clay container used to hold the production pottery while it is fired in a kiln, protecting the finer china from the open flames. A saggar full of dishes weighs 35 to 40 pounds. The saggar toppled off the conveyor belt just as Ron found the nickel.

Had Ron not been so pleased with himself at the prospect of cheating his friends out of 20 cents for the pimento cheese sandwich, he would not have done a little twirl of satisfaction and the saggar would have landed directly on his head.

As it was, the falling saggar caught Ron's right shoulder, scraped down his back, hit his left calve, and chewed out a chunk of muscle the size of a large plum. The saggar settled onto the floor without breaking or chipping a single piece of the fine china inside.

"Nobody was hurt?" Ron asked Sonny when he heard of The Great Bus Ride. "No? Let me show you what hurt is." And Ron pulled off his shirt, pulled up his pants leg and told again the story of the day he cheated death.

Charlie Stadler, Duck's father, wished he had been on the bus himself and made Duck retell the story over and over. Charlie knew danger and accepted it with a grim fatalism. He was sure the mine would get him one day and he was sure that would not be nearly as much fun as riding a school bus down Summit Hill. Whenever Duck told Charlie the story, he never included his part in dismantling the bus seats, but Charlie was pretty sure Duck was involved and he felt, for one of the very few times, pride in his son.

Butchie climbed back up from the steps where he had finished falling. He had lost his glasses and his inhaler. Butchie peered out through the cracked windshield and was immediately aware that his eyesight was now extremely sharp.

He never had to wear eyeglasses again, and his breathing problem got better. He still used his nebulizer even when he didn't need it, just to make the farting sound. But now the children would laugh and ask him to do it again. So relieved were his parents, Twyla and Tim Booker, that they bought Butchie a new bicycle, a red Schwinn Ranger, and Butchie was the envy of the school.

Butchie's eyesight was so good he could count the hairs on Cammy Lynn's left hind leg, now resting on the hood of the school bus. The rest of Cammy Lynn was somewhere out of Butchie's newly improved vision. Tilly James, the town butcher who prepared Cammy Lynn for Walter Gorby's freezer, was very impressed with the surgical precision of Mr. Ethel's cut.

"I couldn't have done it better myself," Tilly said. "Not with a 10-horsepower Hobart."

Walter Gorby was not happy to lose his prize cow but his relief that no child had been harmed was greater than his regret. He pressed no charges and sponsored a barbeque featuring the best of Cammy Lynn.

With the bus now at rest, Butchie heard laughter and turned to look back at the children behind him, most of them squealing and whooping and pushing at each other. Butchie had a very clear view of Ink Ear Ryan, who was not laughing at all. Ink Ear was tight-lipped and wet cheeked.

Ink Ear had quickly wiped away the tears, or thought he had, so that Sonny and Duck had not seen them. But he knew Butchie had seen them and now he had a whole new reason to hate the little creep.

Sheriff John Brown investigated the incident with all the tools of the Perry criminal justice office. That is, he called in those he thought might have done it and accused them of doing it.

He suspected the older boys of Perry High School of pulling the prank. He questioned the ones he usually questioned when things happened, boring in particularly on Dean Ryan, Ink Ear's older brother. But Dean had been out of town for a week helping his father, Woody Ryan, with a road paving job, though his real job was to keep Woody sober long enough to get a paycheck. Dean left his father serving 30 days in the Dayton city jail for drunk and disorderly, but he brought home what was left of Woody's pay.

"The last I saw him, he was curbing it," Dean told his mother Ida. 'Curbing' meant sitting on the curb, too drunk to stand, until the police picked Woody up.

Badgering and bullying got Sheriff Brown no confessions on who was responsible for the Great Bus Ride so he reported to the town council that it was probably the work of those punks from Loganville, a neighboring town and the main rival of Perry.

"I really think it was those Szabo gypsies up at Jericho," Sherriff Brown confided to his wife Laura.

Laura nodded silently, not because she agreed with her husband but because she had heard it before. Whenever anything went wrong in Perry, it was either those punks from Loganville or the gypsies in Jericho.

Loganville had more to boast of than did Perry, since it was the county seat and it had a courthouse, a three-story heap of red bricks and white turrets with long windows and a clock tower poking above the center arch. Next to the extended tier of stone steps that led to the vaulted entrance, a Civil War cannon rested between two huge wheels with a plug in a barrel that was pointed in the general direction of Perry.

Perry had no structure as impressive, and none as picturesque as the Loganville Courthouse. Public business was conducted in Perry from a plain two-story office block, practical but without the least bit of flair. In addition to the clerk's cubicle and the mayor's office, the building also contained the firehouse, the jail and a meeting hall/courtroom that was usually stacked with wooden folding chairs. Sheriff John Brown's office was in a temporary plywood annex that had long since become permanent.

Loganville's fairgrounds staged dirt track stock car races in the spring and held the county fair in the late summer. Perry's only park was barely large enough to hold a traveling carnival or the occasional tent revival.

Loganville was most importantly upwind from the slag piles, thus being geographically more pleasant, both in aroma and appearance. The local newspaper, the Messenger, was published in Loganville. Perry had its own section for news, but the weight of reporting went to happenings in Loganville.

Ethel Ethel, who remained head of the Women's Library Club of Perry, wrote weekly letters to the editor complaining about the lack of attention paid to the goings and doings of the WLCP.

"Dear Editor: Our annual paper drive raised $130 for charity which amount shall be used to help clothe and feed the less fortunate children in our community. I must point out that we have fewer of those in Perry than in Loganville. When Maude Walters of the Loganville Ladies Garden Club gets a front-page picture holding her pathetic geranium and the WLCP's fundraiser is relegated to page 12 below a story on cleaning gutters, I must protest and question your sense of news judgment and fair play. Enclosed is a recent picture of myself which you may use if you have the intestinal fortitude to print my letter."

The Messenger ignored Ethel Ethel's letter as usual but the newspaper did devote several inches of front page space to The Great Bus Ride, emphasizing the destruction of the cow Cammy Lynn under the headline: "An Udder Mess."

The day after The Great Bus Ride, Principal Worthington assembled the children and ordered any child who had any part in it to come to him. If any child knew anything about who had put them in danger, they were to come to him. He said it was their duty. He growled from behind a podium that had been set up in the school cafeteria, "All of you could have been killed. It is your duty to tell what you know."

Darla Hamilton, the class snitch, was tempted to rat out the boys but the hand she would have raised to be called upon was pinned behind her back by Ink Ear Ryan.

"Don't you dare," whispered Ink Ear.

This was the most attention Ink Ear had ever paid to Darla and he was not really hurting her. She could have broken free at any time. Or raised her other hand. Darla liked the touch of Ink Ear's hand gripping her wrist. If Ink Ear had been sensitive to such things he would have felt her pulse beating faster.

"Don't worry," Darla whispered. "I won't say."

"You better not."

"I won't say if you pass through the gate with me."

Passing Through the Gate was the ceremony at the end of each school year that marked the promotion of the children from one grade to the next. As even Ink Ear understood, it represented passage from one time to the next, from today to tomorrow. Ink Ear understood because it meant going from a smaller number to a larger one. One side of the gate, sixth grade. Other side of the gate, seventh grade.

For the sixth graders it served as their elementary school graduation ceremony and each child was given a diploma of completion. The most outstanding student in the sixth grade received the Doerr Prize, named for Frankie Doerr, who had never completed the sixth grade. Frankie became famous for being killed during a high-speed chase of the only bank robbers who had ever bothered with the First Bank of Perry.

Sheriff John Brown, then only a deputy, saw the whole thing. He was waiting to catch speeders when the robbers sped past him. John Brown spun through the gravel behind the large bush where he had parked and turned on the single blue light on the top of the cruiser. The siren was broken so John Brown made the sound himself, leaning out the window of the cruiser and screaming, "Woooooeeee, wooooooeee."

Frankie was delivering the Loganville Messenger on his bicycle when the green Packard sedan driven by Roger Simmons with Larry Boyer and the money, $7122, in the backseat, careened around Three-Mile Turn. The Packard caught little Frankie with the right front fender, sending him into a stile that was no longer needed since it had been replaced by a gate in the fence between Phil Newell's farm and Janice Hoover's garden. Everyone agreed that without Frankie, the robbers would have gotten away.

John Brown's capture of the robbers boosted him into the sheriff's office and his tale of the heroic sacrifice of little Frankie caused the Perry Exempted School District to create the Doerr Prize for scholarship, although what being run over by a green Packard had to do with scholarship was never made clear.

Sonny Tolliver was to get the Doerr Prize because he was the smartest kid in the sixth grade, and that meant he was the smartest kid in the school. Sonny liked knowing that.

Sonny suggested to Principal Worthington that they ought to change the name of the ceremony to Climbing Over the Stile. That would honor little Frankie and there was no actual gate to pass through anyhow. The children walked under an arched trellis that was always covered with spring flowers from Imlay's green house. Principal Worthington patted Sonny on the head and said he would still get the Doerr Prize.

"Why did the moron pass through the gate?" Ink Ear had thought this up all by himself.

"Give up.

"To get to the other side. Ha, ha, ha."

The students passed under the arch in twos, paired by boy-girl when possible, holding hands. Because there were more girls than boys in the school, boy passers through were highly prized. Boys had to dress in clean clothes and comb their hair. The girls wore new dresses and ribbons. The girls liked it more than the boys.

Ink Ear Ryan always avoided the ceremony. All the Ryan children did and there were seven of them, Ink Ear square in the middle of the order. The Ryans had neither the clothes nor the consistent hygiene to be part of such a ritual. Ink Ear had not passed through the gate even one time in all the years he had been in school. If he were better at arithmetic Ink Ear would have known it was half of his life, counting kindergarten. Yet he managed each year to pass on to the next grade. As long as he had Sonny to pass him answers during tests, Ink Ear was certain he could pass through any gate that he needed to.

"What am I going to do?" Ink Ear asked Sonny. "Darla will squeal if I don't walk with her."

Sonny was no better informed on matters involving girls than was Ink Ear but it seemed to him a small sacrifice. Hold a girl's hand for a couple minutes. Even Darla Hamilton's.

"Why did the moron hold the girl's hand?" Sonny asked.

"I give up?"

"To save his friends."

No one ever told who was responsible for The Great Bus Ride, and the final, official judgment was faulty equipment due to the bus's age. Principal Worthington got the Perry Exempted School Board to give him money enough to repair the bus. The bus got a new paint job at the same time, something Principal Worthington had been trying to get done for several years.

As long as no one was hurt, Principal Worthington wished the bus had been more extensively damaged. Maybe then he could have gotten a whole new bus. He had his eye on a Gillig C-180, flat front with air conditioning and automatic transmission. Loganville had nothing to match it.

Chapter 3

Just the Ticket

Another thing that Loganville did not have was a movie house. Not any more. What was once the Logan Theater was now an empty lot. At the back of the lot near the alley, stacks of rubbish had grown into scattered mounds, some of substantial size. A chewed mattress and a set of inner springs leaned again the outer wall of Trotter's Fine Dining. Stained shingles on the building were a reminder of where the Logan Theater had once stood next door.

The fire that ruined the theater was limited to the structure itself, leaving the buildings around it touched only by soot. It was almost as if it were planned that way. But the insurance paid and the owner, Henry Rodenour, took the money and moved to Fort Myers, Florida, with his new wife, Cheryl, once a very good waitress at Trotter's.

For several years, then, the only movie house in the county was in Perry. It was the most distinctive structure on Main Street. The wedge shaped marquee came to a point over the sidewalk providing space on two sides and in two directions for the names of the movie features. The name of the theatre was lit vertically down the front of the wedge, each letter illuminated in small yellow lights, all except for the final letter of the name which never seemed to light up no matter how many electricians fooled with the wiring.

Thus Perry's movie house was The Globe in the daytime and The Glob at night. Everyone had called it The Glob for so long that the owner and manager, Andy Sloan, stopped worrying about fixing the sign.

Andy Sloan was a big man with a big belly and a big voice that could scare any kid at a Saturday matinee into keeping his feet off the seat in front of him.

"Ink Ear Ryan!" boomed Andy, "you kick that seat one more time and you're out for a month!"

For a short time Sonny Tolliver had a job at The Glob. It was not much of a job, sweeping up on Monday mornings after the week's trash had piled too high under the seats. Sonny was allowed to run the projector every once in a while.

For pay Andy Sloan let Sonny keep anything he found of value, even though he was supposed to drop it into the lobby box that had crude lettering identifying it as Lost and Found. Sonny did not keep eyeglasses or gloves or wallets that had no money in them, but loose change was his. Sonny pried the odd quarter off the sticky theater floor. But for pennies, even nickels, Sonny gauged the goo before deciding.

Sonny had found three cigarette lighters, two Zippos and a Ronson shaped like a small pistol. If he ever started smoking, Sonny thought, he was set.

Andy Sloan also allowed Sonny to see any movie for free, as well as allowing him to have a small bag of popcorn. Sonny had to buy his own drink.

Andy himself manned the concession stand at the Glob. The stand was a small space barely large enough for Andy to fit inside. The stand was located next to the left door entrance to the theater with one window opening to the inside of the theater and another opening to the street. Passersby could choose from the collection of Paydays and Milky Ways without going into the movie house itself. Andy made change from a small apron he wore around his middle, an apron that tended to disappear under Andy's very large stomach. Andy's mother, Irene, sold tickets at the box office and, unknown to Andy, kept the money from every third admission for herself.

Irene's little bit of graft was contributing to the bleak future of the movie house. The place had been opened several decades before by Irene's only husband, a small, quiet man who was allowed to believe he was Andy's father. The new drive-in movie down at Three-Mile Turn, the curve in the road roughly half way between Perry and Loganville, was eating into Andy's profits more surely than was Irene. The real killer would be television, of course, and even Andy had one of those.

The Glob was open from Thursday through Sunday, with matinees for children on Saturdays and Sundays and a double feature on Thursday nights. The movies were not first run, or even second run, but the movies did not matter much because Thursday nights between features The Glob offered Skreeno, a low-grade way to gamble.

Each Skreeno card cost an extra fifty cents and players could play up to five. After the first feature, Andy SLoan would announce from the back of the theatre, "Get your cards out. It's time for SKREE-EE-EE-NO." He had no microphone but his booming voice carried well. Andy was what Sonny's mother, Clara, called "theatrical," and Sonny took her at her word.

Clara Miller was at The Glob every Thursday night. Clara walked the mile from the Miller home to the movie house, clutching a purse that contained almost nothing, a compact with a fold out mirror, a tube of lipstick, a small change purse and her mother's heirloom hatpin. Clara did not wear a hat and had not worn one since she was a teenager. She used the hatpin to punch out numbers on the Skreeno cards. Clara did not know how to drive, and even if she had known, there was no chance that she would ever have been allowed behind the wheel of Ron Miller's pride and joy, a nearly new white Dodge Town Wagon panel truck.

Pastors in churches in both Perry and Loganville preached against the evils of Skreeno, not as gambling but because it cut into their crowds for Friday night Bingo. Warren Lund, the radio preacher, called Skreeno "the devil's dice." The Glob gave away actual cash while the Methodists and the Presbyterians only gave coupons.

Sonny hated more than any other part of his job getting up the tiny pieces of paper that were punched out for the Skreeno games. The Glob had no vacuum cleaner and the punch holes resisted every cleaning device available, which would include one broom, a rag mop and Sonny Tolliver's fingers. Over the years the little punch holes were simply ground into the general grime of the theater floor.

Skreeno, Andy Sloan had thought, was the way to save The Glob, and though it was an old movie house gimmick, it was new to Perry. Andy had changed the spelling of the game, substituting a "k" for the "c" in order to avoid copyright and to make it seem as if his Skreeno was Perry's very own game. "Nothing like it anywhere else," Andy boasted.

A large numbered dial, resembling a clock face, was projected onto the movie screen. A spinning needle would revolve around the dial until it stopped on a number. Cardholders would punch out the number on their cards if they had it, using toothpicks that Andy provided or, as was the case with seasoned players, their own personal hatpins.

There were 10 games between features, with a total prize purse of $50, or $5 a game. Clara Miller had never won a Skreeno game, even though she made sure to use her mother's lucky heirloom hatpin.

Clara Miller was an optimist. In a town with horizons lowered by the perpetual slag smoke, Clara could see a brighter day. She was certain she would win. One day, she said, her ship would come in, even though she had never seen a ship nor had she any idea where ships came in.

It seemed to Sonny that not only did his mother Clara not win at all, few ladies—and the Thursday night audience was mostly made up of women—won at Skreeno. Not as many won as should have been the case. Some games would go entirely through the cards with no one having enough numbers, up, down or sideways, to claim the prize.

Of the $50 that could have been won, usually only $30 or at the most, $35, was paid out. And the money not won one week was not carried over until the next. It seemed to Sonny that Andy Snead was holding back $15 to $20 each week.

Once a month The Glob held Bank Night. All movie tickets that were sold during the month

34

were eligible for a drawing and a prize of $100. Patrons were advised to keep their ticket stubs and show up on Bank Night for the announcement of the big prize.

The presentation on Bank Night was more elaborate than for Skreeno. Andy Sloan dressed in a tuxedo, maybe the only tuxedo in Perry. He would draw the winning number from a huge glass fish bowl where the stubs for the month had been deposited. Andy wore white gloves when he fished through the bowl for the winning number.

Just to show everything was on the up and up, Andy would occasionally call a member of the audience to the stage to pick the number, usually a small boy. The kids were not given gloves.

Sonny noticed that at least half of the time, the winning number was not in the audience.

"Oh, my dear. Oh, no," Andy would say. "You have to keep your stubs and you have to show up to win. The more stubs, the greater your chances. Be here for the movies and be here for Bank Night next month."

The money not won was money that stayed in Andy's pocket.

"Something smells at The Glob," Sonny said to Duck.

"Yeah. I think it's a dead rat or something."

"No, I don't mean that," said Sonny. "I think somehow Andy is fixing Skreeno. And Bank Night is just as fishy."

"How did the moron know where to go back to catch a fish?" asked Ink Ear, not waiting for the answer. "He marked an X on the side of the boat. Ha, ha, ha."

Andy kept the fish bowl used for the Bank Night drawing in his office, a cramped room up a twisting set of stairs next to the projection booth. He kept the door locked, not the usual thing to do in Perry.

Door locks in Perry tended to be the kind with keyholes, the kind you could see through. Perry was not a dead bolt kind of place. And any key that fit any similar lock would, with just a little bit of jiggling, unlock any other door. This is how Duck got into his father's liquor, which is another story and the scar across Duck's left cheek tells some of it.

Sonny creaked open the door to Andy's office, pushing back a large mixed Abyssinian cat that was sleeping behind it. Goldy was the reason there was a dead rat smell in The Glob. While a good mouser, Goldy was not a tidy housekeeper. She would kill a mouse or a rat and drag it somewhere to let it rot. Odors leaked from various corners of The Glob, especially near Row D on the right side. Sonny never bothered to clean there and only on Bank Night did anyone sit there. Goldy jumped up, hissed and ran out the door before Sonny could close it.

"Christ," muttered Sonny. "Now I've got to get her back or Andy will know someone has been in here."

The office was not much. A folding card table with a splint on one leg served as Andy's desk. A three-shelf metal bookcase held whatever records Andy kept and a series of numbered file boxes. The wooden swivel desk chair was the nicest piece of furniture in the room. It was the only real piece of furniture in the room. It was very like the chair Mrs. Mears sat in. The fish bowl was on the table, empty. Beside it was the trash bag that Sonny had dropped behind The Glob earlier in the day.

Fished out of the trash bag were ticket stubs that had been discarded. These stubs were thrown away by the kids, mostly, and by anyone who did not care about Skreeno. Sonny would clean up dozens of the stubs each week.

Andy was increasing his odds by adding both halves of sold tickets to the drawing. If both halves were in the bowl, the other half could not be in the audience. Andy could be sure no one would have the winning ticket if, as he fished through the bowl, he picked one that had been on the filthy floor of The Glob.

"That's why he wears the white gloves," muttered Sonny. Sonny said this not without some admiration.

Peeking from underneath the trash bag was a film can. The trash bag had been plopped on top of it. Sonny scooted the can out. Scrawled on a piece of white adhesive tape, the same lettering that identified the Lost and Found, was the word "Skreeno."

Sonny was sometimes asked to be the projectionist, usually for matinees when Andy had to be the theater warden. Sonny could thread the film and change reels, do whatever was needed to get through previews, cartoons, and the feature. Of the film cans he used on the days he ran the Brenkert Deluxe BX-80, he had never seen any film can marked "Skreeno."

Sonny removed the film from the Skreeno can. He projected it onto a piece of gray cardboard instead of onto the theater screen down below. The familiar dial and numbers flickered and moved from game to game. Nothing seemed wrong. The dial would spin, stop, spin, stop.

Before each game of Skreeno a number would flash briefly. Where had he seen those numbers? Back in Andy's office, Sonny pulled out one of several small file boxes from the metal bookshelf. Inside the box were Skreeno cards. Marked on the box in the same Lost and Found scrawl were numbers. They were the same numbers Sonny had seen flash on the Skreeno reel.

And then it clicked in Sonny's head. He realized if you knew which numbers the spinner would stop on, you could know which Skreeno cards had the best chance of paying off.

And which ones did not.

"Scrawkkkk."

Sonny jumped. Goldy the cat was back. She had dropped a half eaten rat at Sonny's feet. Goldy arched her back and rubbed against Sonny's leg. Sonny picked up the cat and scratched behind her ears. The cat closed her eyes and purred.

"You got your rat," said Sonny. "I got mine."

Chapter 4

Pot de Chambre

For as long as Sonny, Duck and Ink Ear had been alive, Perry's town slogan was painted on the tank of the town water tower. "Perry, Happiness, Prosperity" each word getting its own line.

Only one of the words was accurate, the name "Perry," and there are those that would argue that Perry was not the name of the town at all. It should be known as Forge, the name it had gone by after the first kiln was fired up to make the first pot.

It was widely assumed that the name was changed to Perry to honor the hero of Lake Erie, Commodore Oliver Hazard Perry. But it was actually named for Harry Perry, the man who signed the application for a post office. Harry Perry had mistakenly put his last name where the name of the town was supposed to go.

A ladder led up to a metal platform that encircled the water tank. Every so often Sonny and Duck would climb up and sit there, feeling superior to all those little people leading little lives below, and when the slag haze was blown in the other direction they would get a fine view at the same time.

They could see all the way down to Winslow's Bend, the curve that was named for a turn in the Jericho River. Back when the town was still known as Forge, a man named Jeremiah Winslow had lost his mule Jocko in the river. This was when the river's water was clear, before silt had clogged the bottom and the current moved more rapidly. Jocko was pulling a wooden raft up river, walking along the bank while Jeremiah urged him along with a willow branch. Jeremiah's son Lud was on the raft, guiding it with a crude tiller. A player piano was the only cargo on the raft, tied down by rough twine, the same inadequate rope that connected the raft to the mule. The reason the Winslows were trying to float a player piano up river has been lost over time.

At the turn in the river, Jocko stopped to munch on a patch of creeping thyme and no matter how Jeremiah whacked him, Jocko was not inclined to move. The twine from the raft pulled at Jocko's harness and Jeremiah tanned Jocko's flanks but fresh thyme is the devil's own dinner to a mule. The current in the river began to turn the raft around and Lud could not hold the tiller. Jocko's head was wrenched away from the thyme by the tug of the raft as it began to go back downstream. The mule dug in and stretched his neck to get another bite. The rough twine broke just as Jocko was losing his footing on the bank. The raft rocked and the player piano tinkled to life, breaking into a jaunty version of "Dew-Dew-Dewey Day." The raft began floating back down river. Jocko tumbled into the water, submerged and did not reappear. The last glimpse of his mule by Jeremiah Winslow was of a happy animal with a tuft of thyme sticking out of the corner of his mouth. Lud and the player piano made it to shore but Jocko was never seen again.

Beyond Winslow's Bend, the Jericho River squirmed its way to an eventual union with the Muskingum River, picking up additional flows from Stonecoal Creek and Laurel Run. At a point in the center of downtown Marietta, the liquid mixture from Perry would blend with the Ohio River, though the boys could not see that far away.

Two ridges cradled the river and the town—Flint Ridge to the north and Brimstone Ridge to the south. The boys would often explore Flint Ridge looking for Indian arrowheads. The name of Flint Ridge came from discoveries of arrowheads and flint tools generations earlier. Traces of flint mines, dug out by prehistoric tribes, still existed, though they were now entirely overgrown by ash, hickory and maple. None of the boys found any Indian arrowheads, but Ink

Ear had dug out a sharp piece of chert that he imagined once was on the end of a spear.

Brimstone Ridge was sun blessed. Stands of oak and hickory had been cut from it, leaving splotches of open fields. From the Perry Water Tower the treeless spaces looked like stains on a carpet. Brimstone Ridge was named after a rock formation called The Devil's Tea Table, and the boys understood that creepy things happened there. They had been told, or maybe they just imagined, that the immigrant clan known as the Szabos preformed satanic rituals on the flat rock that was the Tea Table itself. They promised each other that they would go some day and find out if the stories were true.

Off to the west, the general clutter of Loganville was sometimes visible from the Perry Water Tower. The boys had to admit, when the sun was setting and a golden glow silhouetted the buildings of their rival town, Loganville seemed to be blessed in a way they could never see in Perry.

Ink Ear did not climb up the tower with them, preferring to stay below and throw pieces of gravel to see if he could hit either Sonny or Duck. Ink Ear did not have Duck's arm nor his aim and Sonny and Duck never felt threatened.

"Come on up, chicken shit," yelled Duck.

"I ain't neither," Ink Ear shouted in return.

"He is," Duck said to Sonny.

The evening before the unveiling of a new water tank, the sun nipped at the tops of trees along State Street. The light fully illuminated the water tower as Sonny and Duck sat on the platform, their legs dangling over. A ceremony was planned for the next day and a small stand of bleachers had been erected over the gravel lot at the base of the tower. A raised platform faced the bleachers with several folding chairs and a podium. Sonny leaned back and crossed his arms behind his head. He was looking straight up under the tarpaulin that hung loosely over the water tank. A slight breeze lifted and wafted the tarp. Sonny had an idea.

"How about this," and he told Duck his plan.

"Jesus, that's great. That's just fantastic."

Perry's water tower functioned as water towers do, storing and dispersing fresh water. Perry's tower was unusual because of its planned new shape. It was to be shaped like a cookie jar, the same as one of the cookie jars made at the Perry Pottery. Cookie jars were the biggest sellers of any single piece of pottery in Perry.

The design was simple, a rounded crock, with foot and lid, covered with a classic glaze the color of sand. Like the Model T Ford, it came in only one color. If you wanted a Perry Pottery cookie jar, you took the tan one.

The new tank of the Perry Water Tower was a copy of the cookie jar. Four angled legs with struts and crossties supported the water tank. A ladder had been fastened to a central shaft, which contained the feeder pipes that brought the treated water from the Perry Reservoir several miles away and the pipes that fed the water into the homes of Perry.

The system worked efficiently and those with indoor plumbing in Perry had no complaint. Those without indoor plumbing sneered at those who had it.

"Won't be any outhouses left by the time you're grown," Clara Miller told Sonny. "You're sitting on history, so to speak."

Sonny hated sitting on the seat in the Miller outhouse. The small shed with a star cut in its door was 40 yards below the Miller house, a cold walk in the winter and generally inconvenient at all other times. What Sonny hated the most were the flies from below that bombarded his bottom and buzzed around his squirter. What other creatures dwelt amongst the Miller deposits Sonny did not want to think about. He had dreams of spiders, deadly black widows, and scorpions. He had never seen a scorpion but he imagined a fierce creature with sharp teeth.

He did not use the outhouse unless he absolutely had to. If Sonny could not do his business at school, and he was regular, after lunch each day, he waited as long as he could until the next day. To urinate Sonny simply stepped out the back door and treated the lawn much the same as did Clara's chickens. A bare slope of dead grass and caked dirt reeked of urine. His mother used a chamber pot and it was Sonny's job to empty it each day.

The idea to shape the water tank like a cookie jar was that of Sid Frash, grandson of the founder of Perry Pottery. Sid had kept the pottery profitable despite competition from Japan and other foreign potters. Perry Pottery was notable not only for its cookie jars, but as well as for its creamers, sugar bowls, gravy boats and mixing bowls.

The more delicate china was made at Gilbert and Trent China Company, on the other end of State Street. Had the GTCC a view of the Perry water tank, the new tank might have become a cup and saucer. But as it was the window of Sid Frash's office looked out onto the tank, sticking up 150 feet above ground, a half mile away.

When Sid looked up from his drawing board, the place where he fiddled with designs for new lines of pottery, the tower was always in his view. The same day that he was designing a new sugar bowl and creamer, the tower seemed to him more prominent than usual, more obvious, almost as if it were trying to tell him something.

It occurred to Sid that the creamer he had just drawn looked very much like the tank on the water tower except for the handle and the spout.

Sid looked down at his design for the creamer, a little bulb of a shape with a handle and a short spout. He looked up towards the tower and then again at the creamer. Was this inspiration or

46

coincidence? Sid held the paper on which he had drawn his cream pitcher at arms length. He squinted. That's it! Inspiration or coincidence, it made no difference. Sid Frash had a new line and a new idea.

Why not shape the Perry water tank like the creamer? What a great advertisement for his pottery and for the town. It would be seen for miles.

Excited, Sid rushed from his office, grabbed his secretary, Nellie Long and kissed her on the mouth.

"I'm going to make us and this town famous. I am. I am," he shouted.

While Nellie Long was used to being kissed by her boss, as well as pinched and rubbed against, she had not seen him this excited.

"What are you going on about?" she asked.

"Look," he said. "You have to look." Sid took her by the arm and led her to the window in his office.

"Aren't you going to lock the door?"

"What? No. Not that. This."

Sid Frash held out his drawing and told her to imagine that the tank on the water tower in the distance could be shaped exactly like that. Nellie looked and imagined and then asked, "What about the handle?"

"The handle?"

"Sure. You can't have a handle sticking out of a water tower. That would look dumb. And probably would be very expensive."

"The handle. But I like the handle."

Sid had drawn two handles on the matching sugar bowl. They looked like ears on a pumpkin.

"Then how about this?"

Sid resketched the bowl, eliminating the handles.

"It looks like your cookie jar," Nellie said.

"We'll make it a cookie jar, then. That's even better. Our cookie jars are our bread and butter."

And that is how the Perry Water Tower became the talk of several counties. Loganville had nothing like it, nor did any town between Athens and Columbus.

The fame of the tower spread just as Sid Frash had believed it would. People drove from miles away to see it, some from as far as away as Canton and Youngstown.

The final design, taken from Sid Frash's own drawings and executed by Signpost Structures of Pittsburgh, varied only slightly from the original plan. To hold enough water and to use the existing supports, alterations had to be made. The lid and the foot were shaped just as designed but the bowl had to be slightly longer than calculated.

The day of the great unveiling came. A rope hung down from the tarpaulin that was draped over the tank. Sid Frash himself would do the honors and pull the cord that would drop the tarp that would reveal the new and distinctive Perry Water Tower.

"My friends, my colleagues, my employees," Sid said, "and you know which ones you are. Today marks a milestone in the history of our town. We can think of this water tower as a symbol of all we stand for. Anyone who sees it will know that this is Perry."

He pulled the cord and …

Sid Frash heard a gasp, several gasps, and a few titters.

"What is that?" asked the mayor, Howard Trickle.

"Is that what I think it is?" asked Howard's wife Ellen.

"What's going on?" asked Herbert Rodenour, who was sharing the platform with Sid Frash. The two men were the only ones wearing suits.

Sonny, Duck and Ink Ear, on the edge of the crowd, laughed and slapped each other on the back. It had worked exactly as Sonny had imagined.

The photographer from the Loganville Messenger would not stop taking pictures. Sid Frash, his back to the tower, frowned at the reaction of the crowd. He looked at Herbert Rodenour, shrugged and they both turned and looked up. From their angle they could only see the bottom of the tank. Sid stepped down from the platform and walked out to see the legacy he had presented to the town of Perry.

Sid Frash's cookie jar, the new symbol and pride of Perry, looked like...well, if everyone had one of Perry Pottery's cookie jars, they also had one of these, even those with indoor plumbing.

All of Perry knew what the new water tower looked like and so would any stranger who saw it. And if they did not see it, they had the front-page photo from The Loganville Messenger to remind them. It was one of the few times the Messenger had put a story about Perry on the front page. Wire services picked up the Messenger story and picture. Perry exile Eldon Burley saw it in Mesa, Arizona. It was also on the front page of his local paper, the Mesa Republic. Eldon agreed that it, indeed, looked exactly like a "pot de chambre." Eldon did not get to use his French much and never passed up a chance to do so.

"I knew I should have used the creamer," said Sid Frash.

And for any who did not know, the handiwork of Sonny and Duck was there to confirm it for them.

The town slogan had been painted again on the new tank, each word on its own line: Perry Happiness Prosperity.

The night before the unveiling, Ink Ear Ryan had crawled through an unlocked window of the town equipment storage garage and had let Sonny and Duck in through a side door. Duck had worked for the town and knew exactly what he was looking for and where to find it. To say Duck had worked for the town is to say he was punished for letting the air out of the tires all along Walnut Street, four of the tires belonging to Sheriff John Brown. His punishment was to help paint the water tower support legs in anticipation of the new tank.

"Yep," said Duck, fishing a bucket down from a shelf just above a collection of saw horses that were used as traffic barriers. "Here it is." He handed Sonny the same bucket of paint he had used to keep rust off the tower.

With Ink Ear kicking gravel down below and Duck holding the flashlight, Sonny crawled under the tarpaulin and painted out the "Hap" and the "ne" in "Happiness." He then did the same with the "r" the "speri" and the "y" in Prosperity.

When Sid Frash pulled the cord that dropped the tarp that revealed the tank, the sign on the new town water tower now read: Perry, pi...ss, P..o.....t.

"Those words I can spell," said Ink Ear Ryan.

Chapter 5

What's That White Stuff?

Duck Stadler was the best athlete of the three of them, a natural athlete. In any playground game, Duck was the first picked. Sonny had the brains, Ink Ear had the enthusiasm and Duck had the muscles. Duck had strong calves, broad shoulders and big hands. Where they all came from was not obvious.

His dad Charlie was a wiry runt, a hard knuckle of a man, his size better for low seam work in the mine. Duck was already taller than Charlie. Duck's mother Sarah was sickly with less reason to be so than her husband. Sarah never got out of her housecoat except for church.

Duck and Sonny had been next-door neighbors on Washington Street since Sonny was three years old. Clara Tolliver became Ron Miller's second wife barely a month after Ron's divorce from Wilma. The first time the two boys saw each other, Duck balled his fist and Sonny stuck out his tongue.

Clara asked Donald his name and the boy said clearly, "Donald."

Sonny heard it and began singing, "Donald Duck. Donald Duck."

The two boys had been born only a week apart. Duck had slipped easily into life, giving Sarah no trouble at all. Sonny seemed undecided, as if considering his options, keeping Clara in labor overnight and half the next morning.

The two mothers were not friends but neither were they enemies. There was no good reason to be either. Sarah was loudly religious, a member of the New Church of the Nazarene, a congregation that assumed that the Father, Son and Holy Ghost were all hard of hearing.

Sarah Stadler was infused weekly with the word of God by Reverend Warren Lund by way of a floor model Bendix radio. Rev. Lund would preach and Sarah would rock in her rocker to the rhythm of his message. To share the joy of the holy word, Sarah would turn the volume up as loud as it would go. The gesture was unappreciated by her neighbors.

Sarah never pried into the circumstances of Sonny's birth. She simply assumed the worst, and the worst was that Clara was a loose woman who slept around until she became pregnant and had an illegitimate child. Clara's father had assumed the same thing about his daughter and had thrown her out of his house as soon as her pregnancy became obvious. Sonny's grandfather did not see him until Sonny was five years old.

Clara used the only bible in the Miller house to balance her GE wringer-washer. The left rear leg of the machine had lost its roller and the New Testament was just the right thickness to keep it level. Over time the good book became indented from Matthew half way through Luke.

The mothers would meet at a shared clothesline on those days when the wind was right and whites could be hung out to dry. They would swap stories about how vexing their sons were to each of them and inevitably finish with, "I wish Donald was more like Sonny," and "If only Sonny were more like your Donald." Neither of them meant it.

Duck was looking forward to Passing Through the Gate because it meant he would be able to play junior high sports, football and basketball, the only two interscholastic games the Perry Exempted School District could afford.

Duck was already better than half the varsity players on the perpetually pathetic Perry teams. He could run faster, hit a baseball better and dribble a basketball without it eventually bouncing off his foot.

"I'm going to be the best ever in Perry," Duck boasted to Sonny and Ink Ear. "I'm going to break all of Wilkie Wilkins' records."

Edward "Wilkie" Wilkins was a name still spoken with some worship in Perry, the only athlete from the town to ever play college football. Wilkie started as a sophomore fullback for Ohio State and helped the Buckeyes win their first Rose Bowl.

On the way back home from California, Wilkie stopped in Las Vegas and missed the entire spring quarter at Ohio State. He was expelled from school for punching an English professor who would not give him the passing grade that would have made him eligible for the next season.

Wilkie went off to play professional football in Canada and was found dead two years later in a whorehouse in Ottawa, the same day that he scored five touchdowns, a Grey Cup record that still stands.

Duck found a Perry town limits sign that had been thrown away after Wilkie was buried in Las Vegas. His parents honored his last wish to be buried "where the lights are bright and the women are not." His parents moved to Las Vegas where his father dealt blackjack and his mother became a waitress at the Dunes. The town limits sign proclaimed Perry as "Home of Wilkie Wilkins." After Wilkie's dishonor and his preference not to spend eternity with the good folks of Perry, the sign was replaced by the original lie: "Welcome to Perry, Happiness and Prosperity."

Duck tacked the discarded Wilkie Wilkins sign to the back of the Stadler house, crossed out

Wilkie's name and painted his own, calling himself Donald instead of Duck.

Russell Hand, the insurance man, had proposed a new motto: "Fewest Suicides in Ohio." Russell argued that of the things that Perry could be most proud, this one had certification. According to official records from the Ohio Survey of Statistics no one in Perry had killed himself since before the war. Per capita, it was the least desperate town in the state. It was true that Perry took a special pride in pushing on, no matter the misery.

Suicides might have been rare but skin disorders were common in Perry, Ohio. Everyone lived with bad water and foul air. A continual haze squatted over Perry, caused by burning coal slag and a prevailing wind. Life, for better and for worse, was linked to the two main occupations of the area—mining and pottery.

The miners, better paid than the potters, would eventually become victims of pneumoconiosis, Black Lung disease, whereas the potters tended to suffer from bronchitis, though lifers like Ron Miller, Sonny's stepfather, could depend on persistent dermatitis.

The miners tended to get diseases ending in "osis" and the potters had ailments ending in "itis."

"An 'osis' is worse than an 'itis,'" explained Clara Miller to her son, Sonny. "But does it matter? It's like chicken shit. You know what that white stuff is in chicken shit is? That's chicken shit, too."

At Shorty's Tavern after work, Duck's dad Charlie would be black from the coal dust and Sonny's stepfather Ron would be covered in white clay powder from the pottery. They would sit side by side like two piano keys--or to use Clara's image, a lump of chicken shit--drinking cold 3.2 beer. Charlie the miner drank Pabst and Ron the potter drank Blatz. No one could explain why but those two beers seemed to be the natural choices of miners and potters. The two men spoke little but because they lived next door to each other, they would walk home together, wash off and be human for the 14 hours of the day they were allowed to be.

They returned to houses where the paint on the south side of each one was being eaten way by the fumes from the slag piles. They breathed the sulfur stench from the New Hartsfield underground mine fire, "Hell's Oven," it was called. It had been burning for as long as any of them could remember. Repeated efforts to quench the fire had failed. Miles of coal seams continued to burn and may be burning still. Every five years or so Charlie and Ron would scrape their houses and repaint, reconciled to the cycle of life in Perry, Ohio.

Sonny's stepfather nightly rubbed medication into his forearms, made raw from an additive in the clay he handled. The glaze that made his arms bleed made Perry Pottery distinctive.

"Well, at least it ain't cancer or diabetes," Ron Miller philosophized. He would contract both diseases before he died, though neither was responsible for his death. Ron would eventually die not from the sicknesses that came with his work and with his life in Perry but because his white Dodge Town Wagon smashed into a concrete mixer that was on its way to Loganville to pour footers for the New Church of the Nazarene. By this time Ron had lost his job at Perry Pottery and was commuting to the Rockwell plant in Newark.

The cement truck, a Mack B-61, one of a fleet of three belonging to Zinn's Quik-Set Mobile Mix, had stopped just around a sharp curve on Highway 91. Thurman Jansen's goat Angus had wandered off and was calmly eating a bag of potato chips that had been tossed the night before into the middle of the road by Dean Ryan or one of his friends.

Ron was digging at the itch on his left arm and didn't look up until it was too late. Ron Miller hit the brakes and jerked the steering wheel to miss the Mack B-61 but slid sideways instead into the back of the truck. The hanging cement chute swung free and poked through the driver's side window of Ron's Dodge Town Wagon. The force of his Town Wagon crashing into the mixer caused the huge spinning drum to tip up and dump its wet load down the chute and through the window onto Ron.

Sonny's stepfather might have survived the collision but the cement slurry coated him before he regained consciousness, firming up so quickly and completely he could not move nor breathe.

"The clay did kill him in the end," said Clara Miller.

Angus the goat was unharmed and the New Church of the Nazarene was built on time, though some suspect a few pieces of Ron Miller, who was not a religious man, are in the foundation.

Any death in Perry created concern with Russell Hand, the insurance man, who worried that Perry's suicide record might be in danger. Maynard Walters, of the Perry furniture store Walters and Wiseman, died in a car-truck "accident" even though the driver of the truck, Bud Gratiot, insisted that Maynard had driven into his three-quarter ton Chevy flatbed on purpose.

"He waved at me just before we hit," said Bud. "We've known each other for years. He sold me our davenport."

Russell Hand, the insurance man, countered the accusation that Maynard Walters had crashed on purpose on two counts. First, the accident had taken place beyond the town limits and therefore was not a Perry statistic and, second, that if it really were suicide, the statistic belonged to Loganville, since Loganville was closer to where it happened. Russell used the same logic to remove

Henrietta Bickley from the suicide list after she threw herself under the coal train nearer to Jericho than to Perry.

Duck's father Charlie constantly coughed up disgusting stuff from his lungs and spit it onto the ground, or at the dog. Coughing was a common kind of greeting in Perry. Everyone coughed. Acne came before puberty to the children. It came early and stayed late.

Perry was more distinguished for making assorted lines of pottery than for the substantial deposit of bituminous coal that was dug from under Jericho Hill, coal that was scoured from dark and dangerous places, each chunk indistinguishable one from another. As Clara Tolliver Miller said to Sarah Stadler, "A piece of coal is a piece of coal but fine china is a place setting."

Thus came the name of the high school football team, the Potters. It remained the nickname after the potteries were long closed and the potters long gone.

There was never any debate over calling the school the Miners because that was Loganville's team name. Loganville's mascot wore a hard hat with a light on the front that blinked on and off. Max the Miner carried a pickaxe with which he conducted Loganville's cheers. He shook the axe at the opponent and menaced their supporters with it. He had once chased a crying child from end zone to end zone.

"Piss!" Max would shout and the Loganville fans would return "Pot!" The chant would echo and little children liked the cadence.

"Piss pot, piss pot, piss pot," sang little Davey Weaver, happy now, as Max carried him back from the end zone. Davey was from Perry, son of Presbyterian pastor James Nance Weaver. At times during Sunday services, little Davey could be heard from the vestry singing to himself, "Piss pot, piss pot, piss pot."

Max the Miner's act was very visual and very dramatic and every Potter, if he had been honest, would have preferred to have so fearsome a figure as Max the Miner leading the team onto the football field or onto the basketball court.

The Potters had no mascot at all. Various possibilities were considered.

"What are our choices?" asked Chad Fulmer, superintendent of the Perry Exempted School District. "A dancing butter dish or a fierce coffee mug? How silly would it be to have a gravy boat leading the team onto the field for games?"

The cookie jar was Perry's signature piece of pottery, but in light of what happened at the water tower, that symbol was instantly dismissed. And thanks to Max the Miner, they were already derided as the Perry Piss Pots no matter who the opponent was. So the Potters were mascot-less and left to find inspiration where they could. They were not inclined to look very hard.

The Potters had no fight song but simply borrowed the school songs of Ohio State. "Fight the team across the field," applied even though their team was on the same sideline as the visitors.

The Potters home field was at the far end of Perry Municipal Park rather than at the high school itself. The football field had once been named for Wilkie Wilkins but it was now nameless. Both football teams used the same sideline. The other side of the field was never fully cleared and no bleachers were ever built. The opposite side was no more than 10 yards away from wild scrub and thick brush. At least once or twice an evening, the game had to halted to search for a football that had been kicked or thrown into the brush, always a risky adventure due to the presence of snakes.

While looking for the football a referee from Reynoldsburg had been bitten in the leg by a copperhead and the game was forfeited. It was a sad incident because it was one of the few times the Potters ever were leading the Miners.

"The other teams put their pants on one leg at a time," football coach Dub White told the Perry Boosters at the annual season kickoff dinner, the one time of year when optimism was given a seat at the table.

"But ours are smaller and more brittle," said Dr. Paul Tedrow, who had given the team its physicals and knew what he was talking about.

The dressing room for the home team was the boys' side of the municipal swimming pool. The visitors were assigned the girls' dressing room but hardly ever used it. Visiting teams tended to arrive fully armored and were deposited at the field. The Potters had to get from the pool to the field on foot. The long walk to the field made every home game feel as if it was on the road.

Inspiring halftime locker room speeches, and the Potters always needed them, were brief and wheezy because most of the time and breath were taken up with walking to the pool dressing rooms and back.

Duck Stadler never missed seeing a game and never got discouraged by the high school's losing game after game. He would trail along after the team from the field to the swimming pool dressing room and back, offering to carry helmets and offering his advice on how to beat the Loganville linebackers.

"Don't be chicken shit," Duck would yell at the Perry Potters.

Chapter 6

Home Again, Home Again

The parallel ribbons of the Ohio Southern Railroad tracks and the Jericho River bisected the town of Perry, Ohio. The top of the pitted iron rails were kept polished by the wheels of the daily trains that served the mine up the river at the tiny town of Jericho.

The river was barely more than a creek, its broadest point no wider than the highway that led into and out of Perry. The river gave the tiny town of Jericho its name and received in return a consistent contribution of sulfur and sludge and acid runoff from the Brighter Day coal mine. The foul, slowly moving water had become the color of carrots and fish had long since given up the river as a home.

Life in the river and along the river faced a constant demand to surrender.

The railroad tracks pretty much matched the route of the river, crossing the water twice, once before Main Street and further down stream just beyond the old train depot. Both railroad bridges were visible from the Main Street bridge, Trestle One and Trestle Two. The old depot was not used as much as once it had been, and it had always been used for freight, never for passengers.

The trains took the coal away but no longer transported the pottery. The demand for fuel kept the coal cars clattering along the river. The pottery business was not as noisy, needing only occasional trucks, or the U.S. mail, in order to dispense its gravy boats and flower pots.

One of the few times a train stopped at the Perry Station, two dead bodies were left to be collected by Roy Cannon, owner and licensed mortician of Cannon Family Funeral Home. Roy was also the Perry coroner, a job that came by default since he was familiar with handling dead bodies. He also had the only morgue in town and no one else wanted the job. Roy was not as punctual as he should have been. It was said that Roy would be late for his own funeral, this judgment being based on the fact that he was nearly always late for everyone else's.

Luckily for Roy he had the assistance of Maude Heskett, who played the organ and arranged the flowers. She did not work with the bodies, except to tell Roy when too much rouge made the dearly departed look like a ventriloquist's dummy.

Services would begin promptly due to Maude's organization but Roy seldom was at the door to greet the mourners as they arrived, only to offer his condolences as they departed, his breath fragrant with the traces of White Horse Scotch Whiskey.

The Ohio Southern engine huffed into Perry, the low sun seeming to push it along on its way as it rose in the east. The train was on its way to the tiny town of Jericho and the Brighter Day Mine where it would collect its Thursday cargo. The engine hissed and grumbled as the line of coal hoppers behind it creaked to a stop. Steam belched from the engine as it idled, the clatter and clanking enough to wake the dead, who happened to be Eldon and Helen Burley, enclosed in separate crates in the lone boxcar.

Perry was asleep, just after dawn, and was, in any case, used to the racket of the Jericho run at that hour. Except for Jim Norton, who was just beginning his milk route for the Wiseman Dairy and for Sonny Tolliver, who was awake because he felt like being awake, the only other Perry soul not sleeping was Gus Shiner, who often slept on the church pew that served as the only bench on the station platform.

Gus Shiner was the town disgrace. He could have been known as the town drunk except there was lots of competition for that title. Nearly every adult male in Perry could qualify as town drunk but Gus was the only one to panhandle on Main Street. He would spend his days in Shorty's Tavern nursing beers and his nights rounding up enough cash for a bottle or two of wine. The best deal in wine for the money was Thunderbird, the champagne of low-end fortified wines.

If Gus had ever had the choice between real champagne and Thunderbird, he might have chosen the champagne but only to resell it to get more Thunderbird.

Gus Shiner was known as "Old Soldier," to Sonny, Duck and Ink Ear. They did not know his real name and they never asked. Old Solider would tell the boys stories of the war and the boys would then go off into the woods along the Jericho River and recreate the battles, using broken tree limbs for rifles and tin cans for grenades. Duck liked the heft and size of the White Rose quart oil can for his grenades, and Duck could throw it further than either of the other boys.

On the day that the Ohio Southern train stopped at the Perry depot, Gus Shiner was awakened not by the noise of the train but by a disturbing awareness that the noise did not diminish as it should have as the train clattered on towards Jericho.

Gus Shiner opened a single eye as the train groaned to a stop. Gus did not need to open his eyes to see things. Sometimes, eyes open or closed, he would see strange things. This might be one of those times. He opened the other eye, and then hoisted himself upright. He felt in his pockets for change and found none. Gus scratched and yawned, rubbed his stubble and stood up as the train engineer approached him.

"Where do you want 'em?" the man wearing an engineer's cap asked.

"Any where is good," said Gus, having no idea what the man was talking about. "Say, do you think you could spare…"

Gus was about to ask for spare change but the other man had already walked away. The engineer, a man named Paul Fortis, had not made the Jericho run very often. Fortis was from Akron with no idea of Perry, its county or its citizens. What he knew of it was from the engine cab. From his driver's perch he saw a hilly landscape with a rust red river winding through it. Fortis was unaware of the local smell until he stopped that morning to deliver the late and unexpected Burleys. He stepped down from the cab, cupped his hand over his nose and waved at a man sitting on a church pew. The man had to be either the station agent or the mortician. It did not matter to Fortis which it was. His aim was to drop his cargo as quickly as possible and get out of there.

Fortis slid open the door of the only freight car among the line of coal hoppers. Gus walked over and peered over Fortis' shoulder. Gus could see two packing crates made of fresh pine. Each box was the size of an upright freezer. Stenciled on the sides of each one were the words, "Perry Ohio Cannon."

"It ain't my job to lift these, you know," Fortis said to Jim. "Here, help me slide them out."

Gus rubbed his stubble again. He frowned. He had not gotten to this point in his life by doing any more work than necessary

Still, maybe there was a buck or two in it. And already Gus was thirsty.

Sonny liked to walk mornings, occasionally all the way to school, a route that could be covered by going along the tracks of the Ohio Southern. To get from where he picked up the tracks near his house to where he stepped off on Main Street to go to school, Sonny had to take 2,441 steps. He had counted the steps several times. His step was about the same length as the space between the wooden railroad ties.

His record for walking on the iron rails without stepping off was 1177 steps. To do that had taken 6 minutes and 42 seconds. He knew the time from the pocket watch he had found under seat F11 at The Glob. The watch needed winding more often than it should and it lost three minutes an hour. But for Sonny's purposes, it was just fine. His goal for balancing himself was 20 minutes. Sonny could not dream that he would ever walk all the way to school on the rails without falling off. People in Perry learned to set achievable goals. Or none at all.

On the morning Sonny saw the Jericho train wheezing at the depot and Old Soldier helping a man wearing an engineer's cap off load two pine crates, Sonny had counted off step number 954. He was half way across Trestle No. 2. His next step missed the rail and he tripped, barely catching himself, but the stick Sonny had been carrying for balance slipped through the ties and fell into the Jericho River.

"Shit," he said.

The man in the engineer's cap took a clipboard away from Old Soldier, snatched back his ink pen, turned and slid closed the freight car door. He walked away from Old Soldier, who stood between the boxes with his hand out.

"Then you can go straight to hell," Sonny heard Old Soldier yell at the other man's back.

The engine hissed and groaned. The wheels slowly ground forward, slipping initially on the rails. The train picked up speed and disappeared up the tracks, already late for Jericho.

Had Roy Cannon been on time that morning, or had he remembered that the remains of two members of Perry's founding family were arriving at the train depot that morning, what happened next would not have happened at all. As it was, Roy Cannon had forgotten or mislaid or altogether botched the notice of the arrival of Eldon Burley and his wife Helen.

Eldon Burley's father Enos had opened the first coal mine near Jericho and named it The Sunset Mine. Eldon had taken over the mine not long after returning from Heidelberg College in Tiffin, Ohio. It could have been Heidelberg in Germany for all the folks in Perry knew and some thought it actually was. Eldon brought back with him a degree in liberal arts and a wife who was taller than he was.

For the first decade that he was in charge of the Sunset Mine, Eldon Burley was considered the leading citizen of Perry. He also owned the bank on Main Street, the telephone exchange and he had an interest with the Frash family in Perry Pottery.

His wife Helen was a gracious hostess and the founder of the Women's Library Club of Perry. The Burleys had no children and tried to treat the town as their family.

Eldon Burley should have been more aware of the dangers in coal mining, but his resistance to the whole idea of mining had led him to study literature and language in college, the literature being mostly Victorian and the language being entirely French. Eldon found little opportunity to speak French in Perry. He worked out of the mine's main office above his bank in Perry. He almost never went to the mine itself. He signed whatever safety reports came across his desk. Eldon had little idea of the perils of firedamp and methane gas and coal dust. He gave no thought to shelves of unstable shale or to the threat of flooding. On a bright morning not unlike the one that returned the Burleys to Perry, nearly all of those things combined to destroy Mine No. 9 of the Sunset operation, killing 36 men, four mules and a blue tick beagle named Roscoe.

Eldon Burley's first reaction was, "*Merde.*"

It remained the greatest single disaster in the history of Perry mining, if not serious enough in fatalities and financial cost to get it ranked with the worst mining catastrophes worldwide. But it was enough to bankrupt and ruin Eldon Burley. He was found guilty of "negligence and malfeasance" and sentenced to five years in prison, where he was out in two for good behavior.

Helen liquidated what she could, including the Sunset seam that was still rich enough to be worked. The new owners, The Eagle River Resource Corporation of Parkersburg, West Virginia, renamed the mine the Brighter Day. Helen managed to pay the court ordered fine of $1.5 million. Almost all of the settlement went to lawyers because the families of the victims argued with one another about who deserved more and litigated the settlement until the award money was nearly all gone. Helen moved away to await the release of Eldon.

The two of them spent the rest of their days in Mesa, Arizona, cursing the sand and the heat and bad luck. Eldon taught night classes in English to Mexican immigrants and worked by day as a bank teller. The only interesting thing that ever happened to him again was when a man claiming to be Buck Barrow, brother of Clyde, robbed his window at the First Bank of Mesa.

Nearly half a decade after leaving Perry, Eldon and Helen Burley died together when the space heater they were using on an uncharacteristically chilly night in Mesa leaked carbon monoxide, the same gas that had done in the blue tick beagle named Roscoe at the Sunset Mine.

Their wills stipulated that they be returned to Perry, the place of their greatest happiness. And that was why they were now resting side by side in the morning sun on the platform of the Ohio Southern Railway depot in Perry, Ohio.

"What are these, Old Soldier?" Sonny asked Gus. Sonny tapped one of the crates with the toe of his right shoe.

"Dunno," Old Soldier Gus Shiner said. "That sumbitch wouldn't give me a nickel for helping him. Even after I signed my name."

"What did you sign?"

"I signed Kiss My Ass. What'd you think? You got any change, Sonny?"

"I mean what was the paper you signed?" asked Sonny. "It will say what's in the boxes."

"I think he kept it on his clipboard," said Old Soldier Gus. "Asshole."

Sonny walked around the crates, examining them from all sides.

"It says 'Cannon'. You suppose they're guns? You think these are big guns?

"I just need fifty cents, Sonny, a quarter, just to get started."

"Maybe they're cannons," said Sonny. "Maybe they're howitzers."

"I seen howitzers," said Old Soldier Gus. "I seen 'em and I shot 'em. These could be little ones, I guess. In parts. Need to put 'em together."

"Maybe they're for display in the park. Next to the doughboy. Maybe they'll be Perry's cannons, like the one in Loganville."

Perry had a doughboy statue with a list of honored dead in the small park in front of town hall. A cannon would fit very nicely next to the statue. This all made sense to Sonny, who much preferred to think of deadly weapons than dead bodies.

Why would Perry need two cannons? Loganville only had one. Perry had only one doughboy. It seemed excessive to Sonny. But he knew who could use an extra cannon. He and Duck and Ink Ear could use a cannon. It would fit just fine in front of the fort they had built to fight their mock wars down along the Jericho River.

Chapter 7

The Clay Hole

For Sonny, Duck and Ink Ear The Great Bus Ride had been the crowning achievement of their elementary school years so far. After they passed through the gate next spring they would be in junior high school, where, as seventh graders, they would go from being kings of the playground to runts in the dirt.

For the first time all of them would be in a new building, in another part of town, with new teachers and some new classmates. Tiny Jericho had no secondary school and joined Perry Exempted School District for the next level.

"The Szabos will be there," Sonny told Duck.

"Yeah, I know," said Duck.

"Save us from the Zebras." said Ink Ear, pressing his hands together as if to pray.

"Szabo. Zabo. Not Zebras," said Sonny.

The Szabos were from Hungary, just as the Ryans had earlier come from Ireland and the

Stadlers and the Millers from Germany. The Tollivers, according to Vernon Tolliver, came from France, or from Scotland or from Italy, depending on how sober he was. If America was the Melting Pot, the Szabos were the spice in the recipe.

The Szabos were what was left over from immigrant labor that had been brought to the Sunset Mine by owner Enos Burley in order to break a miners' strike. The miners wanted a set wage and Burley insisted on paying them on a sliding scale, depending on the price of coal. The strike was settled with the miners agreeing to the same low set wage the immigrants had been paid, just before the price of coal climbed to a record high.

Enos Burley fired the immigrants and most of them moved on. Only the Szabos stayed and were still resented. It was the fault of the Szabos that the miners made less money instead of more. It was the fault of the Szabos that they prospered when they should have suffered. It was the fault of the Szabos that the wine made by the grandfather, Zoltan Szabo, sold better than the moonshine made by Dewey Hall. It was the fault of the Szabos that when the new owners of the Brighter Day mine closed the company store, the Szabos bought it for pennies and reopened it, charging higher prices.

The Szabos controlled all the commerce there was in Jericho, a place that used to be named Tiny

Jericho. The Szabos now owned almost all the land around Jericho and lived in almost all the houses. When it was Tiny Jericho it was tiny, just a few buildings that existed to oblige the miners who worked the former Sunset Mine, now the Brighter Day.

The Szabos had made Jericho into a viable town and they had taken business away from both Perry and Loganville. They operated a food store, a tavern, a service station and a laundry. Zoltan Szabo made both a dessert wine and a fortified wine and sold them through the food store. Dewey Hall had to hide his still and sell his moonshine out of the back of his truck. Zoltan Szabo paid no tax and sold his wine in the open because he labeled his wine as religious. He sold it to the Jews in Columbus as kosher wine and to the Catholics in Cincinnati as altar wine. It was the fault of the Szabos that they were simply smarter than most of the people in Perry.

The Szabos kept to themselves and ventured hardly at all into Perry and not often into Loganville. The Szabos shopped by mail order catalog, favoring Montgomery Ward over Sears, and grew their own food by making fertile fields from the rocky waste around the Brighter Day mine.

The Szabos made up fully two-thirds of the population of Jericho and more than half the student body of the one-room elementary school.

The Szabos were too exotic for Perry and were suspected of being un-Christian. And even if they were Christian, they had to be Catholic, not quite as bad as being Jewish. In fact, the Szabos were both, trading in their Jewish roots in Europe for the Catholic faith in America. They never went to church, not for worship, not for a wedding, not for a funeral. The Widow Ellen Neary, who still lived in Jericho and kept a shrine to her husband and two sons who had been killed when the Brighter Day was the Sunset Mine, was the source of all things Szabo.

"I've heard chanting," the Widow Neary reported to the Women's Library Club of Perry. "I've seen fires at night and I've heard the most awful noises. Like a grinding, followed by a screech. Like something, or someone, being killed."

"You mean like a sacrifice?" Ethel Ethel asked.

"It wouldn't surprise me."

"Pagans."

"Atheists."

"Aliens.

"Lord save us and protect us."

"From the Szabos."

Children in Perry were taught to end their nighttime prayers in such a way. God, please, keep the Szabos away. To make their children mind, mothers told them that if they weren't good, the Szabo would get them.

78

For the most part, Sonny, Duck and Ink Ear ignored the finer points of adult intolerance. They had a vague idea of what a Szabo might be. But they were not frightened or resentful or angry. Instead, they adapted Perry's common hostility for their own purposes. When the boys gave each other Indian burns or twisted each other's nipples trying to bring tears or surrender, they would make the other boy cry "Szabo." It was the equivalent of crying "uncle."

When Sonny, Duck and Ink Ear thought of the Szabos, they didn't think of bogeymen, or of Gregor Szabo, who had spent two years in Perry Junior High before going off to get killed in the war. Gregor had won a silver star for bravery and the medal, a star attached to a red, white and blue ribbon, was in a case behind the bar at the Szabo tavern.

The boys did not think of Nick and Bela Szabo, who were almost their age and had been banned from the Ben Franklin in Perry for stealing one pair of argyle socks. Nick and Bela tried to walk out of the store with each one wearing a single sock over one of his bare feet. Nick wore a sock on the left foot and Bela on the right. They walked out arm and arm. They would have looked suspicious even if they had been a creature with four legs. It was the only case of theft anyone could document involving a Szabo but nonetheless, most unexplained robberies were blamed on the Szabos anyhow.

The boys did not think of the head of the family, Ferko Szabo, who had the darkest, thickest beard any of them had ever seen. Ferko smoked a pipe, not an unusual thing to do, but his pipe was unlike any pipe anyone in Perry smoked, a long, white pipe, with a skinny stem and a fat bowl. The Widow Neary said she thought it was made from the bones of one of the Szabo sacrifices.

No, when Sonny, Duck and Ink Ear thought of the Szabos, they thought of Margarite Szabo.

None of them had ever seen a fully naked girl before and none had seen pubic hair. They had none of their own at the time.

What they knew of girls was that girls were fun killers. Girls didn't spit or cuss or get dirty. You could never be seen talking to a girl, even if she was your sister, maybe especially if she was your sister. Ink Ear Ryan had three sisters, all of them older than he, and they tried to boss him. Girls snitched to the teacher, like Darla Hamilton. You could not trust girls.

You could not go to war with a girl down on the battlefield they had created along the Jericho River. You wouldn't play cards with a girl even if you needed a fourth for euchre. Girls had their place and boys had their place and one of the best places the boys had was The Clay Hole.

No girls ever went to The Clay Hole. Sonny, Duck and Ink Ear all learned to swim there. Duck swam better than a duck. The first time they went to The Clay Hole, Duck just jumped into the water and dared the others to follow. Sonny slipped in feet first and treaded water until he understood how to move. Ink Ear refused and had to be thrown in. Now he could float around and splash like he invented swimming.

"You asssssshooooooooles!" Ink Ear had screamed when Sonny and Duck tossed him into the water.

The Clay Hole was what remained of an abandoned quarry. Much of Perry's pottery started from the rich deposits of high calcium clay that once covered what was now a large pool of water stuck back in a hollow below Flint Ridge, the last hill before Jericho. The clay had been dug out from limestone, exposing a natural spring that filled the hole. And once it was no longer cost effective to pump the water to get at the clay, it was left alone in its seclusion. The water was clear and fresh, not foul with sulfur like most of the streams that ran down the hollows and into the Jericho River.

The hike up to the Clay Hole required a will to get there and a bit of local knowledge. The Clay Hole was on the back way to Jericho off Snake Hollow Road. The road was a gravel single lane that was no longer used much. A mile or so along the road was a broken black walnut tree with a lighting scar streaked into its dark bark. The tree still thrived and dropped the messy green fruit from which it was impossible to extract the nut without turning the hands a sickly yellow. The shell of the nut itself was not that much easier to open. Sonny had developed a method of his own, dropping a cement block onto an arrangement of nuts and then picking out the edible parts, usually getting a bit of grit and concrete at the same time.

A trail was partially hidden at the walnut tree, grown over with sumac and chokeberry bushes. But once past the entrance the trail up to the Clay Hole was worn and clear, another half mile of climbing.

In a clearing, the pond popped out, suddenly and surprisingly, faintly blue and without a natural shore. A swimmer had to climb out using the crude steps that had been chipped out of the rock. There was no level place to rest or to put clothing except for a limestone shelf seven feet above the water. It jutted out several yards from a sprawling wall of lilac that had gotten its way for years.

The boys thought of The Clay Hole as their own private swimming place. Generations of other boys had thought the same. The town provided a perfectly adequate municipal swimming pool and that is where nearly everyone spent their summers. The best thing about the Clay Hole, besides being private, was that it was free and, as Sonny pointed out, every bit as wet.

They had just reached The Clay Hole the last day of summer vacation just before they entered the sixth grade. They were eager to take a last swim before school began again. Duck and Ink Ear always swam naked. Sonny tended to keep his underwear on. Duck had already peeled off his shirt and was carrying his shoes when they got to the final climb up to the diving ledge.

The boys could not see above them and did not immediately notice someone else was already there. Just as Duck pulled himself up to the ledge, he felt a blur rush past him. They heard a splash below and stared at the ripples in the water until a head covered with coal black hair popped out.

"Who are you?" yelled Duck.

"Who am I? Who are you?"

"We're us," said Ink Ear. "Who are you?"

"I'm me. Who are you?"

"This is getting us no where," said Sonny.

"We're from Perry. This is our swimming hole."

"You don't own it. I didn't see your name anywhere."

"Mine's right here," said Ink Ear, pointing to a place on the limestone wall where he had scratched his initials.

"IER," Ink Ear said. "That's me."

All the boys could see of the figure who was treading water below them was the head. Ebony tresses floated out like seaweed. Peering through strands of matted hair that hung down over the face were two very dark eyes. The swimmer seemed to be about the same size as they were, probably the same age. They weren't looking to make any new friends but they were not unsociable.

"We swim here," said Sonny.

"So do I."

"We've never seen you."

"I've never seen you."

Duck had finished pulling off his shirt and shorts. He was about to peel down his briefs.

"Don't do that."

"Do what?" asked Duck. He dropped his underwear, ran to the ledge and did a perfect cannonball, whooping and aiming just to miss the swimmer below.

Ink Ear followed Duck. Sonny waited.

"You need a haircut," Duck said after he surfaced. He was an arm's length away. He splashed water at the swimmer. He was splashed back and a water fight began, Duck and Ink Ear on one side and the stranger on the other. To even out the odds, Sonny peeled down to his briefs and jumped in. It was two on two now and Sonny's side was winning.

"Zebra, Zebra, Zebra," Ink Ear finally cried out.

"You mean Szabo, Szabo," Sonny corrected, continuing to splash.

"Zabo, Zabo," Ink Ear said, sputtering and laughing.

"That's me," said the stranger.

"That's who?" asked Duck, no longer splashing.

"Szabo."

"No, no," said Sonny. "They called Szabo. We win."

"I'm Szabo. I'm Margarite Szabo. I live over the hill in Jericho."

The boys stopped splashing. The four of them treaded water in silence. The three boys stared at the girl. She glared back at them. Margarite Szabo ducked her head under the water, slicked her hair back and surfaced.

They could see her face clearly now. Droplets of water perched on the tips of very long eyelashes. Her dark eyes flicked from one boy to the next. She snorted water from her perfect, slightly sunburned nose. Her full lips stretched in a grin and then opened into a broad smile marred only slightly by a crooked left lateral incisor leaning towards the center of her front teeth.

"And this is my swimming hole."

She slapped Ink Ear on the top of his head and swam away, kicking water back at the boys. She pulled herself out of the water at the steps and climbed back up to the diving ledge.

Margarite was wearing no top. She was unselfconscious about her breasts. The were not fully formed, not large enough to need a bra but definitely breasts.

She was wearing white cotton underwear, girls' underwear with no opening in front.

"Candy asses," she called down to them. She took her place again to dive into The Clay Hole.

The boys stared up at Margarite. None of them blinked. She raised her arms to get ready to dive, stretching up onto her toes, extending her body to its maximum length. There at her crotch, visible behind the wet white cotton, was a startling patch of black hair, matted down by the fabric, a perfect V-shaped wedge. This was completely unexpected by the boys.

"Jesus, Sonny," said Duck.

"Holy shit," said Ink Ear.

"Look at that," said Sonny.

Margarite stood on the diving ledge, the sun beating straight down on her. The surface of her hair was already drying, showing that completely dry it would have the slightest tinge of red. Light reflected back up from the water and lit her as if she were posing for a photograph. She seemed to shine in the sun.

It was possible that the dark spot down there below her navel was a shadow, a trick of light, maybe a smudge from the clay where she had climbed out of the water. It was possible, but it was not a smudge. Some instinct told the boys that it was something marvelous.

"What is that?" asked Duck.

"What is what?" asked Margarite

"There," said Sonny and pointed.

Margarite looked down. Her look followed the line of her body past the budding roundness of her chest, beyond her waist, down her legs and past her knees. She lifted one foot, and then the other, checking the soles of her feet.

"No, no," said Sonny. "There." And he pointed again.

Margarite Szabo sucked in what was suckable of her flat tummy but could still see nothing. She pulled back the band of her underwear and peered down. A clump of black, matted hair peeked back from the intersection of her legs.

She looked up. She looked down. She looked at the boys. They grinned back at her. She looked down again, leaning out to see what was showing through the white cotton.

Margarite peered down at the faces of the boys in the water. These were not the same happy faces that had just minutes earlier laughed with her, not the same little boys who had splashed water at her, treated her as one of their own.

She felt a sudden shame, as if her being there was wrong, that she had done something wicked and she did not know what. What she knew was she had to get out of there.

Margarite jerked around, knelt down and grabbed up the clothes she had left at the back of the ledge. She clutched them to her naked chest and pushed past an overhanging lilac branch and hurried down the path.

That was the last they saw of Margarite Szabo that summer, bouncing down the trail from The Clay Hole, the white cloth stretched across her rear end a hint of a great and wonderful mystery on the other side.

Soon, the Perry Exempted School District was going to bring her back to them.

"Zebras," said Ink Ear, thinking what the others were thinking. "Margarita Zebras."

"You got that right," said Sonny.

Chapter 8

Clara Miller's Ship

Clara Miller never broke a chain letter chain. She assured herself of good luck, good health and good will by sending along letters to people she did not know because she had received a letter she did not ask for from people she had no idea existed. The letter informed her that if she did not continue the chain, horrible things would happen to her.

Sonny was skeptical and took the money Clara gave him for stamps and bought ice cream.

"Did you take my letters to the post office?" Clara asked.

"Yes, Mom," said Sonny.

"You can't break a chain," Clara said. "Your aunt Florence broke the chain and she was bitten by her own dog. You remember King, her dog? In the middle of the night he went into her bedroom and bit her on the arm. She woke up and hit King with a lamp or she might have only one arm today."

Clara fished a Camel from a package on the kitchen table. The oil cloth table cloth, a pattern of red strawberries and green leaves, was splotched with burns from the Camels that Clara had forgotten were lit and had fallen from saucers or ash trays after burning down. Often Clara had more than one Camel going. The kitchen smelled of lard grease and tobacco smoke. She lit her cigarette with a Ronson lighter shaped like a pistol, a gift from "her Sonny."

"King was such a good dog. He would not hurt anyone. Not a child. Not a cat. Certainly not Florence, but she broke the chain and the very next night, she woke up with her arm in King's mouth. She won't have a pet in the house, now. Not even a goldfish."

Sonny believed that King, a mixed breed terrier, had bitten his aunt Florence. Sonny had seen the marks. But his uncle Ernie told him that his aunt had passed out with her elbow in the gravy after drinking too much wine on Thanksgiving and that King was trying to lick it off.

Ernie had put Florence in bed and she was lying on her back with her arm smeared with gravy hanging over the side of the bed.

"She woke up and scared poor King," said Ernie. "He just gave her a nip when she hit him with the lamp. I won that lamp for her at Buckeye Lake before we were married. We had to put King down and I couldn't fix the lamp. What a waste."

"She shouldn't have broken the chain," said Clara.

One of Sonny's chores was to pick up the Miller mail at the post office. Perry had no mail delivery. Sonny came to recognize chain letters because somewhere on the envelope would be a warning: "Do Not Disregard." Sonny would disregard any letter that told him not to, tossing them into the trashcan at the post office. His stepfather Ron would collect the mail from time to time and the odd chain letter would find its way to Clara.

Whatever good luck Clara had she attributed to not breaking the chain. She did not have any more good luck than anyone else in Perry. But Clara thought the absence of bad luck was the same as good luck. And if her ship was going to come in, as she believed it was, she was not about to close the harbor by breaking a chain letter.

Sonny did not understand the reason for chain letters. It seemed to him just some silly game played by adults. All of the letters were the same. A letter came with a list of names on it. Clara would copy the letter, strike off the top name on the list, put hers on the bottom and then mail the letter to the others. Implied was a collective protection, an unbroken chain of faith. Clara was convinced that blessings and special good luck would multiply for her as her name worked its way to the top of the list.

Sonny left the mail on the kitchen table, an electric bill, an Alden's catalog, a post card from Ron Miller's brother Don reminding Ron that Don was successful enough to be sending him a post card from Cedar Point. There was also an envelope that Sonny had forgotten to disregard.

"Sonny, honey, look at this," Clara called.

The envelope had been torn open through the warning "Do Not Disregard." Clara held one of the three pages. The others lay on the table.

"It says to send money to each of the names on the list," said Clara. " A dollar to each name."

Sonny picked up one of the pages and looked at the list of names. They all seemed to have addresses in Racine, Wisconsin.

Sonny dropped the list onto the table.

"Somebody just wants your money, Mom," Sonny said.

"Well, maybe, but look, it says here that when I put my name on the list people will send me money. If I send a dollar to each of these people and they each send a dollar to five more people, I will get...how much would I get if five people sent me money?"

"Five dollars."

"And I would move up the list. By the time I get to the top I would have how much?"

Sonny was very good at arithmetic but this required a pencil and paper. He put down the numbers, scratched them out, put down more numbers, scratched them out and then drew a triangle. He put $5 at the top of the pyramid. He multiplied every level assuming everyone, like Clara, would not break the chain.

"Five people, 25 people, 125 people, 625 people, three thousand..."

Clara had already gone for her "egg money" even before she heard Sonny mumble "three thousand."

Sonny mailed the letters Clara copied to be sent on. The money she included was all in change, quarters, dimes and nickels. It was the money Clara was paid for selling eggs to a few regular customers who would stop by the Miller house. Her chickens used the Miller lawn as their toilet and the hens did not always deposit their eggs in the nests provided for them. Sonny had to hunt down rogue eggs scattered around in secret places. It was like Easter every day at the Millers.

Each of those coins sent off by Clara Miller represented a yard covered with chicken droppings, years of Sonny being chased by nasty roosters, hens pecking his hands as he fished under them for eggs, surprised rats scurrying away from the places the hens tried to hide their eggs from Sonny, Clara washing the eggs, sizing the eggs, storing the eggs in small brown bags, a half dozen in the small bag, a dozen in the larger one.

"My ship is coming in," said Clara as she handed the envelopes to Sonny.

If her ship came it, it came to a different port. Clara received not a single reply to any letter, got back not a single dollar, paper or coin.

"But I did not break the chain," Clara said and lit a new Camel off the butt of the old one.

When Sonny figured out how Andy Sloan was rigging his Skreeno and Bank Night contests at The Glob, Clara Miller's chain letters came into his mind.

"Maybe I can put her at the top of the list," Sonny thought.

It was easier than Sonny imagined it would be. As Sonny suspected, Andy had separated out the Skreeno cards with numbers that would not appear on the movie screen in a particular game. These had the worst chance of winning. Some cards had no chance. Likewise, Andy had separated out cards in a stack identified by a corresponding number to the Skreeno game. These were cards with more numbers that would show on the screen, cards with a much greater chance of winning. Some of the cards had all the numbers of a specific game. These cards were sure things.

All Sonny had to do was make sure the right cards got into the hands of Clara Miller.

"Mom, Mom," Sonny called. Her son allowed the screen door to bang behind him. The spring that managed the door hung uselessly by one end.

"I got you some Skreeno cards to play tonight," Sonny told Clara. He handed her 10 cards.

"Why thank you, honey," she said. "You didn't have to do that."

"Make sure you play these cards," Sonny said. "I've got a good feeling about these."

"Aren't you sweet."

Sonny never attended Skreeno night at The Glob, but he got Duck and Ink Ear to go with him that night. They found seats in the back row. Ink Ear immediately stuck his feet over the back of the seat in front of him.

The first feature was a sappy romance about a woman who falls in love on a boat and promises to meet her lover at the top of the Empire State building in a year. But she gets crippled and can't meet him and he goes looking for her and...

..."wasn't that the biggest piece of crap you've ever seen?" asked Duck. "If you're going to use the Empire State building in a movie you should have an ape hanging off it swatting at airplanes."

The house lights of The Glob came up and Andy Sloan's voice boomed from the back of the theater. "Ladies! Ladies and I see a gentleman. Is that you Howard Trickle? It's time for...altogether, SKREENO!"

The female audience joined Andy in shouting out the name of the game, but not Howard. He had slunk down in his seat. He reached over and pinched his wife Ellen, who had made him come with her.

"Damn you," he said to her.

"Get your cards ready! Here is the first game!"

On the blank white screen appeared the Skreeno wheel, numbered from zero to 60. The wheel began to spin. Around and around. Sound effects had been added to make a clicking sound as the large arrow that pointed at the numbers spun past each one. The arrow clicked past the number 17, then teetered, changed its mind and fell back.

"Seventeen!" boomed Andy. "Seventeen my lovely queen"

Andy liked to adorn each number with his own filigree. "Thirty-two, boo hoo hoo. Fifty-one. Get my gun. Six. Show me some tricks."

"Watch this," Sonny said, nudging Duck.

"Skreeno!" yelled a lady in the fifth row center. "Skreeno."

Sonny could see only the back of her head and it did not look like the same head Clara Miller used for her hats. The voice, also, was not the voice of Sonny's mother.

"We have a winner," boomed Andy Sloan, full of enthusiasm and delight. "Another happy homemaker. What are you going to do with that $5, Edna?"

The winner was not Clara Miller at all. It was Edna Rodenour, wife of Herbert Rodenour, of Rodenour and Wilson, Mortgage and Loans. His company held the leases on half the stores on Main Street. It also held the mortgage on Clara Miller's house.

Sonny could not see where his mother was sitting. She must be disappointed thought Sonny. I bet she was very close.

Another game began. Numbers were called. As soon as the minimum amount of numbers was selected the same voice shouted "Skreeno!" and Edna Rodenour had another $5. And then $5 more, and $5 more, until each time Andy Sloan called out the winner, his voice turned from animated support to barely concealed spite.

"Quite a night you're having, Edna," Andy snarled. "Give someone else a chance."

By the time the second feature had started, Edna Rodenour had won every Skreeno game. She folded the new, crisp $5 bills Andy Sloan had parted with more and more reluctantly. She creased them and stuck them in a side pocket of her purse. Never did a woman in Perry need $50 less than did Edna Rodenour. All the other ladies in the audience of the Glob for Skreeno night were very aware of the unfairness of it all. They were understandably bitter.

"She'll probably buy another jacket for her cat," said the Widow Neary.

"A mink jacket, probably," said Ethel Ethel.

As a result of the Impossible Rodenour Sweep, fewer and fewer women came to Skreeno after that and Andy Sloan had to drop the promotion. Bank Night was cancelled and a few months after that, The Glob was sold.

"Well, that was something," said Duck. "Did you ever see anyone have that much luck?"

"We should steal her purse," said Ink Ear. "We can follow her and when she puts it down, we'll just grab it. There's a fortune in that purse."

"A whole boat load," said Sonny.

When Sonny got home that night, Clara was seated at the kitchen table reading her favorite magazine, "Amazing True Crimes." Recounted in the magazine were stories of murder and sex, stories of white slavers and mob killings and police corruption. The cover of the magazine depicted a blonde woman screaming as dark hands choked her. All the covers, every month, showed a blonde woman being molested in some way.

"Where were you, Mom?" Sonny asked. "You weren't at Skreeno."

"Oh, honey," Clara Miller said. "I didn't go. I know you wanted me to and it was very nice of you to get me some cards. They came in very handy.

"Edna Rodenour came by to buy some eggs and while she was here I asked her if we could be late on our mortgage payment this month. Eggs haven't been selling so well and Ron has been...well, he had to get a tune up for his Dodge. And he's forgotten his Pledge, too."

Ron Miller had taken a sobriety pledge. Sonny had lost count how many pledges Ron Miller had taken.

"So Edna said she would ask Herbert but she didn't think he would let it go without a penalty. I was holding your Skreeno cards in my hand. She saw them and said she was going to The Glob and was I? I said I was but maybe she would like to have my Skreeno cards and we could pay the mortgage next month. She said okay and so I stayed home and read."

Clara picked up "Amazing True Crimes" and flicked the pages until she found the story she was reading, "Secret Sins of Hollywood."

Sonny was not going to tell his mother about Edna. She would find out soon enough.

"Why didn't you play, Mom?" Sonny asked. "Why? I gave you the cards. I told you to make sure you played."

Clara Miller lit another Camel. Her ship, as small as it might have been, would have come in that night at The Glob. She had no idea how many ships came in during a person's lifetime, but Clara had the feeling that this one was hers.

"You're right, Sonny," Clara said. "I should have kept the cards. I broke the chain."

Chapter 9

Fort Corsage

Sonny, Duck and Ink Ear were not in school the day the pine crates arrived at the Ohio Southern depot in Perry. Sonny left Old Soldier Gus Shiner mumbling to himself and went directly from the station to Ink Ear's house. The Ryans lived over the Morgans and the Morgans were not happy about it. The seven Ryan children fought and rattled and kept up a constant chaos in the five rooms over the heads of Richard and Pam Morgan, empty-nesters who thought the extra money that came with renting out the upstairs of their nine-room Victorian would help them save money for their old age. The Ryans were making the Morgans much older much faster than they wanted to be. And there was no extra money.

Woody Ryan was a good father. That is, he was good at fathering children, the count now being seven. He left their care to Dixie, his wife and their mother, who left their care pretty much to themselves. Dixie was pregnant again and stayed in bed most of the day. Dean Ryan took to heart his position as the oldest and was responsible for what little order there was.

Three times Richard Morgan had tried to get the Ryans evicted, citing non-payment of rent, breakage, hygiene and a general unfitness to be around decent folks. Sheriff John Brown had served the official papers. Or tried to. He had banged on the door. He had shouted and threatened. Each effort resulted in slashed tires on his squad car, a Mercury Montclair with a single blue light mounted on top.

Dean Ryan expected to spend a night in jail each time the sheriff came around. Dean didn't mind. He got his own bed and silence. But after the third visit, Sheriff John Brown stopped coming around. The Morgans moved to Loganville to live with their son Cecil and his wife Mona, an arrangement which was not satisfactory to anyone but the Ryans.

'Ink Ear! Ink Ear!" Sonny half whispered, half shouted. He leaned out from the landing at the top of the back stairs that led up to the Ryans living quarters and banged on the window of the room where Ink Ear slept with Dean, his younger brother Larry and, and on the nights that Woody Ryan was home, baby Winston.

Sonny banged on the window again.

"Is that you Sonny?'

Sally Ryan, a year older than Ink Ear, leaned out of the next window beyond. She had the same freckles as Ink Ear but a much smaller chin. She liked Sonny. Sonny tolerated Sally.

"Go wake up Ink Ear," Sonny told Sally. "Go get him to come out."

"I'm not going in that room," Sally said. "I'll die before I go in that room."

"Then knock on the door. Wake him up."

"Okay, Sonny. For you."

Moments later Ink Ear poked his head out the window. His hair stuck out from his head like fingers.

"Come on," said Sonny. "We got us a cannon."

"A what?"

"I'll show you. I'm going to go get Duck. Meet us at the fort."

The fort protected the town of Perry from any invaders and the boys could imagine all sorts, Indians, pirates, Mongol hordes. They were not sure exactly what either a Mongol or a horde was but Sonny, who knew his history, said most attacks came from hordes, and the worst kind were Mongols, so they had to be ready.

They had built their fort along the banks of the Jericho River, digging out the loose, sandy ground and reinforcing the sides with bed slats that used to hold up the inner springs and mattress of the Morgans' bed. The back wall of the fort was a door they had removed from an outhouse no longer used by Walter Gorby. The roof had a

102

single cross beam, an old railroad tie, and they had covered it with tree limbs and brush. The roof provided more shade than protection. To any outsider the fort was more a low-slung hut than a military stronghold but for the boys it was a firm, safe barricade from which they could check on any hordes that might be sneaking up on them or the town of Perry.

Sonny had named it Fort Courage, a name he may have heard in a western movie or read in a book. It sounded like a good name but he had made the mistake of letting Ink Ear paint the sign that identified the place to any enemy, foreign or domestic,

"Help me put it up," said Ink Ear. He was carrying a pole to which he had nailed a board with the freshly painted words, "Fort Corsage."

"Put what where?" asked Duck.

"Here at the corner. We'll pound this into the ground."

Duck held the pole while Ink Ear pounded it into the soft ground using one of the bricks the boys used to rest their guns on when they were shooting back at the hordes.

"Now it's official," said Ink Ear, urinating on the pole. "I christened thee Fort Courage."

Duck looked at the name on the board.

Fort Corsage. Sonny explained that it was not such a bad name, that corsages could be made of thorns and thistles, too, so Duck decided to let Ink Ear live. He would not have killed Ink Ear, of course, because Duck cared little about such things as spelling or the multiple meanings of words, but he liked to have reasons to harass Ink Ear.

"Don't you know anything?" Duck asked. "What kind of name is Fort Corsage? You think any Indian is going to be scared of a fort named after a bunch of posies? Do you think Davey Crockett would have died at someplace named Fort Posy? Do you think anybody ever yelled, "Remember the Posy?"

Having their very own real cannon in front of their fort would intimidate anyone who dared make fun of the name of the fort, even though no one ever did. They were the only boys who ever came to their fort and no matter how vigilant they were, how certain an attack might come at any moment, how proud they were to be the last barrier between Perry and destruction, the hordes never came either.

Sonny left it up to Duck to decide how to get the crate from the Ohio Southern depot to their fort. Even with three of them, they could not carry it. Possibly they could drag it or roll it end over end. But they did not want to damage whatever delicate works might be inside. If there was a gun sight on the cannon, it would not do to have it broken.

"The Flyer," said Duck. "We'll use the Flyer."

Duck no longer played with his wagon, a red Radio Flyer. It had been a present for his fourth birthday from his father Charlie, or so his mother Sarah told him. Presents were not given easily at the Stadlers and never from Charlie to Duck.

When Duck tried to hug Charlie and say thank you, Dad, Charlie Stadler grunted and pulled Duck's arms from around his neck. Duck loved the red wagon more than any other gift he had ever gotten.

The Flyer was used now to carry coal from the pile behind the Stadler house to the back porch. From there the coal would be transferred to a scuttle and carried into the house. Keeping coal ready for the stove was Duck's job. If Charlie Stadler never saw another lump of coal it would be fine with him.

Duck returned to the Southern Ohio depot with the Flyer. If Sonny could hold the crate and keep it balanced, they could move their cargo. They slid the box to the edge of the platform.

"Ready?" asked Duck. "On three."

Duck counted. "One, two, ugggg."

It was not as heavy as they imagined a cannon might be but it was heavy enough for them. Sonny's end sagged but he held it and they placed the box on the Flyer, balancing it across the bed of the wagon.

"You keep it from tipping off and I'll pull it," Duck said to Sonny. "Just keep it balanced. I'll do the hard part."

The crate tipped off only twice on the way to Fort Corsage, but they rebalanced it and continued on.

"Where's Ink Ear?" Duck demanded, after lifting the crate for the second time.

"I told him to meet us at the fort," said Sonny. "I should have said the depot."

"No, shit," said Duck. And they towed their load on.

The soft soil of the riverbank posed a problem. The Flyer's wheels dug in and refused to turn.

"Now what?" asked Sonny.

"I guess we push," said Duck.

They worried the crate off the Flyer onto the ground. Just then Ink Ear arrived, eating a green apple.

"Where you been?" demanded Duck.

"What you got there?" asked Ink Ear. Apple juice was drying on his chin.

"Something great," said Sonny. "We're going to have to slide it. You're going to have to help push."

"Why not use the Flyer?" Ink Ear asked.

"I'm gonna punch him, Sonny," Duck said.

With three of them pushing and tugging and squirreling the crate along, they reached Fort Corsage twenty minutes later.

"What's in it?" asked Ink Ear.

"What's it say?" asked Duck.

Ink Ear looked at the stenciled markings on the side of the crate.

"So?"

"Can't you read either?" demanded Duck. "It's a cannon. Maybe a howitzer. Ain't that right, Sonny."

"That's the plan," Sonny said.

"A cannon. Oh, boy," said Ink Ear. "A cannon. Where'd you get it?"

"They left two of them at the train station. I didn't think they'd miss one."

"And this one's ours," said Duck.

"Let's open it," said Sonny.

"What with?" asked Ink Ear.

Insight did not come naturally to Ink Ear Ryan. His questions were not always as perceptive as this one. Unless the boys planned to tear off the crate with their bare hands, tools were needed.

"Since you asked," said Duck, "you can go get...let's see, a hammer, a crowbar and anything else we might need."

Ink Ear knew exactly where to go. Richard Morgan had a full set of tools in his basement. The Ryans had pretty much adopted the tools as their own since the Morgans had left. The Ryans used the tools more to break things than to fix them.

"We can use this wood to fortify the fort," said Sonny, after Ink Ear had left. "There might be enough here so we can put on a real roof. This is our lucky day."

"Maybe we'll paint it. You know, we'll splotch it up and make it look like camouflage."

107

"They didn't have camouflage in the old West," Sonny said. "They had wood color, just one color, brown. "

"This is now, not then," Duck said. "You have to get up with the times. I say camouflage."

"I say brown."

"Camouflage."

"Brown."

The decorating disagreement had not been settled by the time Ink Ear returned with everything Duck had asked for. The crate rested on a small rise in the ground, a perfect place for a cannon to be.

"Maybe we should put it closer to the river," said Sonny. "To protect our flank from any water attack."

"You mean from pirates?" asked Ink Ear.

"Well, that's where pirates usually come from, the water."

"No, I think where it is gives us a better range," said Duck. "We can cover a lot more territory."

"The mongrel whores will have tanks," said Ink Ear. "They won't come on the water."

"The mongrel what?" asked Duck.

"The mongrel whores," said Ink Ear. "And parachuters and airplanes. I seen it in the newsreel."

"What about the pirate whores?" asked Duck, winking at Sonny.

"Pirates don't have whores. They don't even have a newsreel."

Sonny stepped off a distance from where the box rested. He looked right and left. He walked down towards the river. He looked upstream and downstream. He paced off an arc back towards the crate. This was a command decision and he was the general. He would decide.

"You can accomplish the same thing down by the river," Sonny said. "You can cover the same territory and get all the whores, plus you can get any boats that come by."

There had not been a boat on Jericho River as long as any of them had been alive. And the likelihood of any whore, mongrel or pirate, showing up at Fort Corsage was extremely remote. But Sonny was determined to be ready for anything.

"Who made you the general?" asked Duck.

"I've always been the general," said Sonny.

"What if I want to be the general?"

"Who found the cannon?"

Duck had to admit that Sonny had him there.

"Let's take a vote," said Ink Ear.

Sonny might have been the general but he was not a tyrant. Besides, he knew that Ink Ear always voted with him.

The final resting place of the Fort Corsage cannon would be with a field of fire over the river. The three of them again pushed and shoved the crate to a rise at the top of the riverbank.

They stepped back and studied the crate. Which end to open first? Or maybe open the top?

"Gimme the damned crowbar," said Duck as the two others pondered where to begin.

Duck jammed the beveled end of the crow bar under the top of the crate. He leaned on the bar and they heard a creak as one of the nails slid out of its place. Duck moved the bar down and creaked another nail out. He went around the crate until the top was ready to be lifted off. The three of them took a side and carried it over and leaned against the side of Fort Corsage.

They peered down into the crate. Still another container was inside. This one rested in asbestos wadding that kept it snug against the sides of the crate.

"That stuff is to protect the cannon," said Sonny. "It must be inside this other box."

"It's not going to be a very big cannon," said Duck, sounding disappointed.

Duck pried off a side of the crate and the boys slid the new container out onto the ground. The new container was not made of wood but of fiberboard. It had two latches on the side and one on each end. It reminded Sonny of his uncle Ernie's guitar case.

"Let's open her up," said Duck, flipping the two latches on the sides. Sonny and Ink Ear flipped up the latches on the ends.

The boys had not pushed the lid entirely open before the odor rushed at them, a sickly chemical barnyard smell. It was enough to make Duck cough. Sonny flipped the lid over, opening up the container.

Ink Ear, looking in from what would be the feet of Eldon Burley, screamed. Duck who had turned away to cough turned around and then jumped back. Sonny, peering in at Eldon Burley's head, stared and gulped.

None of the boys had ever seen a dead body before. Ink Ear had a brother and sister die in infancy but he did not see their bodies. Duck was a babe in arms at his grandmother's funeral. Sonny had drawn corpses before in his school notebook, usually with knives sticking them and blood gushing out, but he had never seen a real corpse.

The first genuine dead body any of them ever saw was Eldon Burley, lying in his shipping coffin, arms crossed over his chest, his shiny hair pasted down and one eye open.

It was like he was winking at them.

Chapter 10

Ashes to Ashes

The shipping crate containing the last earthly remains of Irene Burley rested on the platform of the Ohio Southern depot in Perry for three days before Roy Cannon fished an envelope from inside his mourning coat.

"What the hell is this?" Roy mumbled. He was about to toss it away. The envelope was a bit too thick to disregard. And he had saved it, so it had to be important.

When Roy saw the heading on one of the sheets of paper, "Instructions for the Interment of Mr. and Mrs. Burley," the fog in his head began to clear.

Roy had no clear recollection of the previous several days. He remembered telling Sarah Alderman at the graveside of her brother how sorry he was that Henry had passed on to his reward. Sarah said she would join him soon. She just knew it. Roy, already in the bag, told Sarah that was nice.

He finished the bottle of White Horse he had in the hearse, a black Buick Roadmaster with a grill of menacing chrome teeth. Ink Ear was afraid of the hearse. He thought of it as a monster that would chew up children and take them to the cemetery. The boys called it "The Black Beast," and their imaginations were aided by The Beast's snorting smoke from its tailpipe. In any funeral procession, the worst place to be was in the car directly behind The Beast. Mourners would dally and delay so as not to be there. The wisest ones simply took side streets to Perry Memorial Gardens and waited the arrival of Roy, The Beast and their loved one. More than one citizen of Perry had gone to his grave in a one-car funeral.

The boys often played among the tombstones of Perry Memorial Gardens, ducking behind the marble slabs for protection from Indian arrows and enemy gunfire. Ink Ear had once fallen into an open grave and Sonny and Duck had let him scream for 10 minutes before pulling him out.

Roy Cannon did not remember driving back from the Alderman graveside to the funeral home. He became aware of the world again three days later, regaining his senses in the preparation room shivering on the tile floor under a sheet that once had covered Henry Alderman. Roy was completely naked except for a steel and leather brace he wore on his left leg, a souvenir of childhood polio. When Roy drank, the leg did not hurt as much.

His clothes were scattered around the room, in no order, except for his shoes. They were placed neatly side-by-side under a metal folding chair and his black socks had been rolled together and stuck into the left shoe.

Roy picked up his underwear, sniffed, and tossed them away. He pulled on his pants, wriggled into his suspenders and found his shirt balled up in the wastebasket. The shirt was a stiff collared Arrow that took starch well. It was stained down the front. The dull purple smear had pieces of food sticking to the fabric. Roy had apparently had chicken and beets sometime in the last few days. He balled up the shirt and dropped it back were he had found it.

"My favorite shirt," he said.

His coat was half in and half out of the hand sink. It had been caught and kept from falling to the floor by the eye-washing faucet.

Funeral homes had eye-washing faucets to clear formaldehyde and other chemicals that might splash into a mortician's eyes when he prepared the body. Roy lifted his coat off the plumbing and noticed that it was still buttoned; four buttons each firmly in their holes. To remove his coat he had pulled it over his head, obviously, and while he was not a meticulous man, he had never done anything like that before.

114

"What the hell went on here?" he said aloud. He frowned and thought and could not remember.

Roy felt something thick though the cloth of the jacket, a two-ply worsted gabardine with nearly invisible pin stripes. He folded the lapels back and saw an envelope sticking above the left inside pocket. The gabardine was of such good quality and the cut so well done that Roy could carry things inside his coat without unsightly bulges.

The instructions for the internment of the Burleys included their date of arrival. A memo from the Saguaro Transport Company confirmed the method of shipment, by transcontinental rail to Columbus, and then by local rail to Perry. Roy checked the wall calendar next to the washbasin.

"Thursday. That's today," Roy said to himself. "At least I haven't missed it."

Roy had missed a full three days and pieces of two others, so it is understandable how he might foul up the date. He fished through the rest of the papers from the envelope and found a copy of the Burley's will, the bequest of their entire estate to The Mesa Friends of France. Inside a copy of the instructions to the Saguaro Transport Company was a smaller envelope on which appeared instructions written by Eldon himself: "To be opened and to be read at our service."

Without bothering with a clean shirt, Roy pulled his coat over his head, put on his shoes and

115

prepared to take The Beast to the Ohio Southern depot to meet the train.

As usual, he was late, and days later than he knew, but in his mind he was practically on time. The Ohio Southern train to Jericho was rolling on just the other side of Trestle 2. Roy could see a box on the platform.

"Ah," he said. "They're here."

Roy wheeled The Black Beast to a stop at the end of the station platform. He rolled the gurney from the back of The Beast and realized he might need help hoisting the crate. Roy saw Gus Shiner sleeping on the church pew.

"Gus, Gus," Roy poked Gus Shiner. "Gus, help me here with this box."

"Huh?" Gus awoke one eye at a time. "Who's that?"

"Roy Cannon. Now, help me and I'll give you five...I'll give you two dollars."

"Help you what?"

"Help me with this box."

"I already helped," said Gus. "I got nothing."

"You helped how? You helped unload the train? Gus, helped how?"

"Sumbitch didn't give me anything. I got a bad back, you know."

"Yes, yes. Just help me slide it onto the gurney. Two...three dollars if you help."

"Let me see the money."

Roy patted his coat. He felt the letter inside. He reached his hands into this trouser pockets.

Nothing. He patted his right rear pocket for his wallet. Not there.

"Gus, you know me. Roy Cannon. I'm good for it. Help me and I'll drive you back and get some cash."

"Drive me? In that?" Gus pointed at The Black Beast. "You're not getting me in that. I ain't going in that. I ain't going in that even after I've gone."

"Fine. Help me and I'll go bring the money back."

"Bring it first. I learned my lesson with the other sumbitch. Cash up front, that's what I say."

Roy looked at the crate. He eyed the gurney. How high would he need to lift the box? Five inches? Six? Maybe if he did it one corner at a time. Once on the gurney he could use its mechanics to lift the box to the back of hearse, the same as any coffin.

"Gus. If I tilt the crate back, would you at least then slide the gurney under it?"

"You still ain't got no money."

"Gus, I've got more money than you've ever spent in your life. Now, help me and I'll give you three…five dollars."

"Five dollars."

"Five."

With negotiations ended, Helen Burley was finally removed from the Ohio Southern depot platform. Roy Cannon did not return with five dollars for Gus Shiner and Gus decided he needed a new sleeping place if he was going to be taken advantage of every other week.

The Burleys' instructions included a bank draft for the funeral and two coffins, the choice at the discretion of the funeral director. Notice of their deaths and of the memorial service were to be posted in the Loganville Messenger. During the service the pastor at Perry Presbyterian was to read Eldon Burley's last message to the citizens of Perry. If the pastor deemed it newsworthy enough, he was to pass it on to the Loganville Messenger for publication.

Roy fingered the small envelope containing Eldon Burley's message. Maybe he should be the judge of whether it was newsworthy or not. He would consider it later.

The single crate did not seem large enough for two bodies but Roy assumed both of them were inside.

Roy pried off the pine boards very much as Duck had done the crate that held Eldon Burley but Roy was not surprised to find another container inside. He was surprised that he did not find two containers inside. Were the bodies in the same case, entwined in some sort of final, eternal love partnership? The instructions had specified two coffins.

Helen Burley was alone when Roy Cannon opened the shipping case. Whoever had handled her back in Arizona had done a fine job. She looked peaceful and pretty for an old woman, her wrinkles smoothed and her lips painted a moderate red. There would be little to do for Roy except to move her into a presentable casket. He calculated the amount he had been paid and decided that the 18-guage Cottage Rose would be just fine. The Cottage Rose was not the top of the line but it was not the bottom either. Eldon Burley could have a matching design, probably the Churchill Blue. Now, all Roy Cannon had to do was find Eldon Burley.

What were the possibilities? The pair could have gotten separated in transit. Freight to Perry was not something the Ohio Southern was used to handling. Roy called the railroad headquarters in Columbus.

"Yes," said the voice on the other end. "Two crates. Perry, Ohio. Delivered Thursday. Signed for by…I can't read the signature."

"Thursday? What day is this?" asked Roy Cannon.

"Today is Monday, the 21st."

"Two crates. And you don't know who signed for them?"

"It looks like…let's see. It's just a scrawl but I think it's Ray Gannon. Something like that."

"Roy Cannon?"

"It could be."

"You're sure?"

"No, I'm not sure. I told you it's just a scrawl."

"Today is Monday? That was Thursday? No. Today is Thursday. Are you playing games with me?"

"Sir, I am really too busy for this." Roy heard a click on the other end of the line.

Roy clicked his phone, and then clicked it again.

"Yes, Mr. Cannon?"

The local operator, Bonnie Carpenter, had been listening as she usually did. She and Ruth Wilkins placed all calls in and out of Perry though a Kellogg switchboard in an office above the First Bank of Perry.

"What day is it, Bonnie?" Roy asked.

"He was right, Roy," Bonnie said. "It's Monday."

Was it possible? Had he signed for the bodies, picked up one and left the other to be collected later? Gus Shiner had signed Roy's name. Gus had read, "Cannon" on the side of the crate and figured that was the thing to do.

Knowing his name had been forged might have helped Roy Cannon figure things out. Or it might have muddled them more. His mind was mush. Had he already processed Eldon Burley and put him into one of the caskets in the sales room? Jesus, he hadn't buried Eldon Burley with Henry Alderman, had he? Henry had a closed coffin. Eldon couldn't be in the cold room, could he?

Panicked, Roy Cannon covered all the possibilities he had just considered except for digging up Henry Alderman. If Eldon Burley were with Henry, then with Henry he would stay.

Roy opened every casket, looked in the cold room, looked under his own bed. There was no Eldon. Had Roy cremated him? Another possibility. The instructions said two coffins but Eldon would not be the first body Roy had sent to the furnace by mistake. Lionel Cribbs was reduced to ashes during one of Roy's more agonizing hangovers, a day with three funerals. Roy had not been able to remember which of the three bodies was for cremation and which two were not. He went eeny-meeny-miney and chose Moe, who happened to be Lionel Cribbs.

Apologies for burning the wrong body were not enough. A free funeral and a bribe of $500 was enough. The son, Jeff Cribbs, who had run away from Perry as a teenager and had returned for his father's funeral, agreed to a closed coffin with Hugo Sellers taking the place of Lionel. The Sellers family took Cribbs' ashes home where they still rest in an honored place in a curio cabinet with Kate Sellers' collection of porcelain farm animals.

Burned up. That had to be what happened. Roy checked the crematorium and found ashes. Maude Heskett had used the furnace to get rid of the remains of the large turkey Maude had fixed for Roy before he disappeared on his lost weekend. Roy poked through the ashes and bone fragments.

Roy Cannon concluded that he had cremated Eldon Burley.

He need not have fretted. The memorial service for Eldon and Helen Burley was paid for and thus it was held. The only mourner at the service for the Burleys was Gus Shiner, who had begun sleeping under the loading platform of the Cannon Family Funeral Home. Gus threatened never to leave until Roy paid him his $5.

Roy had not bothered to send a notice to the Loganville Messenger. He did not notify pastor Nance Weaver of the Perry Presbyterian Church.

The Burley Affair, as Roy Cannon came to think of it, should have been enough to cause Roy to stop drinking, to make him face his responsibilities, to cause him to become more punctual. But none of that happened. He continued to drink even more than he had and to be even later. However, Roy did have The Black Beast tuned so it no longer belched onto the mourners.

Eldon Burley had written his last message in French. Roy had it translated and decided not to share it with the town.

The empty coffin beside the one containing Helen Burley held only the last communication of Eldon Burley to the town of Perry, three words on an index card inside its own envelope. It was the only explanation for why the Burleys had returned to the town that hated them.

En enfer ensemble.

In hell together.

Chapter 11

Body in a Bottle

Eldon Burley's corpse winking at Sonny, Duck and Ink Ear coincided with the daily blare of the noon siren in Perry. It was hard to tell the sounds apart, except that Ink Ear's scream had a bit higher pitch, and it was interrupted by the deep breaths Ink Ear needed to take in to keep the sound going.

"Whooooooooooneee.   Reeeeeeeek! Whooooooooooneee! Reeeeeeek!"

If it been a contest, Ink Ear would have been the winner, at least for judges Sonny Tolliver and Duck Stadler. Both of them covered their ears and yelled at Ink Ear to shut up. Still, he screamed on.

The noon siren was a clear, non-stop wail, largely ignored by the town, other than to cause a vague awareness that it was officially midday and it was now time for lunch.

Dogs howled and chickens scattered each day at noon but the town carried on without much

124

interruption. The only significant disruption of routine was at the First Bank of Perry where head teller—the only teller, as a matter of fact—Virginia Heffner would close her window and take her lunch. It did not matter how many customers were in line or at what point in the transaction Virginia happened to be, when the noon siren went, so did she for a full half hour.

The eyes of each boy were fixed on the body of Eldon Burley, six eyes among them compared to the single open eye in the coffin.

By the time the siren ceased wailing so had Ink Ear, who was now whimpering, a noise that had nothing in common with the noon siren of Perry.

The original purpose of the noon siren was to alert not just Virginia Heffner but the farmers and town workers that it was time to eat. The purpose of Ink Ear screeching was to notify the world that he wanted nothing to do with whatever that thing was before him.

"Get it away! Get it away!" screamed Ink Ear. He fell back onto his rear end and began kicking at the container.

At other times of the day the siren meant the volunteer firefighters had to rush to the firehouse. Any fire that began exactly at noon enjoyed a good head start, which is what happened to the packing shed of Warner Pottery.

Yet there was a comfort to the daily wail, a shared awareness of the exact time of day, along with a reassurance that all was well. The siren was also supposed to alert Perry of danger, such as approaching tornadoes. Since there had never been a tornado in Perry, the noon noise was justified and considered a worthwhile annoyance.

Even if the siren and Ink Ear had not gone off at the same time, Ink Ear Ryan's reaction to the one-eyed cadaver of Eldon Burley would have seemed no more than the usual hoots and shouts that came from that area along the Jericho River. The boys were always howling and yelping as they held off Indians and pirates and nasty invaders that were out to do harm to the town of Perry. It never occurred to them that most of the harm done to Perry was done by Perry itself.

"Christ! Christ! Christ!" yelled Ink Ear. "Shit! Shit! Shit! Get it away, get it away!"

Ink Ears' kicking had cocked the container more upright so that Eldon Burley seemed to be sitting up. Eldon Burley's single open eye fixed on Ink Ear. No matter how Ink Ear twisted or turned away, it seemed to follow him.

"Get it away! Get it away!"

Ink Ear Ryan continued kicking at the container that held Eldon Burley, causing it to tip away from him and begin to slide from the top of the rise that Sonny had determined was the ideal place to install Fort Corsage's very own cannon.

"Wait, wait!" shouted Sonny. Ink Ear could not hear, or would not hear. Nothing was going to keep him from kicking at the container. It was as if it had teeth and was biting Ink Ear's pants leg. He had to get it off.

Duck slammed the lid on the container, the latches catching automatically, sealing in Eldon Burley again. Ink Ear was no longer kicking. The siren was no longer wailing. The container was no longer sliding.

"My god, my god," said Duck. "What is that? That's not a cannon. That's a dead body."

None of them had ever seen a dead person before. Dead animals, sure. All of them had cleaned squirrels and rabbits. Sonny had killed his share of chickens, chopping off their heads, a chore he did not enjoy. Sonny did not get the same enjoyment out of a headless chicken staggering out of control, as Duck seemed to. The whole chicken killing thing was also messy, all that blood spurting out, with no clue where or when the chicken was finally going to give up. Clara said the scattered blood helped to fertilize the grass but Sonny had his doubts.

Sonny had devised a way to make headless chickens cooperate. He put the chicken under a galvanized metal washtub, pulling the chicken's head out from the edge of tub. Sonny would grab the chicken by the beak and with a clean chop, off came the head. The chicken would then thump around inside the tub, thereby containing the mess. The death rattle of a chicken banging around under a metal washtub was very clearly a rattle. But chickens and squirrels were the extent of knowledge any of them had about death. None had any idea of what death looked like in human beings.

"Well, I guess it isn't a cannon," said Sonny, answering Duck's question.

"It's a zombie," said Ink Ear. "It's a zombie. I said, it's a zombie."

"What are we going to do with it?" asked Duck.

"Get it away! Get it away!" yelled Ink Ear.

"We could take it back to the depot. It must belong to somebody," said Duck.

"Nobody I've ever seen."

"You're right. I didn't recognize whoever that is. I didn't hear of anybody dying lately."

"What about Henry Alderman?"

"That was not Henry. That was not any Alderman."

Ink Ear could not believe he was listening to a calm discussion about the thing in the box. The thing in the box was still there, just under the lid, and it was still looking at him with one eye. He could feel it.

"Get it away! " yelled Ink Ear. "Whatever you do, get it away."

"Whatever *we* do?" asked Duck. "You are in this, too. *We* will do whatever we do."

Sonny nudged Duck with an elbow. He nodded his head towards the container.

"Wanna see it again?"

"No! No! No!" shouted Ink Ear.

"Let's look," said Duck.

The container was perched precariously on the knob of sand after Ink Ear's kicking. It rocked slightly as Duck and Sonny unfastened the latches again. Duck carefully peeled back the lid.

Eldon Burley was as he was last seen, arms folded, eye open. Ink Ear refused to look.

"He has to be somebody," said Sonny. "Somebody must be expecting him."

"Let's take him back," said Duck.

"Let's touch him," said Sonny. "Ever touch a dead person?"

"I ain't never seen a dead person."

"Me, too."

Sonny reached out his hand, one finger extended. He poked Eldon Burley on the shoulder. Sonny jumped back.

"What?" asked Duck.

"He moved."

"What? He can't move."

"Zombies can move," said Ink Ear.

"Let me do it," said Duck. With his fist closed, Duck punched Eldon Burley on the shoulder. Nothing. Again, a little harder.

"I heard something," said Ink Ear. "He said something."

"He said—ooooooooooo." Duck lunged at Ink Ear, his arms sticking straight out, his hands made into claws just like in the movie "The Mad Ghoul." "He said, 'I want some ears, some Ink Ears'."

"Jesus, Duck, Jesus. Get away!"

"He's dead. See."

Duck grabbed Ink Ear and forced him to the edge of the container. Ink Ear shook and squirmed, trying to get away. Ink Ear reached out and grabbed the lid of the container, slamming it down. The latches clicked. The box slid forward, slipping towards the river. Before either Sonny or Duck could stop it, it had slid down the bank to the Jericho River, splashing into the water, nose first. It bobbed and righted itself and began drifting down stream.

"Crimeny sakes, Duck. It's in the river," yelled Sonny. "It's floating away."

"I'll get it!" Duck yelled and jumped into the mixture of sewage and sulfur and acid runoff that was the Jericho River. Duck was a strong swimmer. He managed to get an arm on the container, but there was no easy way to hold it. His arm slipped off. Duck tried to swim it to shore, using the back of his shoulders and kicking with his feet, but the current carried it further out into the river, along with Duck.

"Let it go!" shouted Sonny. "Let it go!"

The boys had to admit that Eldon Burley, a man they had never met officially, was very seaworthy. The last they saw of the container, it was bobbing along towards Shiloh, the next town downstream along the Jericho River.

Duck pulled himself out of the water and crawled up the riverbank, spitting and wiping his eyes.

130

"Don't ever let me do that again," said Duck. He coughed something from his throat and spat it to the ground.

Duck stood dripping silently onto the sandy bank of the Jericho River. Ink Ear looked from Duck to Sonny and back, waiting instructions. Sonny stared after the drifting container.

"Nobody knows we took it," Sonny said.

"What about Old Soldier?"

"He can't remember yesterday."

"So you say let it go? Do nothing?"

"No, not exactly nothing. "

Sonny cupped his right hand and brought it up to his right eyebrow, a perfect military salute.

Sonny had read about Viking funerals and this was sort of like one of those. No fire, of course, but he could see one in his imagination. He had read of burials at sea, and thought such a thing was an honorable and patriotic end. This was like that, too. Sonny snapped his hand down to his side in a final salute to Eldon Burley.

The other two boys did the same.

"Farewell," Sonny said. "You were a brave soldier and we will miss you."

"I won't miss him," said Ink Ear.

"You mean he was a brave sailor," said Duck.

"No. Soldier. He was a member of the troop of Fort Corsage."

"But he came in a boat and he left in a boat. He never got out of the boat."

Sonny nodded, conceding that Duck had a point.

"Sail on, good sailor," said Sonny.

"Good riddance," said Ink Ear. "I still think he was a zombie."

Sonny had read about bottles washing ashore with messages inside, bottles that came from far away places. No bottle Sonny had ever collected at the banks of the Jericho River had anything inside except crud. He had put messages in bottles and tossed them into the water, imagining the journey it would take. Down the Jericho River to the Muskingum to the Ohio to the Mississippi to the Gulf of Mexico to...was the Gulf Stream in the Gulf? I had to be; otherwise it would not be called the Gulf Stream.

He imagined his bottle finding a whole new river in the ocean and going wherever the current and the wind would take it. Sonny now imagined Eldon Burley doing the same.

Eldon Burley never made it to exotic lands or even as far as Shiloh. He barely made it out of Perry. The boys would learn that soon enough.

"Why did the moron kick the casket," Duck asked.

"Why did he?" asked Ink Ear.

"Because he's a moron," said Duck.

After that day, playing war along the river seemed to lose its appeal to Sonny, Duck and Ink Ear. Pretending to shoot each other and pretending to be dead was no longer as fascinating as it once was. Fake death didn't seem as much fun after seeing the real thing. From then on they ignored Fort Corsage, leaving Perry at the mercy of pirates and mongrel whores, none of whom ever came.

Chapter 12

Original Son

It was Duck's idea to find Sonny's father. Neither Ink Ear nor Duck could recommend the fathers they had, yet it seemed to Duck that if they had to have one, Sonny should have one, too.

"You have to know who he is," said Duck. "Even if he's chicken shit."

"I don't care," said Sonny. "I really don't care."

"Sure you do," said Ink Ear. "How can you not care?"

"It just doesn't matter to me. What good will it do to know?"

"Get his side of the story," said Duck.

"I don't know either side of the story," said Sonny.

"Maybe he's a bank robber, or a killer. Maybe he's in prison," said Ink Ear. "Maybe he's a war hero. Maybe he's a cowboy. Wouldn't you want to know what he is?"

"I know he doesn't give a shit about me," said Sonny.

"Jesus," said Duck. "You sound like Jesus."

"What? What do you know? What are you talking about? Jesus."

Without really wanting to be, Duck was the Bible expert among the three of them. His mother Sarah never missed the Sunday radio sermons of Warren Lund, the Man with the Word. Sarah read the gospels aloud, taking various voices and gesturing when necessary. She was particularly passionate on the cross, sometimes breaking into tears. Matthew was her favorite.

"Yeah, Jesus," said Duck. "Why have you forsaken me? Jesus didn't have a dad, not really."

"Yeah, and when he found him, look what happened."

"You guys are both crazy," said Ink Ear. "Jesus."

The easiest thing to do would be to ask Clara about Sonny's father. After all, she was there. And Sonny had asked her at least a hundred times. Ron Miller was not Sonny's father and Clara had never tried to pretend he was. But she told Sonny nothing about his real dad.

"When you're old enough," Clara said.

Sonny had asked those things that Ink Ear wondered about. What was he? Where was he? Did his mother know who he was?

"I know exactly who he is," said Clara. "And he knows exactly who you are. I will tell you all about it when you are old enough."

"When will that be?"

"When you're old enough."

Sonny let the matter rest there. He gave it less and less thought the closer he got to being old enough. From what he saw of Charlie Stadler and Woody Ryan, fathers were not so much anyhow. They were mean or drunk or not around. Maybe all three."

"Let's find him," said Duck.

"Let's find who?" Sonny asked.

"Your dad. Your real dad."

"Sure, why not?" Sonny said.

"Jesus Christ," said Ink Ear.

Being a bastard had been, all in all, okay with Sonny Tolliver. Compared to the gift of life, the inconveniences were hardly worth mentioning.

His mother Clara explained her part in Sonny's existence: "I didn't flush you down the toilet. There's lots of them that did."

The first flushing toilet Sonny came across, in the lavatory of Perry Elementary School, fascinated him. He pulled the handle over and over to watch the water swirl around and be sucked down into the hole at the bottom. Sonny was certainly glad that Clara had not flushed him down one of those.

Through the first and second grades Sonny sat cautiously on the lavatory toilet seat, as unhappy to be there as he was to be seated in the Miller outhouse. Nothing pecked at his bottom as did the flies in the outhouse, but the idea that babies might be down there pushed Sonny to do his business as quickly as possible.

After a while Sonny grew comfortable being seated where babies might have been flushed but he took the precaution of not flushing after himself, just in case a baby might be climbing back up. He did not want to be the one to send it back down the hole. The hole was very small and the babies would have to be very small but babies were small, weren't they?

How did his mother know that lots of mothers flushed babies? Had she watched it being done? Had she thought about it herself and wanted to know how to do it? Was there a place mothers went to do it? Sonny had a picture in his mind of a column of mothers lined up at a common toilet, each one taking turns dropping a baby in and then flushing, the water rushing over the baby and the hole sucking it down.

The final gurgle of the flush, Sonny always imagined, was a baby shouting. Sonny Tolliver could not tell you where babies came from, but he could tell you where they went.

Yes, he was very glad that his mother had not flushed him down the toilet.

Being a bastard mattered little to Sonny then. His friends, Duck and Ink Ear, had no problem with it. They seldom used the term "bastard" in

137

calling him names. Their vocabularies were large enough for their uses. The three of them could happily insult one another with the words they knew and understood. Usually one would call the other an "Asshole," or "Chicken shit," which was Duck's favorite.

Bastard was beyond them, in any sense, personally or officially. Sonny had always been a bastard, from birth, from a time when the term was a legal designation rather than a social slur.

Being a bastard was his father's fault, as is nearly always the case, though his grandfather tended to blame his mother. Grandpa Tolliver never warmed to Sonny much, but the old man became resigned to the disgrace of Clara, his second to eldest daughter, after subsequent bastards arrived, two more of them, Sonny's cousins in shame.

One of Sonny's cousins had the same name as his grandfather, Vernon, an honor that made little difference to either of them. By the time little Vernon came along Grandpa Vernon had withdrawn from parenthood and from grandparenthood as well. He tended to disappear for long periods of time, leaving his wife Alma with the dishonor of her daughters and the growing clutter of illegitimate grandchildren. Alma tolerated the grandchildren, maybe she even loved a couple of them, but, like Vernon, Alma would have preferred that they have fathers.

Vernon Tolliver was the father of seven children, six daughters and one son. The females were known as the "Tollivers," as if they were a collection, or like a table setting from Warren's Fine China, each piece the same and yet with different uses.

The oldest, Evelyn, was a dinner plate, larger than the others. Clara, next in age, was a saucer, the smallest. Florence was a salad plate, Belle a bread dish, Patti a soup bowl, and Sylvia, the youngest, a teacup. They were all of one design, dark haired and brown-eyed, with small pouting mouths and straight thin noses. If they had been china they would have been saved for company. As it was, they were everyday girls and they picked up a few chips and nicks along the way.

The only Tolliver son, Wilbur, was called "Wib" and he left home at 16 to join the Army, lying about his age. Uncle Wib became a career army non-com and remained for Sonny a romantic figure, a comic book soldier holding off the hordes. Wib was, in fact, a supply sergeant who ran a black market of boots and powdered eggs, depending on his posting.

Sonny never saw Grandpa Tolliver laugh, never saw him enjoy himself in any way. Their first meeting came when Sonny was five, two years after his mother had married Ron Miller. Vernon had finally allowed Clara back into his house at the same time Vernon was in the house. Generally

Vernon would be absent when Clara brought Sonny by.

Vernon was in the parlor, fiddling with a large Philco console radio, taking tubes out, putting tubes in. He poked his head out from the back of the console when Sonny bounded up, full of energy and curiosity.

"Hi, I'm Sonny."

Vernon examined Sonny over the pair of half glasses that rested on the bridge of his nose. He lowered his head slightly, the better to see over the glasses. Sonny beamed back at his grandfather. Vernon shrugged, his interest in Sonny not nearly matching the boy's interest in him.

"What you doing?" Sonny asked.

Vernon said nothing. He turned his face back to his task.

"Can I help?"

Vernon leaned out from behind the radio again. He stared at the small boy who had been dressed by his mother in a sailor suit with white knee socks and Buster Brown shoes. Clara had found the clothing at the Little Echo Resale Shop, a second-hand store specializing in children's clothes. Clara had washed, starched and ironed it herself. Sonny thought it scratched him and had already pulled the shirt out of the short pants. Clara had combed his hair, slicking down a cowlick with her own saliva. Sonny's elbows were scabbed and one of his shoes was untied.

"We have a radio," Sonny said.

"A Philco?" These were the first words he had ever heard his grandfather say. Vernon's voice was thin and his throat seemed to need clearing.

"A plastic one," said Sonny.

"Hold this," Vernon said, offering Sonny a screwdriver.

Vernon Tolliver was a handsome man, though Sonny had no way of judging such a thing. Stubble covered a square jaw and graying hair drooped over his forehead. Sonny noticed a tattoo on each of Vernon's forearms, one of a girl in a grass skirt and the other a ship's anchor with a ribbon streaming each way from the top of the shank. On one piece of ribbon was the word "Honor," and on the other was etched the word, "Victory." Even at five, Sonny could read and he sounded out the syllables in his head.

"Take it," Vernon said again, thrusting the screwdriver at Sonny.

Sonny took the screwdriver and immediately pretended it was a sword. He waved it and poked it at Vernon.

"Gimme that," Vernon took back the screwdriver and dropped it to the floor. "Go sit somewhere."

Sonny took one step back. He ran a finger up his right nostril.

"Don't do that." Vernon reached out and smacked Sonny's hand.

Sonny's lower lip began to quiver.

"Don't you cry."

141

Sonny tightened his lips, drawing them into a thin line. A trace of a tear collected in his left eye.

"You gonna cry?"

Sonny chewed at the inside of his lower lip, considering the question. He picked up the same screwdriver Vernon had taken back. Sonny jammed it into the mesh that covered the radio's speaker. The screwdriver handle sticking out made the radio front look like a face with a long nose. The two main knobs served as eyes.

"Funny face, funny face," said Sonny. He began to laugh. Sonny pointed towards the radio, and Vernon thought he was pointing at him.

"Ha, ha, ha, funny face."

Vernon was not a particularly vain man but he was not going to take any sass from this brat. He scrambled to his feet and lurched towards Sonny, trying to grab him by the wide collar of his sailor's shirt. Sonny easily dodged his grandfather's hand and stuck his tongue out. Vernon knelt down, put his left hand on his chest and began coughing. Sonny backed away, his eyes never leaving the man with graying hair and half glasses.

"You little bastard," Vernon yelled at Sonny. "The next thing you know, you won't know nothin'."

Sonny backed until he felt the door behind him. "I'm not little," Sonny said. "I'm five."

Those were the last words Sonny heard his grandfather Vernon say, words that were spoken directly to Sonny. In the few visits Clara made where Vernon was present, he heard his grandfather's voice, generally angry and raspy. Vernon would die of throat cancer before Sonny was seven. His mother cried nearly every time Clara visited Vernon's house, but she did not cry at Vernon's funeral.

Ron Miller tolerated his stepson Sonny and had offered to adopt him. Ron considered the offer more than generous considering that he had not known that Sonny came along with the black-haired beauty he had just married.

Their honeymoon in Atlantic City was the happiest either one of them would ever be with the other. Ron spun tales of his importance not just to the Perry Pottery but also to the whole of the American ceramic industry. Without Ron Miller, the quality and superiority of the American cookie jar would not be what it was. And without Ron Miller, foreign intrusion would be unchecked. Ron Miller was the protector and defender of Perry's place in the world of ceramics.

Clara listened to Ron as if she believed him. She was happy to have a husband and he was happy to have someone who did not mind him being short and balding.

In truth, Ron Miller was just another clay covered worker. He ran the jigger and jolley at Perry Pottery and worked for wages that had not increased in two years. He steamed off wallpaper on the side and delivered groceries on weekends for the IGA in Loganville. Whatever he was not, Ron Miller was a hard worker.

On the way home from their honeymoon in Atlantic City, Clara told Ron they had to stop at Bernadine Sawyer's in Loganville so she could pick up some things she had left there. Ron waited in his Dodge Town Wagon for Clara.

Bernadine Williams had been Clara's good friend since both of them had quit school after the eighth grade. They met the world together, working as house cleaners, looking for love. Bernadine found and married Clint Sawyer, a traveling shoe salesman from Loganville and had yet to regret it. After Vernon had kicked out Clara for being pregnant with Sonny, Bernadine allowed Clara to stay with her in the Sawyer's 33-foot Royal Mansion, an all-aluminum mobile home that was permanently immobile in a trailer park on the outskirts of Loganville. Shoe sales kept Clint away from home much of the time and Bernadine was happy to have the company. She had assisted Doc Tedrow in delivering Sonny, using the fold-down couch in the Royal Mansion as a delivery bed.

Ron Miller knew of Sonny but he thought the boy belonged to Bernadine, so when the little three year old jumped onto the seat beside Ron while Clara said good-bye to her good friend, Ron humored him.

"Got your nose," said Ron, pulling the oldest gag ever.

144

"That's your thumb," said Sonny, unimpressed.

"You go to school?"

"Not yet."

"What do you do?"

"I stay with Mommy."

"Is your mommy good to you?"

"She's okay."

"You better go see her."

"She's coming."

"Go on. Get down." Ron Miller leaned over and opened the door, nearly catching Clara who had just reached to open it.

"Come and get him," Ron yelled to Bernadine. "We're leaving now."

Clara turned to her friend. She waved.

"Good luck," yelled Bernadine, and went back into her house.

Sonny had climbed into the back of the Town Wagon and was inspecting the equipment Ron Miller used for steaming off wallpaper.

"What's this?" Sonny asked, holding the hotplate up to Ron.

"That's what I would like to know," said Ron Miller.

"Ronnie, honey, I have something to tell you," said Clara Tolliver Miller.

Chapter 13

The Dad End Road

Duck's interest in Sonny's father grew and grew once the boys had decided to find him. Sonny could not understand why Duck cared so much.

"Maybe he's a good one," said Duck.

"A good what?" asked Ink Ear.

"I wasn't talking to you," said Duck. "I mean maybe he's a good dad."

"How good could he be?" asked Sonny. "I'm here and he's not. He's never been here and he never will be."

"You don't know that," said Duck.

"Know what?" asked Ink Ear.

"You mean maybe he's a better dad than Charlie," said Sonny.

"Wouldn't he have to be?"

"Is Woody better than Charlie? Ink Ear doesn't think any more of him than you do of Charlie."

"Think about who?" asked Ink Ear.

"Woody doesn't bat Ink Ear around."

"That's because Ink Ear is too quick. Look at Ink Ear's mom sometime if you want to know."

"My mom," said Ink Ear. "My mom."

"Every dad can't be a chicken shit," said Duck.

"What if he's worse?"

"Then we'll know. You'll know. First we have to find him."

Sonny understood. Sort of. To Duck finding Sonny's father was another adventure. And what greater adventure is there than learning who you are, where you came from? But it was more than that. Sonny thought that what Duck really wanted to find was a better father than the one he had.

On the night Duck was born, Charlie Stadler was trapped under 10 feet of slate with just enough air and with just enough hope to keep him from losing his mind. Charlie was used to tight places but he had never been in one quite so tight.

He had heard the creak and the splitting of the support beam behind him. The seam of coal he was working was nearly played out and he had told Gene Welch, his foreman, that it was not worth the effort to crawl back in.

"Don't back talk me," said Welch.

"Then you go, you want it so bad," Charlie said.

"This is what you do you little ferret. It's why you have this job. Now go do it."

Charlie Stadler checked his lamp, hitched his pants, raised his pick and made a chopping motion at Gene Welch. Then, like a weasel down a rabbit hole, Charlie slid on his side back into a tight, black crevice to dig some more coal for the Brighter Day.

Now Charlie could not move. His cheek was pressed against a slab of rough, wet slate. His miner's hat had tumbled somewhere on the other side of him. The carbide lamp still burned and he could see the shadow of his own head dancing on the wall as the light flickered. No part of his body seemed crushed and he had air. Charlie thought, so, I'm going to die for nothing, for a played out seam. I'm going to die with my hands pinned, crud in my mouth, dust in my lungs and shit in my underwear.

Charlie Stadler was not thinking that he would never see his son, the baby that was due any day. He was not thinking of his unborn child at all. He thought only that he had helped dig his own grave, a wasted irony that gave him no comfort. The flame of his carbide lamp still burned, meaning there was enough air and he could hear scrapping and swearing on the other side of the shale wall, meaning someone knew he was there.

His ordeal was much briefer in time than it was in his mind. Charlie Stadler was pulled out in less than four hours and allowed to leave his shift early. On the way out, Gene Welch stopped him and handed him a note. A call had come for him, notifying him that he was the father of a boy. Sarah had named the child Donald. Eight pounds, eight ounces.

"That's a big turd." Charlie said to Gene Welch. He balled up the paper and pitched it in the general direction of the entrance to the main shaft of the Brighter Day.

Little Donald could not be blamed that he forever reminded Charlie Stadler of the day he nearly died, that Charlie could never separate the new life of his energetic, happy little boy from that black and bleak coffin under the ground. Charlie had been saved, yet he was left with the knowledge that the coffin waited for him every day. Maybe Charlie should have been determined that no son of his would ever have to go into the mines, to never have to face what he had survived. But Charlie Stadler did not think that. He thought, if it ever came down to the two of them, better the kid than him. If he could sacrifice Donald he would and until he could he would chip away at him with the broad miner's belt that hung on a hook by the basement door.

Neither Charlie nor Donald understood the ache between them. They only knew a pain was always there. Charlie reached for his belt and Donald stopped crying when he was seven years old.

Charlie asked for the riskiest jobs at the mine and he took the hazard pay that came with them to stock a liquor cabinet that always seemed to need restocking.

"I bet your real dad wears suspenders," said Duck Stadler to Sonny Tolliver. "Not a belt."

Sonny had read about the need to know, about the quest for knowledge. Needing to know was in every other book he picked up. He was all for it, all for knowing. He thought to himself, what if Columbus had not needed to know what was on the other side of the world? Or if the Wright Brothers didn't need to know if man could fly? The need to know was responsible for progress, for the advancement of civilization, for the development of man over beast.

"All except the cockroach," said Sonny out loud.

"What are you talking about?" asked Duck.

"The cockroach doesn't need to know where the sugar is. He just does."

"You think your dad is a cockroach? If anybody's dad is a cockroach, it's my dad. He crawls around in the dark all day."

"What I mean is you can get along just fine without knowing things. Look at Ink Ear."

Ink Ear Ryan knew what he knew and what he didn't know didn't matter. He always knew where to find the sugar.

"You're right," said Duck. "If anybody is a cockroach, it's Ink Ear."

Ink Ear Ryan put his hand up the side of his head and wiggled his fingers as it they were the antennae of an insect.

"Your dad should see you get your prize," said Duck. "He should see us Pass Through the Gate. He should be there for that."

"Us?"

"I mean you. Me, too."

"Will Charlie be there?" asked Sonny. Charlie Stadler was never anywhere for any success Duck had at anything. Duck broke the Perry Little League record for home runs without Charlie seeing a one of them.

"Your dad can be there for both of us."

"I'll tell you what," said Sonny. "If we find my dad, you can have him."

But where to start? Clara had all the secrets and she wasn't talking. Ron Miller maybe knew, but considering he had not known that Sonny was Clara's boy, he was probably a dry well. Grandpa Vernon and Grandma Alma wanted to forget what they knew.

"Ask an aunt," said Duck.

"Which one?"

"The one who doesn't like your mother the most."

That would be Evelyn, the oldest and the largest. She had resented Clara since childhood because all the attention that was supposed to go to her as the oldest girl went instead to Clara, the cutest girl. Vernon Tolliver would bounce Clara on his knee but only pat Evelyn on the head. Evelyn had to wash and clean and Clara only had to dust. Because Evelyn was chubby, her clothes had to be resized in order to be handed down to Clara. Their mother Alma did the cutting and sewing without complaining. What was worse for

Evelyn, what really chapped her already chapped thighs, was that the clothes always looked much better on Clara than they ever had looked on Evelyn.

Evelyn had married a good man, a better man than Clara's Ron Miller. He was bigger than she was, and even Evelyn made fun of his weight. Dan Weller had always been fat and he had always been kind. Evelyn only saw the fat and could not get past the fact that she had to settle for Dan Weller, one of the few men who had ever given her any serious attention.

Evelyn's great advantage over Clara was that Dan was successful, much more successful than Ron Miller. Dan Weller was one of the few men in Perry who met the second half of the town slogan of Happiness and Prosperity. Clara, in her own way, met the first half. Clara always seemed happy for no apparent reason. Evelyn could not forgive her for that either.

Dan Weller owned the Matterhorn, a combination restaurant, dance hall and bowling alley. The 'Horn served as the social center of Perry, a lunchroom for school children and mothers in the daytime, a 12-lane recreation hall on league nights and an address for fine dining and dancing on weekends.

The Matterhorn was also the meeting hall for the Women's Library Club of Perry, a group that Evelyn was hoping she would be asked to join.

Evelyn presided over it all from a glass-walled office at the back of the dance floor, triple glazed and soundproofed to muffle the noise of clattering bowling pins.

Dan Weller had not given Evelyn any children, which is the way Evelyn looked at it. If she had permitted a medical examination into the reason, Evelyn would have discovered that she was the cause, not Dan. After several years of marriage, and after assuming positions that allowed two fat people to try and make a baby, positions Evelyn found degrading, Evelyn simply stopped allowing Dan to try. Her attention was given to the Matterhorn and her affection now was directed at two small dogs, a Bichon Frise and a Brussels Griffon, each of which wore sweaters Evelyn had knitted.

Whenever Sonny had visited Evelyn and Dan Weller the two dogs would not stop yapping, not even when he gave them the meat treats that he always brought.

"Bitches, just like Evelyn," Clara Tolliver would say.

If anyone was going to spill the secret of Sonny's birth, it would be Evelyn. She cared almost as little for Sonny as she did for her sister. She had forbidden Dan Weller to give Sonny a job setting pins in the bowling alley, though Dan gave him the job anyhow. Evelyn never visited the bowling side of the building and she certainly never went down into the dark noisy pits where the pins were reset and the bowling balls were returned.

"This is just between us," Dan reminded Sonny each time he paid Sonny the going rate for pinsetters, seven cents a line and a quarter a set.

"I wish my mom had married you," said Sonny.

"Me, too," said Dan Weller.

On the day that Sonny decided to ask his aunt Evelyn about his mother, Dan was at the shoe counter at the Matterhorn. The shelves behind him were lined with bowling shoes, blue and green and orange. The shoe size was indicated on the tan back heel in red paint. Dan was spraying disinfectant into the shoes, turning his head away each time he spritzed. He replaced a 7 on a shelf and took down a 7-½ woman's.

"I need to talk to Aunt Evelyn," Sonny told Dan.

"I'm not sure that's a good idea," said Dan. "She's been a little bit cranky lately."

Sonny thought he understood why Evelyn was cranky. It was Ink Ear's fault. Evelyn had barred Ink Ear from the Matterhorn because he had unscrewed all the caps on the saltshakers before a luncheon of the WLCP and ruined every salad except that of chairwoman Ethel Ethel, who was restricting her sodium. Ink Ear would not have been caught but he had to stay and see the results of his deed. He was hiding behind the jukebox when Edna Rodenour dumped salt all over her iceberg lettuce with Thousand Island dressing. Six other members of the Perry Women's Library Club had piled their vegetables with mounds of salt when Ink Ear's high-pitched giggle brought Evelyn Weller directly to him. She grabbed him by the very ear he had once inked and dragged him into the street.

"And don't you ever come back," shouted Evelyn.

"It was worth it, you bitch," yelled Ink Ear, agreeing with Clara Tolliver.

The reasons for Evelyn's general unhappiness were more complicated than Sonny could imagine, but he did not care about any of that. He knew he had to start his investigation into the identity of his father someplace and Aunt Evelyn seemed as good a place as any to begin. He could see Evelyn in her glass-walled office, filling her desk chair completely, her elbows on her desk, her head in her hands, her fingers scratching under the edges of a jet black wig she thought no one knew she wore.

Sonny knocked on the door. Evelyn looked up. She immediately pointed a finger at Sonny and began wagging it at him. He could not hear her because of the triple glazing and soundproofing but her lips moved rapidly and the fat under her right arm jiggled as she waved her finger. The two small dogs had woken up from the beds Evelyn had for them and the Griffon began yapping. Sonny pushed the door open just slightly.

"...and your whore mother, too!"

Sonny pulled the door shut and backed away, just as he had from Grandpa Vernon. Why was he always backing away from his relatives? Sonny concluded that Aunt Evelyn might be a treasure chest of information, but like a nickel stuck to the floor of The Glob, it was hardly worth the trouble of getting.

"Then we're just going to have to look some place else," said Duck when Sonny reported the Evelyn Incident to him. Duck was more disappointed in Sonny's failure than Sonny was.

"To hell with it," said Sonny. "Just forget it."

"Did Audrey Murphy forget it?" asked Ink Ear.

"What? Who? Audrey who?" Duck was very close to giving Ink Ear a noogie.

"To hell and back," said Sonny, proud of Ink Ear.

"If we have to, then that's where we'll go," said Duck. "But I think we ought to start in your mom's bedroom."

Clara Tolliver was not an immaculate housekeeper. Not in her own house. Maybe it was because she had cleaned so many other houses that she allowed hers to display a natural clutter. She emptied her ashtrays at the end of each day but any other routine depended on her whims. Baskets of clothes to be ironed sat on a trunk in her bedroom. Sonny knew that the trunk was not locked even though a metal latch plate with a keyhole seemed designed to keep the lid secure. He had seen his mother whack the plate with the heel of her hand. It would fall out and hang, leaving the lid to be opened easily.

Sonny had never seen inside the trunk but he was sure that any evidence of her life before Ron Miller had to be kept there. Sonny thought of it as their trunk, not just Clara's trunk, and it took very little urging from Duck Stadler to agree to search it.

"I bet it's all there. Who he is. Where he is. I bet there are pictures," Duck said.

"Then you do it," said Sonny. "Only don't steal anything."

"I'm not doing it. You do it. She's your mother," said Duck. "It's your life. I bet everything we want to know is in there."

"We? Everything *we* want to know? I don't want to know anything. I'm happy knowing nothing."

"Sonny, he's your dad. You have to know about him."

"He knows about me," Sonny said. "It's up to him."

"Shit," said Ink Ear. "I'll do it."

"No you won't," said Sonny.

"I don't mind. I'll do it."

"I'll do it," said Sonny. "I guess I have to."

Opportunity is never convenient. For days the boys kept alert for a time when Clara Tolliver would be away or when she was occupied with the chickens or with the washing so that Sonny could keep his promise to see what was in Clara's trunk.

157

"You keep her busy and I'll go do it," said Ink Ear.

"You're not doing anything," said Sonny. "I said I'll do it. I'll do it."

Clara was only slightly curious about why the three of them, who never hung around the Tolliver house, came directly home from school and hung around the Tolliver house. They played marbles, using the dead zone where Sonny and Ron urinated nightly, scratching out circles and lines in the dirt and then smelling their fingers.

"Smells like piss," said Duck.

"You would know," said Sonny.

They played mumblety-peg, using Sonny's Kutmaster pocketknife. The knife had a stag handle, one long blade, a bottle opener, a screwdriver and a leather punch. Sonny had used all of the blades except the punch. Duck won every game because he dared to throw the knife the nearest to his own foot. He could drop the knife from the top of his head, from the back of his hand, even between his teeth. Duck was fearless. And the knife always stuck into the ground for Duck.

Finally, Clara announced that she needed to take some eggs to Margaret Clory, a shut-in who lived a half mile away. She usually asked Sonny to do it but Clara said she needed to make sure that Margaret had been taking her pills.

"You boys stay out of the house," said Clara. "I just cleaned it."

What Clara meant was that she had done the dishes and picked up Sonny's clothes from where he had tossed them. Otherwise the Tolliver house looked as it usually did, like an unmade bed.

"Where's the trunk?" asked Ink Ear after Clara had left. "Which room is it?"

"Chicken shit," said Duck.

"I'll do this," Sonny said. "It's my job."

Sonny entered his mother's bedroom, a room that was even more disheveled than the rest of the house. The chest with the secrets was covered with baskets and loose piles of ironing yet to be done. Sonny shoved the clothes onto the floor and whacked the latch with the back of his hand. It popped open and Sonny lifted the lid to his mother's past.

Chapter 14

Eldon Burley Returns

The destiny of the late Eldon Burley faded from the concerns of Roy Cannon, the town mortician and Perry coroner. Sonny, Duck and Ink Ear were occupied with the new adventure of finding Sonny's father. They did not speak of the day at Fort Corsage when they had knocked a dead body into the Jericho River. Roy simply did not care, and if the boys imagined anything, it was Eldon bobbing along the Mississippi River and out to sea.

For a little while, Ink Ear Ryan had nightmares and would cry in his sleep or wake up shouting "Zombie!" Ink Ear slept in the same bed with his younger brother Larry and the first couple of times Ink Ear shouted "Zombie!" Larry woke and yelled, "Where, where?"

But by the fourth time, Larry simply cracked Ink Ear in the head with a shoe that he had put under his pillow for just that purpose. The thought of zombies diminished, as did the bruise above Ink Ear's eye where Larry had cracked him. Larry told Ink Ear that their dad Woody had come into the room during the night and smacked him. Ink Ear not only believed it possible but probable. The life of the Ryans continued as did life in the rest of Perry until news arrived that a body had been fished out of the Jericho River not more than three miles from where the boys had last seen it.

"It can't be our soldier," said Sonny.

"You mean our sailor," said Duck.

"Yes, okay, our sailor. Our sailor was in a box. This one wasn't in a box. And this one was naked. It has to be somebody else's soldier."

"Sailor."

"Okay, okay. Sailor."

"Zombies can get out of boxes, you know," said Ink Ear.

"Maybe he was a zombie," said Duck, not kidding this time. As much as he hated to agree with Ink Ear about anything, Duck had to admit that a zombie was a possible answer.

"He was not a zombie," said Sonny. "He was a dead guy in a box and dead guys in boxes don't get out of the box and take their clothes off."

"But if he was a zombie…"

"He was not a zombie. He was not our sailor. He was somebody else."

"Maybe he wasn't dead," said Duck. "Maybe he was just sleeping and he woke up and got out of the box and took his clothes off because…"

"Because what? Because he was hot? Because he wanted to take a bath? Because what?"

The only thing for the boys to do was to see for themselves. None of them would ever forget the face with one eye open. The body had been taken to Cannon's Family Funeral Home and was being held in the cold room pending an official inquiry to be headed by Sheriff John Brown.

Gus Shiner was the first to find the body. He was searching along the Jericho River for empty bottles to sell. Gus got two cents for soda bottles and a nickel for beer bottles. On a good day he could get enough money for a bottle of Thunderbird. The Thunderbird bottle itself had no value and Gus would usually toss it into the Jericho River when he was finished.

Gus had strayed a little beyond his usual range. He seldom went as far as the Swinging Bridge, an improvised contraption of cables and boards that had been strung between two hickory trees, one on each bank of the Jericho River. On the side next to the railroad tracks of the Ohio Southern a ramp led up to the bridge. On the other side boards were nailed to the tree to serve as a ladder.

Even Duck, the bravest of the boys, was apprehensive about the Swinging Bridge. Many of the wooden planks had rotted and the cables were frayed and rusted. When anyone tried to cross the river on it, the bridge would swing.

"That's why it is called The Swinging Bridge," Duck explained.

162

Duck would cross the bridge and pretend to be brave about it, but the bridge's instability kept his attention all the way across. Once on the other side, Duck would yell back at Sonny and Ink Ear that they were chicken shits until they, too, crossed carefully. Mostly the boys, as did nearly everyone else in Perry, avoided The Swinging Bridge.

Against his better judgment and usual habits, Gus Shiner had decided to cross The Swinging Bridge, carrying a shopping bag from Young's Grocery with two Coke bottles, two Blatz beer bottles and a Hudepohl beer bottle.

The bottles clicked against one another and Gus Shiner adjusted the bag. Halfway across the bridge, he heard a crack. He dropped the bag with the bottles and they bounced off a plank and into the river, the Hudepohl bottle tumbling out, followed by one Coke bottle. The rest stayed in the bag that hit the water with a splat.

"Shit! Shit! Shit!" shouted Gus Shiner.

Gus Shiner's left leg dangled through the plank he had just stepped on and broken, and the rest of him lay flat, afraid to move. The Swinging Bridge swung and Gus, his chin perched upon one of the unbroken boards, waited for it to stop. As he waited he stared down river. The swaying of the bridge brought something along the south bank into and out of Gus Shiner's view. Under an overhanging weeping willow tree and tangled in a clump of sedge grass was …what? Something.

Gus pulled his leg free, ripping the only pair of pants he owned, and warily crept across the Swinging Bridge on his hands and knees, testing each board ahead before he put his weight onto it.

He climbed down the other side, using the boards that had been pounded into the hickory tree and made his way towards the weeping willow. Gus broke a hickory branch to use as a grappling rod and poked at something half submerged along the bank. Eldon Burley rolled over and, still with one eye open, stared back at Gus Shiner.

The fiberboard container that once held Eldon Burley had since disintegrated in the chemical bath that was the Jericho River. No trace of it was around. Eldon had floated up and over to the edge of the river and had become tangled in sedge grass, one of the few plants hardy enough to grow near the water of the Jericho River.

Gus' reaction to meeting Eldon Burley was much more unruffled than had been that of the boys. He did not flinch or squeal. He hooked the broken end of his branch under one of Eldon's arms and pulled him up onto the bank under the weeping willow.

"Hello, my friend," said Gus Shiner. "Nice suit."

It was a nice suit and sturdy, too. While the water of the Jericho River had made short work of the fiberboard container that held Eldon Burley, it had little effect on his clothing. Gus could imagine the jacket and pants drying out and fitting him pretty well. Gus was not one to look a gift corpse in the mouth, or in the eye. He reached out and closed Eldon's eye. Eldon's skin was mushy, but solid enough. The fact that Eldon Burley was embalmed and the irony of a river so dead that neither bacteria nor any of the usual instruments of decomposition could live in it had allowed Eldon Burley to remain generally in tact. Gus reached under Eldon's arms and pulled him entirely free of the water.

"Shit," said Gus Shiner, seeing that Eldon was wearing no shoes. He had hoped to replace his shoes, certainly the left one which had a piece of cardboard jammed in it to provide a makeshift sole. Florsheims would have been nice. Gus reached into the pockets of Eldon's jacket and found nothing. In order to get into the pockets of Eldon's pants, Gus had to first remove them. He slid them down Eldon's hips, wiggling the wet cloth until they came off. Eldon Burley was wearing no underwear. No shoes, no underwear. Well, thought Gus Shiner, he wasn't from around here.

Once Eldon Burley was completely undressed, Gus Shiner decided he could use the pants and jacket but the shirt had been slit up the back and was useless. Eldon's tie, a dark silk Van Heusen with a faint white stripe, was of no use to Gus either. He balled up the shirt and tied it into a bundle with the tie. He threw the bundle into the

165

Jericho River and watched it float away. Gus slid the body of Eldon Burley back into the murky water of the Jericho River assuming it would float away just as the bundle had done and become someone else's problem. Gus watched it submerge instead of float away. Eldon Burley came to rest with his bare feet wafting up out of the water and the rest of him not visible at all. Gus Shiner gathered up his treasures and left. This time he walked the long way around to get back to Perry, refusing to re-cross the Swinging Bridge.

Floyd Hickman, the brakeman of the Ohio Southern, spotted Eldon Burley's feet the next day. Floyd had thought he noticed something when the coal train was making its morning run up to the Brighter Day mine in Jericho. On the return trip with the sun at a different angle, Floyd was sure that what he had seen was, indeed, two naked feet sticking up out of the water. Rather than have the engineer stop the train and get off schedule, Floyd waited until it had arrived at its next stop in Newark and placed a call to the Perry telephone exchange.

"Have your sheriff look down by the river, past the Swinging Bridge," he told Perry telephone operator Bonnie Carpenter. Floyd then hung up, satisfied that he been a good citizen.

Bonnie was befuddled by the message. It had come from a Newark exchange. What did it mean? Was it a prank? She wrote down the message: "River. Swinging Bridge. Look." She folded the

166

paper and put it aside, preferring to listen in on a call between Oscar Willis and Carol Nelson, both married but not to each other.

Two days later, Bonnie Carpenter was cleaning her workstation and came across the folded piece of paper on which she had written the odd message about the Swinging Bridge. She plugged into the number for Sheriff John Brown.

"Bonnie," said the sheriff. "Some business for me? It's been slow."

"I got a call on Tuesday telling me to tell you to look down by the Swinging Bridge."

"Two days ago? Look for what?"

"I don't recall exactly. It did not seem important. More like a prank. Usually pranks come from Loganville. This was from Newark. Did the Swinging Bridge finally fall into the river?"

"Not that I know of. I'll go see what it's about."

Sheriff John Brown did not go see what it was about. He sent his part-time clerk and janitor, Slobbering Silas Ashbaugh, to see what it was all about. Silas was not entirely normal, even by Perry standards, and had worked for the sheriff since John Brown arrested him for looking in the window of Rebecca Baker. Rebecca did not mind men looking in her window and she left her shades up for that purpose. But Silas had not only looked in her window, he had begun licking it, leaving drool marks from sill to sill. Silas had been known as Slobbering Silas ever since. Upon

167

reflection, even after she had called the sheriff to report Silas, Rebecca Baker considered it the greatest compliment she ever received.

Silas tended to lick anything shiny, so it was not Rebecca Baker he was drooling over, but his own reflection in the glass of her window. Sheriff John Brown, a lazy but not a cruel man, never told Rebecca he had learned this about Slobbering Silas.

John Brown called Silas from his duties, cleaning the kitchen, catching Silas licking the silverware. He told Slobbering Silas to stop slobbering on the cutlery and to go down past the Swinging Bridge and see if he could see anything unusual.

"Ride your bicycle and be quick about it," Sheriff John Brown said.

Slobbering Silas mounted his blue Firestone Cruiser with carrier seat, headlight, chain guard and white wall tires and pedaled down the gravel path between the tracks of the Ohio Southern and the Jericho River, past the Swinging Bridge and stopped, not knowing exactly what he was supposed to be looking for. Except for one broken slat in the middle, the Swinging Bridge seemed to be as durable as ever, though Silas was not going to test it. Slobbering Silas looked down at the water, which was as dull and orange as ever. He saw nothing. He leaned his Firestone Cruiser against a signal box beside the railroad tracks and moved further down the bank. He peered under a weeping willow tree. Nothing unusual there. He turned to climb back up the bank and saw them. Two bare feet sticking up from the water. He blinked and rubbed his eyes. He looked again. Two feet. Yes.

Slobbering Silas hurried up the bank, jumped onto this bicycle and pedaled back to the sheriff's office. He rushed inside, leaving the door open.

"Mr. Brown, Mr. Brown, I seen 'em," Silas reported, panting.

"How many times have I told you, Silas, about leaving the door open? Close the door and tell me what you saw."

Slobbering Silas turned, pulled the door closed and turned back to Sheriff John Brown. He pulled at his crotch to ease where his pants had bunched during the bicycle ride.

"Now tell me, Silas," said Sheriff John Brown, "what did you see?"

"Two of 'em," said Silas.

"Two? Two what?"

"Feet. One foot and one foot. Sticking up out of the water."

"Two feet sticking up out of the water. Are you sure? Are you absolutely certain?"

Slobbering Silas considered the question. "Yes. I think so. Feet. Two of 'em."

"You think so. Listen to me Silas, I want you to go back there and look again and make sure what you saw is what you think you saw. And then come back and tell me."

Sheriff John Brown turned his attention back to the copy of National Geographic he had been reading, a story with pictures of pygmies in the Belgian Congo.

Again Slobbering Silas hopped onto his Firestone Cruiser and pedaled to the spot where he had seen Eldon Burley's feet sticking up out of the water. He leaned his bicycle against the signal box, climbed down the bank, looked at the feet and counted, "One, two," climbed back up the bank, remounted his Firestone Cruiser and pedaled back to Sheriff John Brown.

"Two, just like I said," said Slobbering Silas Ashbaugh, remembering to close the door this time.

Chapter 15

The Coroner Reports

Roy Cannon pulled the heavy rubber embalmer's apron over his head. Some traces of earlier use still clung to the front. Roy flicked off a piece of gristle, either human or yesterday's lunch. He pulled open the handle of the door to his cold room, not a room as much as a large refrigerator. Four sliding racks were available, three more than were usually needed. Roy was surprised to see that two of the racks were occupied.

He slid the covered corpse on the second rack onto a portable gurney and rolled it above the floor drain. Roy secured the wheels, connected the suction hose and wheeled over the cart with his tools. Laid out for use were three pairs of scissors, a scalpel, an extra nozzle and a syringe. He scooted up the stool on which he would sit. He fitted his goggles over his glasses and pulled on a pair of rubber gloves.

"What's he going to do?" whispered Ink Ear Ryan.

"Shhhh," said Sonny Tolliver.

Duck Stadler said nothing but craned his neck for a better look.

The three boys had squeezed between a filing cabinet and a coat rack when they heard the outer door to Cannon's Family Funeral Home creak open. They had come through the same door several minutes earlier, surprised to find it unlocked. They had seen no trace of their discarded sailor when they entered Roy Cannon's preparation room. They had supposed that bodies would be lying around with tags on their toes.

"This is creepier than chicken shit," said Duck.

"Let's get out of here," said Ink Ear.

"Not yet. He has to be here somewhere," said Sonny.

Duck had walked directly to the large refrigerator and was ready to pull the handle when they heard the outer door. The three scurried for the best hiding place available on short notice.

"Get off me," Duck said to Ink Ear, shoving him sideways. The metal filing cabinet teetered but settled back. Ink Ear knelt down, Sonny bent slightly and Duck stood behind both of them, his hands on Sonny's shoulders.

"Well, Amy, let's make you look half your age, whatever it is," Roy Cannon said aloud before pulling back the cover from the body on the embalming table.

"What the…" Roy Cannon was stunned to see staring back at him, the pesky left eye again open, the face he had last seen in the framed picture that had been placed beside the empty coffin for the Burley services. The man was Eldon Burley. And Eldon Burley was supposed to be lying in a plot of ground in Perry Memorial Gardens. Eldon and his wife had no headstones, but Roy planned to get around to that sooner or later.

As confused as Roy was the day he could not find Eldon Burley's shipping crate, he was more bewildered now. A body that disappears and reappears is not a common occurrence in the mortician trade. They tend to stay where they are put. Roy Cannon had lost track of clients before. Usually they were merely misfiled, stuck in the wrong box or left in the Black Beast. Sooner or later they would be found, usually by Maude Heskett but found nonetheless.

This was a new one for Roy. He had come to work with only a slight hangover, expecting to find only Amy Wright in his cold room. She had been the oldest citizen of Perry and had been lying about her age since she was 91. In order to be the oldest person in town, she had to be four years older than Earl Byers, so when she was 91 she said she was 95. Some say that Earl was so stunned to discover that he had lost his status as the eldest elder that he simply quit living. Amy was stuck with her lie and not unhappy to be so. She had had no other distinction in her life until then.

173

Earl's death had made her lie into the truth. It was recorded in her obituary in the Loganville Messenger that she was 97 instead of 93, yet she was the oldest person either way.

The right eye of Eldon Burley popped open, making a matched pair glaring at Roy Cannon and even Roy, used to such things, flinched.

"Whoa," said Roy Cannon. "Is this some kind of joke?"

Eldon Burley said nothing. As if to answer Roy's question, the phone rang. Again Roy flinched. He pulled off his rubber gloves, walked over to the wall phone and picked up the receiver. Roy stretched the phone cord from the wall, cradled the receiver between his neck and shoulder and sat back down on the stool.

"Roy." It was Sheriff John Brown's voice. "We dropped a body off that we fished out of the Jericho. We couldn't reach you. Maude let us in. Looks like the poor duffer drowned trying to swim naked in the river. Don't people do the damnedest things? You do up a report and we'll accept that."

"What?" said Roy Cannon. "Drowned. Naked?"

He removed the sheet that was covering Eldon Burley to confirm the sheriff's diagnosis.

"Unless there's foul play," the sheriff said. "Unless you find he was shot or knifed or some damned thing. We didn't see any wounds. We didn't look real hard. He was getting kind of ripe."

174

"Do you have an identification on him?" asked Roy Cannon.

"Nope. Looks too old to be a miner, looks too soft, too. Maybe he was a drifter or one of them Szabos. My theory is he fell in the river up by Jericho and floated down here. Maybe somebody pushed him in but why push a naked man into a river? Don't make no sense. He might be a suicide but that's a lot of paper work. And Russell Hand would foul it up trying to prove otherwise for his damned statistics. And if someone killed him, well, he probably had it coming since we don't know who he is."

The investigative curiosity of Sheriff John Brown had never been what could be called enthusiastic. On the rare occasions that it came into contact with the confusion of Roy Cannon, it worked out well for both men. The coroner's report would reflect what was easiest for the sheriff and this one was going to be accidental death while swimming.

The truth was that Roy Cannon was more concerned about who was going to pay for Eldon Burley's second funeral than the truth of why there would be one.

"I'll take care of it sheriff," said Roy Cannon and Bonnie Carpenter, who was listening in, could almost hear the wink on each end of the line.

The boys were only able to hear Roy's half of the conversation and they had yet to see clearly the face of Eldon Burley.

"Is he ours?" whispered Ink Ear.

Sonny flicked Ink Ear's ear and said nothing.

"Ow, ow," said Ink Ear, loud enough for Roy Cannon to hear.

"What? Who's that?" Roy Cannon turned toward the noise. Ink Ear tried to scrunch back but instead caused Sonny to tumble over him. Duck, holding onto Sonny's shoulders fell, too, and the three of them gathered in a pile on the tile floor of Roy Cannon's preparation room.

"It's just us, sir," said Sonny. "We didn't take anything. We just wanted to see a dead body."

"Yeah, a dead body," said Duck.

"Any dead body," said Ink Ear. "No particular dead body. Just a dead body. Like that dead body."

Ink Ear Ryan pointed at Eldon Burley.

"Is that the body they found in the river?" asked Duck.

"We wanted to see that dead body," confessed Sonny.

"Oh," said Roy Cannon. "Do you think you know this man? Have you ever seen this man?"

The boys had edged towards Roy and Eldon, but as yet, they could not see Eldon's face. Roy moved from blocking their view and there glaring at them, accusing them, was their brave and honored sailor.

"Jesus Christ," said Ink Ear. "Now both eyes are open."

176

"Both eyes? You've seen this man before?" Roy Cannon demanded.

"No, no. I mean, he means his eyes should be closed," said Sonny. "Shouldn't they?"

"Don't lie," said Roy Cannon. "You've seen this man. Where did you see this man?"

Duck looked at Sonny. Sonny looked at Ink Ear. Ink Ear looked anywhere but at Eldon Burley. Sonny raised his eyebrows and shrugged.

"We saw him...." Duck began.

"We saw him in Jericho," Sonny said. "We saw him get off the train in Jericho. He was riding in a coal car. He was probably looking for work."

"Yes," said Duck. "We hitched the train to Jericho and saw him get off."

"This man is embalmed," said Roy Cannon. "How did an embalmed man get off a coal car?"

"You tell us," said Duck. "You're the embalmer."

Roy Cannon considered the three boys before him. They knew something. Duck began fiddling with the scissors on the cart. Ink Ear shifted his weight from one foot to the next. Sonny regarded Roy Cannon, noticing a bead of sweat on his upper lip. The boys knew what they knew but they did not know what Roy Cannon knew and Sonny knew that Roy knew something.

"Will you tell Sheriff Brown what you just told me?" Roy asked.

"About Jericho?" asked Sonny.

"Exactly."

"But not about the embalming?" Sonny was not exactly certain what embalming was or how it worked but some instinct told him that it was important to Roy and that somehow it gave the boys an advantage.

Duck picked up the scalpel from the cart. The blade glinted in the cold light of the room. Duck thought that it would make a dandy knife for mumblety-peg. "Can I have this?" he asked Roy.

"That's very sharp. Put it down."

Duck slid his fingers down the handle to the blade. Blood immediately gushed from his forefinger.

"Shit, shit, shit," yelled Duck. "Shit, shit, chicken shit."

Roy Cannon reached into the pocket of his rubber apron and pulled out some gauze. He handed it to Duck. "Wrap your finger. I'll get some tape," Roy said.

Roy walked over to a cabinet and opened a door. Sonny whispered to Duck. "Something's fishy. He wants us to lie."

"Well, hell, we want to lie," said Duck. "What's the problem?"

"Here," said Roy, holding out a spool of white adhesive tape. Sonny took the tape and peeled off a strip, tearing it with his teeth. He wrapped Duck's finger. None of them said anything. The silence seemed to bounce off the walls.

"Boys," said Roy Cannon, "here's the thing. Sheriff Brown wants this to be an accident. It probably was an accident. The embalming, well, I could have done that. If he was in Jericho, and you say so, everybody's happy."

"Except our sailor," said Ink Ear.

"Your what?"

"Nothing."

Duck's finger was throbbing. The gauze was getting red, even through the tape.

"You may need stitches," said Roy.

"What do you say, Sonny?" asked Duck.

"Yeah, you probably will."

"I mean about...about him." Duck motioned with his head to Eldon Burley.

"Well, the first thing I say is...can't you close his eyes?"

Roy Cannon reached over and pressed the lids of Eldon Burley's eyes down over the eyeballs. "Got any coins?" Roy asked.

"Coins? Like money."

"Any coin. Penny. Nickel."

"I got these," said Ink Ear. He fished into his pocket and pulled out five lead washers, each the size of a nickel, each with a hole in the middle. Ink Ear was going to use them to stiff the Coke machine at Neff's.

"They'll do," said Roy. He placed a washer on each eye. But because of the holes in the centers of the washers, it still seemed as if Eldon Burley was staring at them.

"Jesus," said Ink Ear, "he even looks more like a zombie."

179

Roy Cannon pulled the cover over Eldon Burley's face.

"Do you know who he is?" asked Sonny. "I have an idea you know who he is."

"Boys," Roy said. "Let me explain something. I am the coroner. I have to make a report. I am not going to ask you where you first saw this body and you are not going to ask me why I don't ask you. I know you know that nobody killed this man. I will tell you that his name is Burley and that's all I'm going to say about him."

"Burley?" asked Sonny.

"Whirly Burly," said Ink Ear.

"Get on with it, get on with it," said Duck.

"I am going to report that you boys saw him in Jericho and that more than likely he jumped into the river up there and drowned. Not a suicide. No, he was swimming. He was unfamiliar with the quality of our water and he went swimming. And then he was overcome by the elements or by the current or something. But he drowned and he was washed down to where he was found in Perry. That's going to be my report. I am going to ask you to witness it and you are going to sign your names. I am going to send the report to Sheriff Brown. I will cremate the body and that will be the end of it. Is that agreeable to you?"

Sonny considered the offer. Ink Ear waited for Sonny to tell him what to do. Duck, his finger dripping through its bandage, had nothing to consider.

180

"Where do I sign?" Duck asked.

And thus ended what the boys would always call the Whirly Burly Adventure.

"Can I have my washers back?" asked Ink Ear.

Chapter 16

Clara Tolliver's Souvenirs

Sonny Tolliver could not believe how neat and organized his mother's trunk was. It reminded Sonny of the items that were on display in one of the glass jewelry cases at the Ben Franklin, the ones that had to be opened from the back with a key.

Clara Tolliver might not keep a tidy today but her yesterday seemed to be in excellent order. The past is always easier to arrange than the future and the present is a constant adjustment.

The trunk was made of wood covered by worn and splotchy leather. The brass corners and hinges were tarnished. The lid and bottom of the trunk were crossed by raised strips of wood, splintered by time and use. A handle on one side was made of the original leather and the handle on the other side was a replacement rope, bound together by black electrician's tape.

The shabbiness of the trunk fit in with the general shabbiness of the room. And yet, as with Clara herself, and maybe all human beings as far as Sonny knew, what was on the outside did not always reveal what was inside.

A series of four lift out trays were inside the trunk, each covered with patterned silk, a faint landscape scene outlined in white against the cream colored cloth. The lining on the sides, on the top and on the bottom of the trunk was of the same design and of the same material. Sonny lifted out the top tray and placed it on the bed that Clara sometimes allowed Ron Miller to share.

The tray was partitioned in two halves by a stiff divider. Filling the left half of the tray and arranged smartly from top to bottom and left to right were pieces of jewelry, cheap bric-a-brac that would be ignored at a yard sale. Pins, brooches, earrings and several strings of beads were all made of glass or plastic. They were fixed to the lining of the tray by what Sonny had to believe was paste or glue. Clara did not plan to be wearing any of her jewelry again. The realization made Sonny suddenly sad, and he felt guilty for poking into his mother's past.

"What do I need to know?" he asked himself. "What if I really am not old enough?"

Underneath each piece of jewelry on white adhesive tape Clara had written in ink a description of its significance to her. She wrote in an exquisite cursive hand. Sonny recognized it instantly as Clara's. It was the same writing she used to answer the chain letters.

The pattern seemed to be chronological, the first pin being a yellow, plastic star. It was identified on the piece of tape that was used as a label as "Third-grade spelling." Other pieces were labeled with dates, some with places, some with names.

The yellow star was the only kind of award there. Maybe third grade was the pinnacle of Clara's academic achievement. Maybe they didn't give pins for scholarship then as they did now. Sonny himself already had a drawer littered with them. He had never worn one and he never would wear one. Only candy asses wore scholarship pins.

Sonny's eyes moved over the display as if he were picking out one of the items for a gift. In fact, one of them had been a gift from him.

The last item in the collection was a faux silver pin Sonny had given to Clara. The pin was a block lettering of the word "Mom," with an angel sitting on the "O." Sonny had never seen her wear the pin but it pleased him to know that it was safe and treasured. "From My Sonny," read the label.

Sonny had almost forgotten why he was there. He was looking for clues. A clue might be right in front of him, a clue that only a scholarship pin winning smart boy like himself could see.

Calculating the years between his mother's third grade star for spelling and his own gift of the "Mom" pin with the sitting angel, Sonny figured that an oval, pink cameo brooch would have coincided with the year he was born. He knew little about birthstones or he might have recognized that it was supposed to be a ruby, the stone for July. Clara was born on July 5th, and she told Sonny when he was younger that all the fireworks the day before were to announce her birthday, to make sure people did not forget it. Sonny believed her then. Maybe he still did.

The carved face on the pink brooch seemed to resemble Clara, a younger Clara with the same loose hair and sharp chin. Clara had written "19" on the piece of adhesive tape under it and Sonny supposed it was for her 19th birthday. She was 19 when he was born.

Maybe this little pink brooch was the only souvenir of that year in her life. Other than Sonny himself, of course.

The edge of the tape label under the brooch was not stuck securely and Sonny was about to smooth it down. Instead he picked at it and peeled it back. One piece of tape was covering another. Sonny carefully removed the top piece. On the one underneath, in his mother's fine cursive hand, was the word "Bob."

He knew no "Bob." He had never heard his mother mention a "Bob." Nor had any of his aunts mentioned a "Bob."

Okay, thought Sonny, let's suppose this "Bob" gave his mother this brooch in July on her 19th birthday. Sonny was born in September. He knew enough about where babies came from to know that the term of a human pregnancy was nine months.

He had often heard his aunt Florence count backwards to the wedding day when someone they knew, or even someone they didn't know, had her first child.

"In under the wire," Florence said of her own sister Belle when his cousin Larry was born.

Sonny did the math in his head. He was good at math in his head. He was always telling Ink Ear exactly how much change to expect when he bought something. The math in his head told him that if Clara received a birthday gift in July and Sonny was born in September, then his mother was already seven months pregnant. Sonny knew that it was very difficult to hide being seven months pregnant. Clara would already have been kicked out of the house by Grandpa Vernon and she would already have told Sonny's father of her condition. And if she didn't, hell, all he had to do was look at her. Right?

Right? Of course. There would have been no hiding the approaching of the future Sonny. Sonny felt like a real detective, like one of the Hardy Boys. If his math was correct and his assumptions accurate, and if this "Bob" was his father, then he cared enough about Clara to give her a birthday present when she was already as big as a barrel, right?

But what if "Bob" was just another name among his mother's souvenirs?

Sonny smoothed the original tape back over the one that had announced the mystery of "Bob." Other pieces of jewelry that Clara had saved had the names of males under them, likely donors of the items. He did not see Ron Miller's name under any of them, but maybe Ron was not the jewelry gifting type, whatever that was. Sonny could think of no other reason why a "Don" and a "Thad" and a "Martin" would be there and not a "Ron," not the man Clara married. Sonny might not understand why the label "Bob" was the only one that had been covered over, but he was sure it was important.

Sonny tried to visualize the girl who had accepted the gifts but he could not see her. He could not see the happy, flirty girl who tossed her hair and her smiles at men. His mom was his mom and that's what she was, wasn't she?

Or was she? In just one half of one tray of Clara's trunk Sonny had seen in glass and rhinestone that his mother had not always been the dowdy housewife who sat around chain-smoking Camels at her kitchen table while she read gruesome stories of murder and white slavery.

On the right half of the tray were assorted ceramic things, an ashtray shaped like Pennsylvania, a coaster painted like the American flag, three fake seashells, two small china figurines, a boy and a girl, each playing a mandolin. Sonny picked up a snow globe depicting the Steel Pier at Atlantic City with a horse that floated up and down when Sonny shook it.

"What did you find?"

Sonny jumped when he heard Duck's voice behind him, a harsh whisper that was entirely unnecessary.

"Jesus, Duck. Where's Ink Ear?"

"He's keeping watch for your mom. He'll whistle. What did you find? Anything we can use?"

"You know Ink Ear can't whistle."

"Yes, he can. I taught him."

"When did you teach him?"

"I don't remember. But he can whistle. Trust me. Did you find anything we can use?"

"Maybe. Maybe not. There are some more trays in there. Lift them out and let's see what's in them."

Sonny and Duck removed the next two trays, one filled with neatly folded clothes, linens, doilies and a tea towel embroidered with two kittens. Sonny remembered when his mother had done that. The other tray was more scattered, filled with stuff that made no sense to Sonny. A wooden fishing spool with line. A box of dominoes. A shot glass with a shamrock on it. A plastic baby, no more than eight inches long, without clothes, with eyes that opened and closed. A kaleidoscope. Duck picked up the kaleidoscope, put it to his right eye and began turning the revolving band at the end.

"Maybe your dad's in here," Duck said.

"Put that down. Let's see the last tray."

They did not pull the final tray from the trunk. They could see what was in it. The tray contained envelopes, some tied in bundles, obviously letters. Sonny could see on the edges of some of the bundled letters the red and blue markings that indicated airmail. Who did his mother know who would send her letters airmail? Other envelopes were loose, lying one on top of the next. A piece of sheet music had been creased and stuck between the tray and the side of the trunk. Sonny pulled the sheet music out of its resting place and folded it out, smoothing it until it was flat.

The sheet had five sets of lines marked with little symbols like flags that Sonny did not recognize. Song lyrics were written under the stanzas. In larger type at the top of the page was the title of the song: "We're Having a Baby, My Baby and Me." Clara, or someone, had used a red crayon to strike a line through "and Me." Sonny creased the paper and returned the sheet music just as he had found it.

In one corner of the tray was a hard cover book, "The Secret of Tree Cottage, a Dana Girls Mystery." Sonny picked up the book and opened it. On the inside of the cover was an inscription. "To Clara from your loving father." Vernon Tolliver had then signed his full name.

So, that's where her interest in detective stories began, thought Sonny. But he doubted that either of the Dana Girls, whoever they were, had to rescue each other from a white slaver.

Sonny replaced the book and selected one of the loose envelopes. He shook out a handful of black and white photographs onto the floor. He knelt down and spread them out. Duck stood at the window, looking down the lane for Clara, just in case Ink Ear missed her. And Duck knew that Ink Ear was always missing something.

Several pictures were faded and grainy, mostly pictures of old people standing next to one another. He did not recognize any of them. Sonny thumbed through the photos, all black and white with a border around them. A very pretty young girl in a one-piece bathing suit posed for a photo with one hand on her right hip and the other arm raised and crooked behind her head. Her hair was cut short and spit curls laced her forehead. She could have been one of those women in a magazine or in the movies. Sonny then realized the girl was his mother. He turned the photo over. The number "15" and "Lake Hope" was written on the back. Sonny spread the pictures around on the floor, sliding them apart so he could see them better.

Another picture was of his mother holding a baby, obviously Sonny. Sonny recognized a photo of himself in the same sailor suit he had worn the first time he met his grandfather. He did not remember when it was taken, but it was a studio photograph with no border around it.

Sonny picked up a picture of a man he did not recognize, a man with a cocky grin standing beside a small headstone in a cemetery. One foot was raised and placed on the stone and his hand held a cigarette. He wore a sailor suit, too, but this one was clearly the real thing. The man was in the Navy. Sonny turned the picture over. On the back, in his mother's cursive hand, was the word "Bob."

"Look here, Duck," said Sonny. "Do you think it's him?"

Duck took the picture and tipped it right and left to get the best light. He looked at the grinning face in the photo and then at Sonny. Then back to the photo.

"Grin," said Duck.

"I don't feel like grinning," said Sonny.

"Do it anyhow. I want to see something."

Sonny cocked his head slightly to one side and grinned.

"Could be," said Duck. "I bet it is."

Ink Ear Ryan's whistle was not as shrill nor as high pitched as his voice could be but it was, as Duck had promised, a whistle and it was useful enough to warn Sonny and Duck that Clara was on her way back.

Sonny stuffed two pictures, the one of "Bob" and the one of himself and his mother, into the back pocket of his jeans.

"Let's put this back together," said Sonny. "Careful or she'll know."

They slid the trays back into the trunk, closed the lid, slapped the lock back into its place and shoved the ironing back onto the top of Clara Miller's trunk.

They had just made it to the bottom of the stairs when Clara pushed open the screen door and stepped into the house.

"You boys behaving yourselves?" Clara asked.

"Yes, Mom," said Sonny.

"Yes, Mrs. Miller," said Duck.

Clara put her purse on the kitchen table, got down the accounts book she used to keep track of her egg sales and entered the day's transaction.

She then lit a Camel, pulled a half-filled ashtray towards herself and opened her latest copy of "Detective Confidential." The magazine had a picture of a blonde on the cover, screaming with the hands of an unseen assassin around her neck.

Sonny stood across the room, staring at the one person he had known longer than any other person in his life.

As little as Sonny knew about his father, he realized he knew almost as little about the woman who had not flushed him down the toilet.

Chapter 17

Two Becomes Three

Sonny and Duck lived next to one another and made a natural connection because they were neighbors. Ink Ear was from the other side of Perry, not nearly as nice a side of Perry as Sonny and Duck, but to be honest, Perry did not have many nice sides.

The Jericho River had flooded one spring, one of the very few floods any one could remember. The high water came from unusually heavy rainfall and from the Perry Reservoir. The first cause was a result of nature and the second the result of stupidity. Whenever stupidity was the root cause of anything, Perry looked to its mayor Howard Trickle.

Perry kept electing Howard as its mayor mostly because no one else wanted the job, and being the mayor of Perry did not require a lot of ability. Howard's job was mainly to bang his gavel at town meetings and say no to anything anyone wanted to do.

Politics in Perry were practically nonexistent, so whether Howard was a Republican or a Democrat or a Free Soil Ventriloquist did not matter. Had he been a Catholic, or a Jew, or an immigrant, that would have been a different matter, of course. The Szabos, who had converted to Catholicism after coming to America, were all three.

Really, the only thing that mattered was that Howard Trickle was a Presbyterian and not a Communist and he was willing to take the job.

Perry was probably more conservative than liberal even though there was more labor than management in the town. Unions had not made their way into the potteries and only recently and barely into the mines. Organizers who had tried to get unions into both could not explain why.

The one collective stand that the mineworkers had taken brought them less money than they had been paid before and it put the Szabos in Jericho. Fool them once, shame on you. Fool them twice and it was probably just as easy.

No matter how often it was pointed out to the workers of Perry that there was strength in numbers, they refused to join together. Not even reminders of the Burley settlement when they pissed away almost all the money by arguing with one another could change their minds. They went their own ways chiefly because the people of Perry just did not trust one another enough to join in a common cause.

The United Mine Workers had made a feeble connection to the Brighter Day Mine, an "auxiliary" connection. The miners had voted to think about it and had agreed to allow labor literature to be sent to Allen Charles but Allen never read it or passed it on.

They were proud Americans. Make no mistake about that. Patriotism was the one unifying agreement among them. They fought and died in wars and they listed their honored dead on the monument of the doughboy in front of the town hall. They really did need a cannon to complete the tableau. The subject of a cannon was brought up periodically and was always gaveled down by Howard Trickle. If Howard loved to do one thing, it was to gavel.

July 4 was a very big holiday and every household had an American flag. The Potter high school band would march in the parade, sweltering in wool uniforms that were made to be worn in cooler weather. Bobby Metcalf, who carried the tuba, had to be carried off the street one year. Sonny and Duck took Bobby and Ink Ear took the tuba. The tuba was never seen again and everyone agreed the band sounded better without one.

The two fire engines of the Perry Volunteer Fire Department were washed and polished and led the parade. Even The Black Beast of Roy Cannon was festooned with patriotic banners, looking almost hospitable.

The main float was sponsored by Wiseman Dairy and the Summer Queen sat on a throne of fake milk bottles that looked more like bowling pins. She waved and blew kisses at her subjects.

Clara Tolliver had once dreamed of being the Summer Queen. Her father Vernon told her often that she was "as pretty as a summer queen," and if she had not quit school in the eighth grade in order to work for enough money to buy her own Camels, she might very well have one day ridden down Perry's Main Street on her throne of milk bottles. As Vernon said, she was pretty enough.

And Howard Tickle might have been Clara's summer king. They were the same age and Howard was not as goofy looking as the goofy things he did or the goofy things he let happen.

"Yes," Clara told Sonny, "I knew Howard very well. We went on a few dates."

Could Howard be Sonny's father? He certainly hoped not. And all the evidence was against it. First of all, his name was Howard and not "Bob." You can't make "Bob" out of "Howard." You can make a "Howie," or a "Hal," maybe, but definitely not a "Bob." Howard Trickle had never been a sailor. He had never been in the military at all according to Dan Weller, who had become the main source of confirmation for any information picked up by the boys in their search for Sonny's father.

Sonny had told Dan what they suspected about his real dad, that he was a sailor and that he was named "Bob." Sonny asked Dan if he would verify this with Evelyn and Dan said he would. But Dan, like Sonny, avoided confronting Evelyn with anything he did not have to. And so he avoided it and apologized each time Sonny asked, saying that he had not found the right moment to ask.

The Matterhorn was spared any damage the year of the big flood because it was at the head of Main Street instead of at the foot. Aunt Evelyn saw the flood as a blessing, not only because it increased the business for their restaurant/bowling alley/dance hall but also because it dumped fresh water into the Jericho and for most of the rest of the summer the town was without its usual stench.

"It is just things like this that convince me to vote for Howard Trickle," said Aunt Evelyn.

The Jericho River flooded and Ink Ear joined Sonny and Duck in their gang or their band or their crew, whatever it might be called. They did not call it anything. Had the flood not happened very likely they would have remained two instead of three.

Sonny had always thought that the two of them needed a third. Duck was happy the way things were.

"We can't both be Roy Rogers," Sonny said. "We need a Gabby Hayes."

"I thought you were Gabby."

"No, I'm Roy."

"You can't be Roy. I'm Roy."

"See that's exactly what I mean," said Sonny. "We need a Gabby."

"But both of us would still be Roy," said Duck. "There would just be two Roys and a Gabby."

"Let me explain this another way," said Sonny. "It's like rock, paper, scissors. See?"

"No, I don't see anything."

"We need a tie breaker."

"Why not just flip a coin?" asked Duck. "Heads I win, tails you lose."

"That's still possible," said Sonny, "but we really could use a tie-breaker. Like I want to do something and you want to do something. How do we decide"?

"Like I said. Heads I win..."

"No, come on. This just makes sense. Three makes more sense than two."

Ink Ear Ryan did not think it odd that he should be listening to the discussion between Sonny and Duck about whether he was worthy to join them or not. He was holding the sleeve of his shirt up to his nose to stop it from bleeding. It was bleeding because Duck Stadler had punched him in his nose. Duck had punched Ink Ear because they both wanted the same can of pears.

The flood waters had come to Perry because Howard Trickle had ordered the sluice opened in the Perry Reservoir. He wanted the sluice open so that the reservoir would not overflow from the rain and cause a flood.

198

"Where did you think the water was going to go, Howard?" asked Henry Rodenour.

"I thought the river could handle it," said Howard. "I'm not an engineer, Henry.

"You're an idiot," said Henry, who suffered more than anyone else in Perry from the high water because he owned most of the property in Perry, especially on Water Street, which ran along the Jericho River.

One of the flooded businesses was Rodenour's Grocery, located on Water Street. The water came in from Water Street and ruined all the produce and meat in the store. It swept the canned goods out through the broken front window to where two feet of water had collected on Water Street. Cans and bottles bobbed or sank. Many of the cans were there after the water receded. One of the cans, wet but with the label still on it, was a 16-ounce tin of Faultless Pears.

The children of Perry had been sent by their parents to collect what they could of the non-perishable goods that had been washed out of Rodenour's Grocery into Water Street. Duck Stadler had brought his Flyer and had filled it nearly full. Sonny had used his undershirt as a bag, tying a knot in the tail. Ink Ear Ryan had only what his arms could carry.

Even though he was in their class, neither Sonny nor Duck had paid any attention to Harry Ryan. What little they knew of him was he always held up class when reading out loud and that he picked his nose. They didn't hold nose picking against him but they hated to sit there while he stumbled from the beginning of a sentence to the end of it.

Both Duck and Ink Ear reached for the can of Faultless Pears at the same time. Ink Ear got there first. His right hand barely fit around the can while he held the other cans in the crook of his left arm, pinning the cans against his chest.

"Mine," said Duck.

"Not so. It's mine," said Ink Ear. "I was here first."

"I say it's mine," said Duck.

"You got a whole wagon full. This one is mine."

"Let him have it," said Sonny. "It's pears. You don't even like pears."

"Nope," said Duck. "It's mine. Give it to me, runt."

Ink Ear Ryan had been called "runt" many times. Sometimes it bothered him. Sometimes it did not bother him. This time, it bothered him.

"You want it? Here," said Ink Ear Ryan, and he jerked the can from under Duck's grip and threw the can of Faultless Pears at Duck Stadler. Duck easily dodged it.

"Did you just throw a can of pears at me?" asked Duck. "Did you?"

"I did. And now I'm going to throw…" Ink Ear looked at one of the cans he was cradling. "I'm going to throw a can of pork and beans."

"You like pork and beans," Sonny said to Duck.

"How do you know it's pork and beans?" asked Duck. "It's not got any label on it."

"I remember it," said Ink Ear. "It's Van Camp beans."

"It's what?" asked Duck.

"He means Van Camps," said Sonny.

"I mean what I say when I say what I say," said Ink Ear. He drew back the can.

"You throw that and you're a dead man," said Duck.

"Not if I hit you first," said Ink Ear and flung the can. Duck again easily stepped aside and the can flew past, landing with a clunk on the wet paving bricks of Water Street. The can's side seam split and bright orange peaches shot out, skittering and splashing down the street.

"It wasn't beans," said Duck. "It was peaches."

"I like peaches," said Sonny.

"What a chicken shit," said Duck.

"One of them is beans," said Ink Ear, picking another can from its cradle. Ink Ear began throwing one can after another at Duck. A can finally caught Duck on the shoulder. Ink Ear ran over to Duck's Flyer and picked up another can, this one with the label on it. This one had pineapple chunks in their own juice.

"I like pineapple," said Ink Ear. "Can I have this one?"

"You can have this," said Duck Stadler and punched Ink Ear in the nose.

201

"Ow, ow, ow," said Ink Ear. "You didn't have to do that."

"Sure I did. Now we're even," said Duck.

"We're even?"

"Even steven," said Duck.

"My name's Harry," said Ink Ear. And his name was Harry at the time. Only later would the legendary adventure of the blue ballpoint change it to Ink Ear.

"What do you think?" Sonny asked Duck.

"About what?"

And thus began the discussion about Roy and Gabby and about rocks and papers and scissors and about the need for a tiebreaker.

Ink Ear Ryan watched and listened and eyed all the cans in Duck's red Flyer. Maybe he should just grab the wagon and go.

"Rock, paper, scissors," said Duck.

"You're on," said Sonny.

Duck's hand flicked out. A fist. Rock. Duck was always rock. Sonny knew that Duck was always rock. Sonny's hand flew out, palm up. Paper.

"Paper swallows rock," said Sonny. "He's in."

Duck, rubbing his shoulder, looked at Harry, too small, too homely and too much trouble. Duck could just sense it. "Okay," Duck said. He picked up the wagon tongue of his Flyer and started off. Sonny motioned Harry to follow and the three of them sloshed down the flooded Water Street of Perry.

202

Still holding his sleeve against his bleeding nose, Ink Ear asked Sonny, "Am I rock, paper or scissors?"

"You're paper," said Duck.

"I want to be scissors," said Ink Ear.

"Sonny is scissors."

"Then I want to be rock.

"I'm rock. You're paper."

"I'm afraid you're paper," said Sonny.

"If you say so, Sonny," said Ink Ear. "But I'd rather be scissors.

"Anybody would," said Sonny.

Chapter 18

The Devil's Tea Table

Judging by the crude map that Sonny held in his hand, the hike to the rock formation known as The Devil's Tea Table was not going to be any longer and not any more difficult than the one to The Clay Hole. At the end of the journey there was not likely to be any reward, no swimming and not any Margarite Szabo. Sonny was sure of that. But since the abandonment of Fort Corsage, the boys were looking for another place. And, as Sonny explained, they had to go for no other reason than to see what a tea table for the devil looked like.

"What does any tea table look like?" asked Ink Ear. "A table just for tea? That sounds stupid."

"Some people have a table just for tea," said Duck. "Tea is very important to some people."

"Name some," said Ink Ear.

"Well, the harbor people," said Duck. "If you paid attention in school you would know the harbor people were not very happy when the Indians dumped their tea in the harbor."

"Was it their harbor?"

I think so."

"Then they could just drink the harbor. They wouldn't need a table at all."

"That's stupid," said Duck. "What about sugar?"

"Maybe they didn't like sugar in their tea," said Ink Ear.

"Nobody drinks tea without sugar."

"Maybe the harbor people did."

"They didn't drink the harbor…oh, shit. You tell him, Sonny."

Sonny knew the story of American patriots throwing tea into Boston Harbor. He did not know all the reasons they did it, but he knew that it was a very big deal for America and that it helped to cause the Revolutionary War. Without tea there would be no America. He started to explain all of it to Ink Ear, but then just shrugged. If Sonny did not understand, he was sure that Ink Ear would not understand either. And as for Duck, well, a little knowledge was good enough.

"Why isn't it the Devil's Coffee Table?" asked Ink Ear. "I bet the devil likes coffee better than tea."

"I bet he doesn't," said Duck.

"Who knows?" said Sonny. "I guess we'll have to wait and ask him."

The boys had heard the stories of strange sounds and weird lights coming from the place. The Szabos were suspected of holding bizarre rituals at the Devil's Tea Table, maybe even sacrifices.

"What's a sacrifice for, anyhow?" asked Ink Ear.

Duck knew the answer to this one. His mother Sarah had explained it to him when he asked why Abraham would want to kill his only son, Isaac.

"He was trying to please God," Sarah said. "But it was only a test, you know, to see how much Abraham loved God. When he saw that Abraham would sacrifice the one he loved the most, God told him to burn a sheep instead. It was a test of faith."

Duck told Ink Ear the story of Abraham and Isaac. "And ever since they use sheep or goats instead of kids."

"I bet it still scared the shit out of Isaac," said Ink Ear.

"Dads will do that," agreed Duck.

Sonny had misjudged the time it would take to get to the Devil's Tea Table. He was not sure exactly where it was. He had gotten directions from high school senior Marion Legarde during a pause in setting bowling pins at the Matterhorn.

"Why do you want to go there?" asked Marion.

"To see it. I've never seen a devil's anything before."

"It's just a rock," said Marion.

206

"What kind of rock."

"To tell you the truth I think it looks more like a mushroom. It's kind of a bigger flat rock on top of a skinnier rock, like a mushroom on a stem."

"Can you climb it?"

"No problem. There's a view but not much. It's kind of on the side of a hill at the top of a clearing. I wouldn't bother if I were you."

"Can you draw me a map on how to get there?"

Marion's map gave no perspective on distances. The boys had to make their way through a thick woods, down into a hollow, across a narrow creek and up to another woods, through the trees, across a long flat field, down into another hollow and halfway up the other side. The tea table was around the hill and hidden from above. That was the long way from Perry. From Loganville it was a short climb to the other side of Brimstone Ridge.

"Shit, are we ever going to get there?" asked Duck.

They had started after lunch and Sonny figured they would get there by early afternoon and have plenty of daylight left to get back to Perry. Already the shadows of the trees were stretching into the final field on Marion's map.

"It's not far now," said Sonny.

"This better be worth it," said Duck. "We better see the devil himself having tea."

"We better not," said Ink Ear.

Rounding the final hill to where Marion had drawn the X on his map, Sonny could hear a low, steady murmur. A soft breeze moved the leaves of the trees and flickering through the branches they could see a soft glow.

"Maybe the devil is having tea," said Duck. "Goody, goody."

The three of them made their way through a small grove of pawpaw trees down the hill to a ledge of rock that ran across the hill. The waning day and the chill of autumn made Sonny shiver.

"I should have worn a coat," said Sonny. "This is going to feel like the Devil's Iced Tea Table."

"What? Iced Tea Table?" asked Ink Ear.

"Forget it," said Duck.

"There it is," said Sonny in a whisper, not knowing exactly why he was whispering.

Below them, less than 50 yards away, just as Marion had described it, was a toadstool shaped rock formation, flat on top, held up by a thinner formation from below. The rock was nearly the size of the chicken coop at the bottom of Sonny's yard. The weathering of wind or of water had cut away the lower portion of the rock but left the larger area above. It might have been a table if tables had one leg.

It was not the shape of the rock that drew the attention of the boys but the shape on top of it. Standing in profile to the boys seemed to be the figure of a man, covered in gold, from a hood on his head to his feet. Only the toes of his shoes peeked from beneath the hem of his robe. His arms were folded across his chest, his hands hidden inside the folds of the sleeves.

"Is that the devil?" asked Ink Ear.

"You idiot," said Duck. "The devil wears red."

The boys moved further down to see beyond the Devil's Tea Table. In the clearing, a couple dozen, maybe 30, figures were all dressed in robes, some of the robes white, some of them blue, and some red. The colors appeared to designate the status of the wearer with the whites nearer the rock and the reds furthest away and the blues to one side. The arrangement gave the impression of an American flag. The figures all wore cowls, like those of medieval friars, the faces inside nearly hidden. Only noses and a few chins, peeked from beyond the folds of the cowls. Leaning against the base of the rock were several rifles and a shotgun.

"Shit, look at that," whispered Duck. "It's the Szabos."

The figure on the tabletop was covered in a tailored robe made of glistening gold satin. The hem and the sleeves of the robe were trimmed in a purple border. Kerosene lanterns had been placed around the edges of the rock table like footlights for a stage. The light from the lanterns reflected from the shiny fabric making the figure in gold appear to be a burning flame.

"That guy's wearing a dress," whispered Ink Ear.

Instead of a loose cowl, the figure in gold wore a hood that covered his head and face. Eyeholes

209

were outlined in bright purple. He raised his arms and stretched them up towards the darkening sky. A symbol was sewn over the heart of his garment, a purple Christian cross with an open eye stitched at the crux.

A soft, steady chant began. "Prune, prune, prune."

"What are they saying?" whispered Duck.

"Sounds like poop, poop, poop," said Sonny.

"No, it's boom, boom, boom," said Duck.

"It's prunes," said Ink Ear.

"That doesn't make any sense. Prunes?"

"Why is he wearing a dress?"

"It's not a dress. It's a robe."

"It looks like a dress."

Dress or robe, the figure in the gold garment lowered his arms. Sonny could see a gold watch on the wrist of his left hand. Few in Perry wore wristwatches. They carried pocket watches or relied on the noon siren to mark the day. The chant died down.

The sun had settled on the tops of the trees on the far hill and soon it would disappear entirely. Too soon for Ink Ear.

"I'm getting out while the getting's good," whispered Ink Ear.

"No, wait. You stay exactly where you are," said Duck.

The gathering below the rock table grew silent. The tut-tut-tut of wood thrushes calling to each other was the only sound until the figure in gold spoke.

"Welcome, Pruners!"

"Amen," called back the figures below the rock.

"Gardeners of Faith!"

"Amen." Again.

"Tillers of Truth!"

Again. "Amen."

Sonny had heard the voice before. He knew the voice.

"Harvesters of Brotherhood."

That sounded okay to Duck. Faith and truth and brotherhood. If this was a club, when he grew up Duck thought he would like to join. He had his eye on the gold robe. That's the one he would wear.

"The weeds increase among us. They thrive under our noses. They grow without limit. The weeds will overtake our garden if we do not prune them out!"

Where had Sonny heard that voice?

The low murmur began again, the chant of "prune, prune, prune."

"We gather again under the eye of almighty God, in this holy place…"

Holy shit! It was the radio preacher. What was his name? Reverend Warren. Reverend Warren Lund.

Sonny had heard this sermon, or something very like it, on the radio one Sunday morning. Sarah Stadler always listened to the Reverend

Lund. Clara Tolliver would not have the radio on during the reverend's broadcasts, but Sarah turned up the volume on her Bendix so that all the neighbors could hear the weekly message.

The sermon from the Devil's Tea Table covered much the same material as the one Sonny remembered from the radio. God's garden needed constant tending. Tiny seeds may grow into nourishing plants or into wicked weeds. The wicked must be pruned from the righteous.

"What's he talking about?" Ink Ear poked Sonny. "Are they the Szabos or farmers or what?"

"I have seen the eye of God…" The figure in the gold robe clutched the symbol over his heart. "I have looked through the eye of God. I have seen the garden that God sees. I have seen the garden that God wants. I have seen the garden as it first was, as it should be. Look with me! Look with me!"

The gold-gowned leader cupped his hands and held them with fingers touching, shaping his hands into the form of an eye. He drew his hands to his eyeholes and peered through the opening his fingers made, like someone holding binoculars.

Each member of the robed audience cupped his hands under his cowl, making the shape of a human eye. They turned their faces to the darkening sky and peered through. One of the cowls fell back from the head of one of the figures and in the torch light Sonny saw Andy Sloan.

212

Andy quickly pulled the hood back and reshaped his hands and gazed through God's eye to heaven.

"What are they looking at?" asked Ink Ear, looking up.

"God's garden, idiot," said Duck. "Didn't you listen?"

"There's a garden in the sky?" Ink Ear cupped his hands and stared up. He saw clouds tinged with the orange of the setting sun. One cloud looked like a potato. He pointed it out to Duck.

"All clouds look like potatoes," said Duck.

"Do you know who these people are?" Sonny whispered to Duck. "The one in the gold, that's the radio preacher. And I saw Andy Sloan's face. What are they doing here? Is this a revival meeting or something? I thought Andy was a Lutheran. And the radio preacher is from Loganville."

"That's your dad," Duck said to Ink Ear.

"Where?"

"The little guy in the blue robe. I saw him take a drink from a bottle. I saw his face. That's your dad."

As far as Ink Ear knew, Woody Ryan had few friends, few old friends at least. Woody was outgoing and sociable but he tended to wear out his friendships by borrowing money he never repaid and by always being absent when it was his turn to buy the next round. If these people were putting up with him it was because he had just recently joined them or they did not recognize him in his costume.

"Think of that," said Ink Ear. "Pa with buddies."

"I guess they're buddies," said Sonny. "I guess it's like the Eagles or the Elks."

The gathering did seem to be some kind of men's fellowship, like the Eagles in Perry or the Elks in Loganville. Ron Miller belonged to the Eagles and twice a year he took Clara to the lodge, once for dancing and once for dining. The Eagles in Perry had nothing to do with the Elks in Loganville so whatever this was it broke boundaries that had been set for a long time.

"Do you see the weeds?" The gold-gowned figure asked.

"No weeds, no weeds," the gathering responded.

"Do you smell the weeds?"

"Stink weeds, stink weeds."

"They're not farmers," Duck said to Sonny.

"I don't think they like weeds," Sonny said.

"Why don't they just piss on 'em? That's what I do to weeds," said Ink Ear. He concentrated on the figure in blue, waiting to see if he would take another drink, waiting to see if he could see his face.

"Weed the garden! Weed the garden!" A low chant began. The figure in gold lowered his hands. Those below him in the clearing did the same, continuing to chant, "Prune the weeds." The chant died away until again the wood thrush was the only voice in the dusk.

214

Ink Ear heard the figure in blue belch, a sound he knew very well, a rolling belch from somewhere deep inside the small body. It was Woody Ryan, for sure.

"Our garden will be pruned!" boomed the figure in gold. "We must prune our garden."

"Prune, prune, prune."

In a more reasonable voice the figure in gold said, "The Fraternal Order of Eden will gather again next month. Those of you who did not bring tools please remember them the next time. Those who are behind in dues will not be able to take part in the pruning." He pointed at Ink Ear's father.

"Remember that God is watching. His eye is everywhere."

Dusk had turned to darkness. A rising moon cast enough light to define the Devil's Tea Table where two figures in blue robes helped the man in the gold robe down from the rock. Others collected the lanterns that had lit the ceremony. With darkness now serving as a mask, others pulled back their hoods and several slipped off their robes entirely. In the scattered light, Sonny, Duck and Ink Ear could see Sheriff John Brown, mayor Howard Trickle and Woody Ryan. Many of the others they did not know.

One of them took a miner's helmet from under his robe, lit the carbide light and put it on his head. In the flicker of the miner's light, Sonny thought he caught the face of Dan Weller, his aunt

215

Evelyn's husband, the proprietor of the Matterhorn and the only male adult Sonny had any respect for at all.

Lanterns and miner's lights illuminated the way from the Devil's Tea Table. The procession moved down the hill like a glowing snake towards the town of Loganville.

Sonny, Duck and Ink Ear followed, keeping a distance and keeping quiet.

They had seen the table. And they had seen the devil.

Chapter 19

The Burden of Legendship

Halloween was a challenge for Sonny, Duck and Ink Ear. Halloween was no longer a night when little boys dressed in silly clothes and wore masks and begged for candy. Halloween had become an obligation for adventure. They missed the masks and the costumes and they especially missed the candy. But that was all behind them. They had a reputation to maintain. They could never go back.

Sonny and Duck sat on the platform at the Perry water tower. The autumn palette spread across the hills, reds and oranges and greens. Ink Ear was down below, throwing gravel up at them. A stone clanked off the water tank.

"He's getting better," said Duck.

They sat and they studied and they looked out over the roofs of the homes and the stores of Perry. Down there somewhere was the adventure.

"It will be hard to top the piss pot," said Sonny. He looked up at the tank that still resembled a piss pot but the lettering had been painted over. And now the tank said simply "Perry."

"That was great, wasn't it?" asked Duck. "That's the best one ever."

"But that wasn't Halloween," said Sonny.

"Yeah. It doesn't count."

"How about tipping over some out houses?" asked Duck.

"Start with mine," said Sonny.

"You'd just have to put it back up," said Duck. "And I'd have to help."

"How about we paint all the white wall tires in town orange?" asked Sonny. "Orange for Halloween."

"Do you how many tires that is?"

"What are you guys talking about?" yelled Ink Ear Ryan. "I can't hear you."

"Okay. Let's just paint the mayor's tires, and Principal Worthington's. And Reverend Norman's. Just the big shot's tires. No, I know. Let's paint the tires on the sheriff's car pink."

"Didn't someone already do that a few years ago?"

"Oh. Wait. Yeah. You're thinking about when the Loganville basketball team painted the wheels on our school bus red. You remember. To match their school colors."

"Yellow and red. Sure. They beat us by 30," said Duck.

218

Both Sonny and Duck agreed that, while not the same, painting white walls was too derivative. Being a legend was not easy work.

"I can't hear you guys," yelled Ink Ear. "Talk louder."

"Eggs," said Duck.

"What eggs?"

"We could egg Max the Miner's house. I know where he lives," said Duck. "He's chicken shit that Max is."

"Eggs? You're talking about eggs?" Ink Ear Ryan put one foot on the ladder to climb up and join his friends. "Let's egg the doughboy. You got plenty of eggs, Sonny. Rotten eggs, too, I bet."

Egging on Halloween was so...well, so ordinary, so beneath the architects of The Great Bus Ride and The Perry Piss Pot. Not to mention The Sailor in a Bottle, as they remembered Eldon Burley. And they never mentioned him. Even to each other.

Ink Ear Ryan decided against climbing up the ladder. He picked up a piece of gravel and threw it. The stone clinked off the central feeder pipe of the tower, way short of its mark.

"I don't want to egg the doughboy," said Duck. "Somebody is always egging the doughboy. Maybe we ought to hide and beat up anybody egging the doughboy. I like the doughboy."

"We could steal the doughboy," said Sonny. "We could keep him safe."

"We could put a dress on him," yelled Ink Ear.

219

"That's worse than egging," said Duck. "Nobody is putting a dress on my doughboy."

"Your doughboy? Since when?"

"Since I said so. We shouldn't do anything to the doughboy. He's the only hero we've got."

Sonny considered what Duck had just said. Duck was right. The male figure they all admired the most was a replica of a man, not a living, breathing role model but a fake depiction of one. Maybe all heroes are better that way.

"Sure," said Sonny, "we could take him and put him...let's see. We could put him in the Matterhorn. We could tape a bowling ball to his hand. That would be great. Wouldn't that be great? The Bowling Doughboy. They'd put his picture in the Messenger, I bet. That might be better than the Piss Pot."

Duck dismissed the idea instantly, guessing that Sonny was just feeling the strain of legendship.

"Nobody's messing with the doughboy," said Duck.

"Then what? What will it be?"

Again they fell into contemplation, Sonny and Duck up above on the catwalk of the Perry water tower and Ink Ear down below, now sitting cross-legged in the gravel imitating Sonny and Duck.

"Besides," said Duck. "He's too heavy. How much do you think he weighs?"

"Who weighs?" asked Sonny.

"The doughboy."

"He's hollow," yelled Ink Ear.

220

"He's what?"

"He's got a hole in his ass. You can see inside him. Clear through him."

It was true. Ink Ear had seen the hole one day when he was waiting for his dad, Woody, to be released from the town jail. The Perry town hall was a combination office building, firehouse and jail. The jail occupied the back side of the building, and the firehouse took up one of the sides. A gravel parking lot ran the length of the other side of the building. A traffic light hung above Ceramic Street at the intersection of the entrance to the parking lot.

The town offices were recessed from the street beside the firehouse, leaving an open space in front. A small park occupied the space, with enough room for two benches, a pole to hold the American flag and the Perry Doughboy. Visitors to the town hall using the parking lot passed by the doughboy on their way into the building.

The statue was nearly six feet tall, perched on a small concrete pedestal. He was known as the "Perry Doughboy" but he represented all soldiers of any war, past or future. As Howard Trickle pointed out, if the town erected statues to every war, they would not have enough room nor enough budget. The one doughboy would do for them all. He wore the "tin hat" that placed him clearly in the Great War. His eyes were fixed, his jaw was square and his brow was strong.

"What is a doughboy, anyhow," Duck asked Sonny.

"He's a soldier that fights for dough," said Sonny.

"He doesn't fight for his country?"

"Yeah, sure, but he has to see the dough first."

"Smart," said Duck.

Other towns had their own doughboys, most commonly the famous "Spirit of the American Doughboy." The "Spirit" doughboy was throwing a grenade with his right hand as he raced forward, his bayoneted Enfield rifle in his left fist. His mouth was open in what was an obvious challenge to the enemy ahead. The "Spirit" was a doughboy to be proud of.

The Perry Doughboy was a much less aggressive figure, not to mention less expensive. He stood at ease with his elbow bent and right hand on his hip. His left hand barely held his rifle, using only the thumb and forefinger to steady it against his left leg. His weapon had no bayonet. He might have been guarding chickens, or keeping watch while someone stole their eggs. He seemed to show a disdain for either job.

The Perry Doughboy wore the same wrapped leggings as the more famous "Spirit" statues and he had the same utility belt and gas mask pack. His rifle was the same Enfield, the model used by Sgt. Alvin York, but the Perry Doughboy was not cast in bronze. He was an alloy of the finest Mexican zinc and aluminum, much less expensive

222

and just as durable, as Henry Rodenour's father had explained to the American Legion.

The low afternoon sun was about to dip below the roof of Arlen's Lumber across the street from the Perry town hall. The angle of the sun's rays gave the Perry Doughboy a golden glow instead of his usual olive drab.

Names of those from Perry who had been killed in action in all the wars were commemorated on brass plates on each side of the pedestal. Ink Ear walked around the base looking to see if anyone with the name of "Ryan." had ever given the last full measure of devotion.

Among the R's were Russell and Riggs and Robinson and Roberts, but no Ryan. As Ink Ear ran his finger over the space between Riggs and Simpson, having concluded that it was the space where "Ryan" would have been, a beam of light caught him in the left eye. He turned his head, and then turned it back. Again, light in the left eye. Ink Ear climbed up onto the cement base, stretched to his tiptoes, wrapped his arms around the Perry Doughboy's waist and pressed his face into the right cheek of the Perry Doughboy's ass. He could see through to the other side.

"It's like a peep hole," yelled Ink Ear. "I seen it."

"What is it, a gunshot hole?" asked Duck. "Maybe it's authentic. Maybe our doughboy was shot in the ass and they were just being realistic."

"What it means is the doughboy isn't solid like we thought," said Sonny. "He might not weigh so much."

"Who would shoot our doughboy?" asked Duck. "I never would. Would you, Sonny?"

"If it was him or me, yes I would," said Sonny.

As it turns out, it was him or Harry Raines, the Loganville sheriff. Sheriff Harry Raines was driving past the Perry town hall very late one night, returning from a meeting of the Law and Order Sheriff's Lodge, an organization that had yet to invite Perry's Sheriff John Brown to join. The meeting had been held at the Big Apple roadhouse on the other side of Perry. Hard liquor could not be served within the town limits of Perry or any other town in the county. The limit inside the town limits was 3.2 beer, and yet Perry had more beer joints than churches. Sheriff Harry Raines had a "snoot full," --his own description-- and would have been arrested for drunken driving if he had not been the officer in charge of arresting drunken drivers.

Sheriff Harry Raines stopped at the traffic light that was used to manage the traffic into and out of the parking lot of Perry town hall. The traffic light was entirely unnecessary except after town meetings. To put it another way, it had a real function only twice a month.

On the night that Sheriff Harry Raines pulled the Loganville law wagon--his description--to a halt, the traffic light was red. The light had been red all night. The people of Perry knew that the light sometimes was stuck on red and rather than repair it, they expected it to sort itself out and they simply ran through it until it did.

Sheriff Harry Raines of Loganville did not know about the quirks of Perry traffic lights. He was the law and the Law of Loganville did not break the law, even the law in Piss Pot Perry. He sat and waited. The light remained red.

Sheriff Harry Raines felt eyes on him. Someone was watching him. He looked out the window of the black Plymouth Satellite with a full rack of lights across the top and a safety screen between the front seat and the back. The Perry Doughboy, in his jaunty pose, one hand on his hip, stared at Sheriff Harry Raines. Sheriff Harry Raines was certain the doughboy was smirking at him.

"What are you looking at?" demanded Sheriff Harry Raines.

The Perry Doughboy said nothing.

"You looking at me?" asked Sheriff Harry Raines. The light remained red but even if it had not, Sheriff Harry Raines was not going to let some Perry punk get away with sneering at him.

"Wipe that smirk off your face," said Sheriff Harry Raines. The sculptor of the Perry Doughboy had meant the look on his creation's face to be one of purpose and courage. But for the price, truth was with Sheriff Harry Raines on this one. The Perry Doughboy did look like he was smirking.

With the light still red and the Loganville law wagon in neutral, Sheriff Harry Raines got out of the car and walked over to the Perry Doughboy.

"I said what are you looking at?" demanded Sheriff Harry Raines.

The Perry Doughboy looked straight on, a figure of nonchalance, his gaze now over the head of Sheriff Harry Raines.

"Where'd you get that rifle?"

The Enfield leaned against the Perry Doughboy's leg, hardly a threat to life, limb or the Law of Loganville. The Perry Doughboy held the tip of the rifle with his thumb and forefinger almost as if he didn't want to touch it.

"Gimme that gun," said Sheriff Harry Raines. "I said give it to me."

The Perry Doughboy ignored the order.

"So, smart ass are you? I'll show you."

Sheriff Harry Raines pulled his 38-caliber Smith and Wesson pistol from his holster and, without further warning, shot the Perry Doughboy in the groin, the bullet exiting through the right cheek of the Perry Doughboy's buttocks, sailing into the brick wall of the Perry Town Hall before coming to rest in the boxwood hedge under the window of Mayor Howard Trickle's office.

The crack of the shot startled Sheriff Harry Raines. Nothing sobers a man quite like a gunshot. He felt his pistol in his hand. He raised it and looked at it. He looked at the Perry Doughboy, still standing, still smirking. Sheriff

Harry Raines realized it was he who had pulled the trigger. The Law of Loganville had just violated the Hero of Perry. He had just killed a statue. He spun around, expecting someone to be there. Sheriff Harry Raines saw the unchanging red light and heard the soft purring of the finely tuned eight-cylinder engine on the Loganville law wagon.

Sheriff Harry Raines holstered his pistol, hitched his pants and crept quietly back to his car. Ignoring the red light, Sheriff Harry Raines slipped the Loganville law wagon into gear and motored out of the town of Perry.

Running the red was the least of the laws he had broken.

The wounding of the Perry Doughboy might have become a unifying incident for the community had anyone noticed it. But no one did until Ink Ear Ryan kissed the doughboy's ass. And Sonny and Duck were the first ones he had told.

"He'd still be heavy," said Duck.

"So, then, we'll do it. We'll take the doughboy bowling."

"I like the doughboy," said Duck. "I don't think we should be messing with him. He'd very hard to move."

"If we can move a corpse all the way to Fort Corsage from the train station, then I bet we can move a hollow doughboy to the Matterhorn," said Sonny.

Desperation had pushed Sonny into bringing up Eldon Burley. Duck said nothing. Ink Ear down below could not hear too clearly so he was unaware of Sonny's breach. Sonny and Duck did not look at each other.

Ink Ear called up from below.

"We can use The Flyer," Ink Ear yelled.

"Think about it, Duck," said Sonny. "The Flyer."

"Can't. The Flyer's broken," said Duck. "Charlie smashed it up with a crowbar."

Duck Stadler's red Radio Flyer, the last happy trace of his childhood, was now folded in the middle, creased by Charlie's blows. Two wheels were missing and the tongue was broken off. The Flyer was no more.

"That chicken shit," said Sonny.

"Let's get Butchie," yelled Ink Ear.

"What's that? Why don't you come up here so we can hear you," said Duck.

"You come down."

"We're coming down," said Sonny.

The three of them reunited on solid ground, three heads not necessarily better than two. Sonny asked Ink Ear what he had said.

"I said we should get Butchie."

"Butchie Booker?"

"Yeah. I never did like him."

"What did Butchie ever do to you? He's the reason we had the Great Bus Ride," said Sonny. "Without Butchie we would not be legends."

"I got my reasons," said Ink Ear.

Chapter 20

Butchie Booker, Again

Butchie Booker had become nearly as big a deal as Sonny, Duck and Ink Ear after the Great Bus Ride. He no longer wore glasses and his asthma was hardly a problem. He used his inhaler to make fart sounds and it always got a laugh. Teachers could do nothing about it. He needed his medicine and whenever things got boring, Butchie would rip one off. Only the smell or lack of it, would determine if Butchie was joking or farting.

Sonny, Duck and Ink Ear had nothing to match the fart, nor anything to counter the reward Butchie received for surviving the Great Bus Ride.

Butchie's parents, Twyla and Tim Booker, were so happy with the improved health of their boy that they bought him a bicycle, a shiny new Schwinn Ranger, a red beauty with shiny chrome handle bars and white wall tires.

The bike had orange reflectors on each side of its central tank and a larger red reflector on the carrier that rested above the back fender. Inside the tank a large dry cell battery gave power to a horn and to twin lights in front of the handlebars. The tank opened with a key that Butchie kept on a string around his neck, the same key that locked the steering column to discourage theft.

No child in Perry had anything to match it. Butchie would give rides but only he was allowed to pedal the bike. The school bus did not need to climb Summit Hill any more because Butchie rode his bike to school. In any case, the new bus driver, Rudy Holcomb, would not have given the children the same thrill around the curve at the bottom of Summit Hill that Mr. Ethel had because Mr. Holcomb did not like children, did not like them to have fun and would scold any child who laughed too loudly on the bus or sat in the wrong seat. The Great Bus Ride to school had become a dreary punishment, just like school itself. And it was all, in Ink Ear Ryan's mind, Butchie Booker's fault.

Ink Ear made his case to Sonny and Duck, citing all of it. The real reason he wanted some payback from Butchie had nothing to do with bicycles or gloomy school bus transportation, of course. The real reason was that Butchie had seen Ink Ear's tears during the Great Bus Ride. But all the other stuff was sufficient to draw in Sonny and Duck.

"Let's take his bike," said Ink Ear.

"We're not thieves," said Sonny, though sometimes they were, if only the occasional pack of Neccos from Neff's and the beer bottles they would take from the rear of Shorty's Tavern so they could sell them back to him in the front. Shorty knew their scheme but played along mostly because he could see in Duck great things ahead for the Perry Potters.

"We'll give the bike back," said Ink Ear. "Or we'll tell him where to find it. Where should we put it? I know. Let's put it where everybody can see it. I know, hey, let's put it under the doughboy."

Of the workable ideas Ink Ear had ever come up with, this one was at the top of a very short list. It could work. The question was whether the doughboy's legs were apart enough to slide a bicycle between them. The right leg was bent slightly at the knee and was a bit ahead of the left. It might look like he was pedaling.

"Maybe it would work," said Sonny as he pictured the possibility. "The Pedaling Doughboy. I don't like it as well as The Bowling Doughboy. But it could work."

"I said we're not messing with the doughboy," said Duck.

"We're not messing with him. We're helping him. We're giving him a ride."

"What about his gun? Doughboys don't ride bicycles with guns," said Duck.

"How do you know what doughboys do? Have you ever seen a real doughboy?"

"My granddad was one," said Ink Ear.

"For the other side," said Duck.

"No, for the right side. I have a picture of him wearing a helmet and holding an American flag."

"He was probably a spy," said Duck.

"Take that back," said Ink Ear.

"I ain't taking back anything."

Ink Ear remembered the punch in the nose and he did not want another one. "If he was a spy he was a spy for us," Ink Ear said.

"That's all I meant," said Duck.

"Spies don't wear helmets," said Sonny.

"How do you know what spies wear?"

"I know as much about spies as you know about doughboys."

"Okay," said Duck. "We'll give him a bicycle."

It was settled, then. The Perry Doughboy would get Butchie Booker's Schwinn and their legend would be satisfied.

The three boys sat on one of the two benches in the small park in front of Perry Town Hall. They studied the Perry Doughboy. Sonny got to his feet and walked around the statue. He stopped and peered between the Perry Doughboy's legs. He gauged the width and height of the opening. It would be a tight fit.

Ink Ear joined Sonny in his examination. Duck remained on the bench, still reluctant to do anything to the doughboy.

"How are we going to get the handle bars under his legs?" asked Ink Ear. "The handle bars are too wide. Everything else would fit, but not the handle bars."

"Don't be stupid. We'll take them off," said Duck.

"No," said Sonny, "we'll back the bike in. We'll have to lift it up and back it in. This is going to work. It is going to work."

Butchie Booker considered Sonny, Duck and Ink Ear his heroes. They did not know they were his heroes and they would not have cared. Butchie was a little creep and beneath their caring about. Just as without Butchie they would not have been the authors of the Great Bus Ride, Butchie knew that without them, he would not have the Schwinn and without them he would still wear glasses and without them he couldn't rip one off whenever he felt like it. Butchie had them, three to one.

But more than any of that was the Swinging Bridge Incident, and for that, Butchie may have owed one of them his life.

Why Butchie Booker tried to take his Schwinn across the Swinging Bridge, even he did not know, except it seemed the thing to do at the time. The bridge was not made for bicycles. It was not made for human foot traffic unless the human was particularly courageous, someone at least as brave as Duck Stadler.

The boards that spanned the two cables and provided the floor of the bridge were uneven in size as well as in wear and in safety. They were strong enough to hold a small boy but, as Gus Shiner could testify, not so much for a grown man or for anything of greater weight than your average sixth grader.

Butchie had followed Duck Stadler after school one day, asking him if he wanted a ride, if he wanted to pedal the Schwinn, if he wanted to do anything with Butchie Booker.

"Get lost, creep," Duck said. "Get the hell away from me."

Butchie Booker and his Schwinn represented to Duck everything he did not have and everything he wished he had, a loving mother and father, money to buy Neccos, clothes that did not smell of the coal mines as his did because Sarah washed his and Charlie's clothes together.

As good a friend as was Sonny and as big a pain in the ass as was Ink Ear, they were the same as he was. The comfort in that did not match the envy that came whenever he saw Butchie on his Schwinn.

"Come on, Duck. Take a ride," said Butchie

"Don't call me Duck. My friends call be Duck. Don't talk to me. Get away from me."

Duck had no real destination, but he knew wherever it was it had to be where Butchie Booker could not take his Schwinn, that outrageous, wonderful bicycle. Duck walked along the tracks of the Ohio Southern beside the Jericho River. He could hear the tires of Butchie's Schwinn crunching the gravel behind him.

The railroad side of the Swinging Bridge had a ramp that led up to the entry of the bridge. The other side had a crude ladder made from boards pounded into a hickory tree. Duck sprinted up the ramp and bounded across the bridge, making it sway and creak.

Butchie Booker had never been on the Swinging Bridge, not alone and certainly not with a shiny red Schwinn bicycle with twin lights and horn. Butchie pushed his bike up the ramp. Duck had already crossed and was out of sight. Duck was rid of the little creep and his red bicycle.

Duck had turned the corner of the path that led back to Perry when he heard Butchie scream.

"Aaaaagh! Aaaaagh! Aaaaagh! No! No! No!"

Duck ran back to the Swinging Bridge. He could see Butchie in the middle, hanging on to one of the guide ropes with one hand onto his Schwinn with the other. The front wheel of his bicycle was already off the boards, its two chrome headlights staring down into the Jericho River. The weight of the bicycle was pulling at Butchie. The bridge was swinging and Butchie's grip on the guide rope was slipping.

"Leg it go! Let it go!" yelled Duck. "Let the bicycle go!"

"I ain't! I ain't!" yelled Butchie.

"Then you're going in, too!" yelled Duck. "Can you swim?"

"No! No! No I can't and no I ain't."

Duck scrambled up the board ladder on the hickory tree. He had to be careful not to cause the bridge to swing any more than it already was. He put his weight on the side of the bridge opposite the hanging bicycle and that seemed to settle the sway. Duck reached Butchie just as his grip on the guide rope was breaking. He grabbed Butchie's wrist and reached out and seized the Schwinn just under the seat. He had them both. The bridge settled into a barely noticeable roll.

"What in the hell were you doing, you little creep?" asked Duck.

"I was following you."

"You're nuts."

"I guess it wasn't very smart."

"How did you expect to get down the other side?"

"I don't know."

"What a creep."

Sonny examined Butchie Booker. His brown eyes were large and clear. Not a tear. The little creep would not have let go of that bike. He would have drowned.

"I'll say one thing. You're not a chicken shit," said Duck.

So it was that Duck had two reasons to resist sticking Butchie's Schwinn under the Perry Doughboy. He had a patriot's affection for the

236

statue and he had a grudging admiration for Butchie. Sonny and Ink Ear knew only about the first one. Duck never mentioned the second one.

"Now, we've just got to steal the bike," said Sonny.

"I know where he keeps it," said Ink Ear. "It'll be there after Beggar's Night, I bet."

As did most towns in that part of Ohio, Perry divided its Halloween into two nights. The last day in October was Halloween and the night before it was Beggar's Night, the night when younger children would dress in costumes and trick or treat.

The children did not know why Halloween had two nights instead of just one, and it was not clear to most adults. But that's the way it was. One night for candy and one night for mischief. Butchie Booker was still on the candy side of the line and Sonny, Duck and Ink Ear were on the mischief side.

Butchie's Schwinn was just where Ink Ear said it would be, down a paved driveway next to the back door of the Booker house. It rested on its kickstand, backlit by a soft light from somewhere inside the house. It was after midnight and most of the mischief was done. Sheriff John Brown had gone home. Only two outhouses had been tipped and no one had egged the Perry Doughboy. A peaceful Halloween, all in all.

"You get the back and I'll get the front and we'll carry it off," whispered Sonny to Duck. "Ink Ear you watch out for us."

"Do they have a dog?" asked Duck.

"No," said Ink Ear. "They got cats."

How Ink Ear Ryan knew so much about the Bookers did not occur to either Sonny or Duck. But Ink Ear had made a study of the Bookers ever since the Great Bus Ride. He knew he had to be prepared for a night just like this.

Twyla Booker was a nurse, working at the Bethesda Hospital in Newark and Tim Booker owned a Studebaker dealership in Columbus. Twyla's widowed aunt Betsy Andrews kept the house and watched Butchie. Tim traveled back and forth every day, a practice considered stupid by those who lived in Perry. Going to Jericho was enough of a commute. Why didn't they just live in Columbus? Or in Newark?

Good questions if anyone had cared to ask. The Bookers liked the view from the top of Summit Hill. They liked the idea of a small town experience for their son. They had built the house from blueprints and that, too, seemed a bit excessive to the people of Perry. The house had not only a full porch across the front but also a back balcony that led from the second-floor bedroom of Twyla and Tim. The Bookers had paid to extend the town water to their house and they had not only indoor plumbing, but also a separate bathroom just for Butchie.

238

Ink Ear thought of his own living arrangements and was determined more than ever to get even with a boy who had never done anything to him.

"We're not stealing this bike," whispered Sonny. "We're only borrowing it."

Duck and Sonny carried the Schwinn to the road and then wheeled it below the crest of the hill before Duck got on it to ride it to the bottom.

"Let me ride it," said Ink Ear.

"I'm riding it," said Duck.

"Jesus, can we just get out of here?" asked Sonny.

Duck allowed Ink Ear to sit on the back carrier and they whizzed down Summit Hill, Ink Ear making much too much noise. Sonny trotted along after them, unaware of the steady steps of Butchie Booker behind him.

The Ceramic Street traffic light was permanently red when Sonny got to the Perry Doughboy. Duck and Ink Ear were already waiting. Between the red glow of the traffic light and the muted yellow illumination from the street lamps, there was enough light for the boys to see and enough light to be seen by Butchie, peeking from behind the corner of the firehouse.

"Let's fit it in there," said Sonny in a husky whisper. Duck climbed onto the pedestal that held the doughboy, reached down and took the back of Butchie Booker's Schwinn. He pulled the bicycle up and Sonny pushed from below. Duck fitted the back fender between the Perry Doughboy's legs

239

and they wiggled the bike backwards. It moved easily until the pedals caught one of the doughboy's leggings.

"I think this will have to do," said Sonny.

Duck jumped down from the pedestal and they stepped back to survey their work. Well done. Nothing could top this. Sonny had thought of putting a newspaper delivery bag over the doughboy's shoulder but that seemed a bit excessive. No use repainting the outhouse.

Sonny, Duck and Ink Ear were certain that when Perry woke in the morning, they would see the best Halloween prank of them all. The best this year, for sure. The best until they could think of a better one next year. They were very pleased with themselves and went home whistling.

When the folks of Perry awoke the next morning this is what they saw. They saw Butchie Booker in the crook of the Perry Doughboy's arm, his legs dangling through the space between the doughboy's arm and his hip. Butchie's head was behind and above the doughboy's right shoulder and Butchie's left arm was wrapped around the doughboy's neck. Butchie was laughing as if he had just won first prize at the fair. The Perry Doughboy not only looked like he was sitting on a red Schwinn bicycle but it looked as if he was taking Butchie Booker for a ride. And if the people of Perry didn't see it the next morning they saw it the next day. That was the picture that made the front page of the Loganville Messenger.

Butchie Booker had won again.

"The little creep," said Duck, not without respect.

Chapter 21

On the Daddy Trail

The photograph Sonny had taken from Clara's trunk had been in an out of Sonny's back pocket at least a dozen times a day. Sonny had done nothing about the picture except to look at it. It was not much of a clue but it was the only one he had. He studied the picture, examining the face of the man in the picture with a magnifying glass. Ron Miller had given Sonny the magnifier when Sonny had collected stamps.

A cocky asshole, Sonny thought. What right does he have to be grinning like that? How dare he be happy. Sonny held the picture next to his own reflection and did not see what Duck saw. This was just some guy in a sailor suit. Wasn't it? Sonny ran his finger along the bridge of his nose and touched the nose on the man in the picture. His nose? The same nose? He felt the indentation in his chin, something he had never paid a bit of attention to. He studied the chin of the man in the picture. Same chin.

Damn it. Sonny would have hated the man in the picture even if the man was not his father. He would have hated the man in the picture for coming into Sonny's life when Sonny's life had been just fine without him.

Why did a guy need a father, anyhow? To bat him around like Charlie did Duck? To embarrass him the way Woody did Ink Ear? Of the fathers Sonny knew, none were worth a shit. Sonny was the lucky one. He had a half father, a step father, no father at all.

Ron Miller paid no attention to Sonny, and that was just fine with both of them. Sonny could stay out late or get up early or piss in his own yard and nobody would tell him not to.

What did fathers do? Did they teach a boy how to tie his shoes? Sonny knew how to tie his shoes. Did they teach him how to throw a ball? Sonny could throw a ball. Did they take a boy fishing? Sonny hated fishing. Try fishing in the Jericho River and all the fathers in the world couldn't catch a fish where there was no fish.

Duck Stadler was a great ball player. No father, certainly not Duck's father, made him a great ball player. He just was.

"Did your dad ever take you fishing?" Sonny asked Duck.

"Why would he do that?"

"Because fathers are supposed to do crap like that, play games, go fishing, camping, building things together."

"Like what things?"

"You know, toys and shit."

"What toys?"

"I don't know what toys. Toys. Or a tree house. Or a soap box derby car or something."

"A tree house?"

"A house in a tree. You know, a place to play. Up in a tree."

"Do you see any houses in our trees?"

"Jesus, Duck, I'm just trying to find out what you do with your dad. If Charlie ever taught you anything. Did he teach you to whistle? How about how to tie your shoes? Did he ever show you anything you can use? What about shaving?"

"Shaving. Jesus, Sonny, shaving?"

"That's one of the big things dads are supposed to do. They teach their kid how to shave. Did you ever see Charlie shave?"

"I don't shave," said Duck. "You don't shave."

"But we will shave."

"So, we've got to find your father before you shave. We better get started. I see some fuzz there on your lip."

Duck flicked a forefinger above Sonny's upper lip.

"You're full of shit," said Sonny. "There's nothing Charlie ever showed you how to do?"

"I never learned to tie my shoes. I just tied them. I can whistle. I always could. Nobody taught me," said Duck.

"Well, he must have shown you something. There must be one thing at least."

Duck thought about it. So few things had ever been shared with Charlie Stadler. They did almost nothing together.

"Once we painted the back door," said Duck.

"There you go. How was that?"

"Charlie whacked me for slopping the paint on the floor."

"Ah, shit, Duck. You're no help."

"But he did teach me one thing."

"What, to duck, Duck? Ha, ha," said Sonny.

"He showed me how to keep the paint from slopping out of the can. If you drive a nail in the rim of the can, make some holes all the way around, then the paint can drip back into the can. It's neater and the lid doesn't stick when you put it back on."

"That's it? Nails in a paint can?"

"That's all I can think of."

"Jesus, Duck, that's awful. One thing. One stupid, lousy thing."

"How many things has your dad taught you?"

Duck had a point. But Sonny figured that since he now knew the secret of the paint can, he had another reason not to need a father.

The problem was that damned picture. There was a real person in that picture. And he had a

245

name. Before the picture there was only the idea of a person. Sonny could think about him or not think about him. Ideas were great that way. You can keep an idea or you can throw it away. Now there was an actual man. Sonny liked the idea of a man better than a real man. Like the Perry Doughboy. Sonny could imagine anything he wanted to about all the heroic things the doughboy had done. A real man had to be what he was. He could not be more than he was. And what was a real man, anyhow, if he didn't have anything to do with his own son?

Having the picture was like having one piece of a jigsaw puzzle and not even a corner piece. And no box with a lid to know what the puzzle was supposed to look like. How was Sonny supposed to find a father with just one piece?

"I've only got one piece of the puzzle," said Sonny.

"You've got his name," said Duck. "His name is Bob. You've got his picture and his name. That's two pieces."

"Half a name."

"And he was a sailor. You've got three pieces. A picture, a name and a sailor."

"And a cemetery," said Ink Ear.

"What cemetery?"

"The one in the picture."

Sonny handed the picture and the magnifying glass to Duck.

"See, he's got his foot on a tombstone."

246

"I know this cemetery," said Duck. "It's the one in Loganville."

"How do you know that?"

"Look. See that building through the trees there? That's where they keep the ashes of people. My aunt Rosalie is in there. My mother goes there every year on Aunt Rosalie's birthday and puts new flowers in a thing on the wall. Now, we've got another piece of the puzzle. How many pieces is that?"

Ink Ear was weary of the deliberations of Sonny and Duck. He sided with Sonny. The unknown father is better than the known one. Anything further was beyond him. There was nothing Ink Ear could contribute. Still, he offered the logical question.

"Why don't you just take the picture and ask Clara?" Ink Ear asked.

"Then she would know I was in her trunk," said Sonny.

"So what?"

"So...so...oh, shit, Ink Ear. You don't understand anything."

"Besides," said Duck, "it's more fun this way."

"I wouldn't call it fun," said Sonny. But in its own way, it was fun. It was another adventure.

Duck thought the first thing they should do was go to the Loganville Cemetery. They could find the exact spot where this so-called "Bob," had stood when the picture was taken. They could not read the name on the headstone in the picture because the shadow of the man's leg blacked it out. But with the magnifier they could see one of the dates. It was three years after Sonny was born.

"That means he was there and saw your mother and you when you were little," said Duck. "Maybe he didn't like what he saw and he just took off. Maybe he was scared away by your big ears."

"It's not my fault," said Sonny.

"You mean your ears?"

"No. All of it. The whole thing."

One thing Clara always stressed whenever Sonny badgered her was that it was not Sonny's fault that his father abandoned them. She never used the word "abandoned," or even the word "left." She just said it was not Sonny's fault and that she would tell him about it when he was old enough.

"It's somebody's fault," said Ink Ear.

The boys could walk to Loganville or they could hitch. They might end up doing both. Or they could ride with Jim Norton on his milk route. They did that sometimes and pretended they were going off to war or off to anywhere but Perry. They were going in a circle, of course, and always ended up back where they started, at the parking lot of Wiseman's Dairy. Still, they got to hang out of the side of Jim's milk truck because it didn't have any doors and Jim never told them not to do that. Sometimes they ran the full bottles of milk up to a house and brought the empties back. Jim sometimes stayed longer than was necessary at a house, usually the house of Muriel Spillman. Muriel never ordered more than a pint of cream or a pound of butter.

"The cream is for her cat," Jim explained. The boys did not care what the cream was for and they did not know why Jim bothered telling them. "And sometimes we have to look for it, for the cat."

Jim always took Muriel's order to the house himself and when he did, the boys would chug down chocolate milk from the truck until he got back.

They had to get up very early to go with Jim. He always finished his route in time for them to get to school. This time they decided to hitch to Loganville and got a ride right away from Tank Schumaker, a man shaped like his name, a man they all knew. Tank had a hauling business and a three-quarter ton, flat bed Chevy. Tank moved almost anything to almost anywhere. That day he was hauling rolled sod to the Loganville Cemetery, to patch some places that needed new grass. Sonny rode in the cab with Tank. Duck and Ink Ear sat on the sod in the bed of the truck. Ink Ear had yelled, "Shotgun," when Tank slowed down to give them a ride, but Sonny had already won a game of rock, paper, scissors. Wrapping up Duck's rock and breaking Ink Ear's scissors.

When Tank told the boys he was going to the Loganville Cemetery, Sonny felt that some higher power was at work. It could not be a coincidence that the ride they hitched would be going to exactly the same place that they were going. Sonny would learn something today, he was sure of it.

Tank had a hula dancer with a grass skirt on his dashboard. She wiggled as the truck moved. It reminded Sonny of his Grandpa Tolliver's tattoo. The hula dancer connection couldn't be a coincidence either. Something was going on. Fate was going to give him some answers.

"Why is a young kid like yourself going to a cemetery?" asked Tank. "You ain't dressed for a funeral."

Sonny was dressed his usual way, jeans, tee shirt and blue sneakers, the rubber on the left shoe needing to be glued. His jeans were rolled up one turn from the bottom. They were in need of a wash. He liked Levi's but no matter how many times he told Clara, she bought him Wranglers. Most of the other boys wore Levi's but that is not why Sonny preferred them. He did not like Wranglers because Ron Miller wore Wranglers.

"Do you expect me to shop for pants for my two men in two different places?" asked Clara. "Don't be silly."

He wondered what kind of jeans his father wore.

Sonny's tee shirt had a hole at the left shoulder. Sonny had made it bigger by mistakenly sticking his arm into the hole.

"What do people wear at funerals?" Sonny asked Tank.

250

"Suits usually and black dresses. Neckties."

"Even kids?"

"Sure."

"I don't ever want to go to a funeral."

"You won't have anything to say about it," said Tank Schumaker.

Sonny was reminded of what Clara had said to him once. He did not remember the reason or the occasion. "There are no survivors," she said. "Only strivers. Be a striver, Sonny."

Tank and Sonny both sat in silence the rest of the way to Loganville. Sonny could hear Duck and Ink Ear wrestling on top of the sod in the bed of the truck. He wished he had let Ink Ear have his "shotgun" when he called it.

The Loganville Cemetery was on the edge of town, closer now than when it was first used. The town had grown towards death rather than away from it. Two large cement pillars supported a black wrought iron entry gate. The words, "Eternal Rest" were scrolled into the arch of the gate. Oak trees shaded the lane beyond the gate that led through the collection of graves and tombstones and monuments. Some of them had stone crosses, some were plain, some were decorated with carved wreaths and some were topped with marble angels. From his seat in Tank's flat bed Chevy, the cemetery reminded Sonny of the town of Perry as he saw it from the water tower. These people at least know they are dead, thought Sonny.

"Good hunting," said Tank Schumaker after he had passed through the gate and stopped to let the boys out.

"What did he mean by that?" asked Ink Ear.

"I don't know," said Sonny. "I didn't tell him anything."

Sonny removed the photograph from his back pocket. It was beginning to wrinkle and fray along the edges.

"You should take better care of that," said Duck. "You should put it in a frame or something."

"It gets what it deserves," said Sonny. He put the photo on the top of a small tombstone that advised the boys that "Love Lives On." From the picture Sonny figured they had to walk towards a very large marble crypt shaped like a tobacco tin. Somewhere between there and the mausoleum that stored the ashes of Duck's Aunt Rosalie would be the headstone they were looking for.

Sonny turned and walked backwards, trying to keep the line.

"The trees are bigger," Sonny said.

"Look out!"

Duck grabbed Sonny just before he would have tripped over a small headstone. "Saved your life."

"Wait a minute," said Sonny. "I think this is it."

Sonny moved away and held the picture at arms length, trying to match the trees and Aunt Rosalie's mausoleum and the other stones.

"Here, let me see it," said Duck. "You go over there and put one foot up on the stone."

Sonny did as Duck asked. He assumed the pose as best he could remember of the man in the photograph.

"Now put on a sailor suit," said Duck.

"Knock it off, dammit. What do you think?"

Duck looked at the picture. He looked at Sonny. He squinted. He frowned. He tilted his head to one side and then the other.

"I think we have a match."

"Let me, let me," said Ink Ear. He put his foot on the headstone and tried to assume the pose.

"Not a chance," said Duck. "Here, let me."

Duck handed the photo to Sonny and they traded places. He pushed Ink Ear aside and took the same pose. He even tried to imitate the grin on the man in the picture. Sonny had to admit that this was the place. And so what? What had they learned? At one time a man had stood there and had his picture taken.

Sonny had been sure that this was the day he would learn something. There were too many coincidences. Why would the man in the sailor suit have been there? Why would his mother have been there? Did she take the picture? What brought both of them to this place? He still had questions and no answers.

"Look at the writing," said Ink Ear.

"The what?"

"On the stone. Look at what it says."

Duck took his foot off the headstone and stepped back. Sonny moved closer.

Chiseled into the face of the stone was an angel holding a baby. The date of birth and death were the same year, the year when Sonny was three years old. The writing said, "Our beloved daughter, Judith Ellen Tolliver."

Said Duck, "We may not have found your father, but I think we found your sister."

Chapter 22

Clara's Old Story

The gravestone in the Loganville Cemetery had to be explained. As reluctant as Sonny was to complicate things with information, as hesitant as he was to gain knowledge that he was certain he did not need, as disinclined as he was to add another layer of slag to the pile that was his young life, he knew it had to be done.

The need to know is always stronger than the need to tell. Now Sonny's need to know would force Clara Tolliver to tell.

"You've got to ask her about it," said Duck Stadler. "About all of it. You can't tell me you don't have to. Now you've got a dead sister. A dead sister, Sonny. Even if you don't want to know, I sure do."

"Me, too," said Ink Ear Ryan.

"Shit," said Sonny Tolliver.

It had to be done, Sonny knew it. No more random wandering around; no more hit-and-miss adventure; no more guesses; this required actual facts. And Clara is the one who had them.

Why didn't he know before now? Sonny could have already learned the story in bits and over time. Now he had to get it all at once. Like medicine. One gulp. Shit, thought Sonny Tolliver.

What had kept Clara from telling her story was the same thing that had kept Sonny from insisting that she tell it.

Shame.

Shame is an intruder, a nasty trespasser, an uninvited guest that won't leave. Shame comes without being asked and it stays forever.

Shame controls society, and it has done so from the Garden of Eden on. Religions are founded on shame and religions function on shame. Shame is a renewable resource. Shame does its best work in the dark and the quiet.

Sonny was not conscious of the shame that hid behind his reluctance to know. It was not the same with Clara. She knew shame and she felt it. Her own father had made sure of it. Clara was reminded of it every time she saw Sonny. He was shame's scab and no matter how she consoled herself, no matter how she congratulated herself for not flushing him down the toilet, it was a sore that was never going to heal. Clara had known and felt shame since before Sonny was born.

"Mom," Sonny said, the afternoon after the trip to the Loganville Cemetery, "Can I talk to you?"

"Sure, sweetie. Just a minute."

Clara was washing eggs and separating them by size into the brown paper sacks that had customers' names already written on them in Clara's fine cursive hand. Clara set aside the brown eggs in a separate bowl. She sold only white eggs, not because she liked to keep the brown ones for herself but because some customers considered brown eggs to be cursed. Witches' eggs. Sonny thought they tasted just fine.

Clara placed the last of her paper sacks into the cardboard carton she used for storing the eggs until they could be picked up or until Ron delivered them for her. Ron had an arrangement with Carl Lawson. He gave Carl eggs and Carl gave Ron milk. Otherwise, everything was cash.

"I think I'll have enough to buy you a new shirt and pants for the ceremony," Clara said. "I'll buy you Levi's if you like. It's not every year my boy is...what are you? The door prize?"

"The Doerr Prize, Mom, D-o-e-...never mind. A new shirt is not what I want to talk about."

"You can pick your clothes out yourself," said Clara. "You can go with me."

"Forget the clothes, Mom. I want to talk about Judith Ellen."

Clara stopped creasing the fold at the top of a sack of eggs. Sonny had her full attention.

"Where did you hear that name?"

"I saw it."

"How did you see it? Where did you see it?"

"I saw it on a grave."

Clara Tolliver sat down at the kitchen table. She pulled an ashtray towards her, sliding it across the oilcloth with the strawberry design. She reached for her Camels. Her thin lips, which she dressed with red lipstick daily, were pulled into a straight line, nearly disappearing from her face.

Sonny held the photograph of the sailor in front of her.

"And I want to know about this guy," Sonny said.

Clara Miller had not noticed any disturbance to her trunk and she had not missed the pictures that Sonny had taken. She had decided that Sonny would be old enough to know about his beginnings after he was out of elementary school. She would tell him who his father was and leave it up to Sonny to do what he wished with the knowledge. She had not decided if she would tell him about Judith Ellen.

"Maybe I'm not old enough to hear it," Sonny said. "Maybe I'll never be old enough. But I want to know."

"Maybe I'm not old enough to tell you."

Clara lit her Camel with the pistol shaped Ronson Sonny had given her. She drew the smoke into her lungs and exhaled loudly, her face being cloaked by the blue haze of her habit. She did not look at Sonny, nor did he look directly at her. They spoke to each other with eyes lowered. Shame.

"Why don't you just ask me your questions and I'll answer them," Clara said.

"That's bullshit, Mom" said Sonny, smacking his hand on the oilcloth. "I'm just a kid. What do I know? You tell me. You were there. I wasn't."

"Honey, I…"

"Tell me his name."

Clara lit another Camel off the butt of the one she was already smoking. She mashed the first one into the ashtray.

"Wait," said Sonny. "First tell me why he didn't marry you."

"Or I didn't marry him," said Clara.

"Tell me that. Either way."

"I thought he was dead," said Clara.

"How could he be dead? Here he is. I was three years old when this picture was taken." Sonny slid the picture across the oilcloth so that his mother had to look at it. She picked it up.

"Is that him? Is that my father?"

Clara nodded.

Neither of them said anything. Clara continued to stare at the picture. Sonny sat down at the table, folded his hands and waited.

"I kept this in my trunk," she said. "You were in my trunk."

"I was," said Sonny.

"I took this picture," Clara said. "I used his camera. I'm not very good with cameras. I never know what to push. This one had a slide on the side you had to push down. He sent the picture to me. I didn't ask for it. He looks happy. He wasn't happy. Neither of us was happy."

"Not ever?"

"We argued all the time."

"That's not new. You argue with Ron all the time."

"I guess it must be me, then."

Sonny did not want to feel sorry for his mother. And she did not seek his sympathy. But that's the way it was working out. Sonny looked at the woman he knew so little about, his "mommy," from the time she would change his diaper and tickle his tummy. "Whose little boy are you? Whose? Whose?"

That was the question, wasn't it? That was the question he was asking. How much more uncomplicated was the time when the answer was "yours, Mommy."

"Bob Lund."

"What?"

"That's his name. Bob Lund. Robert Allen Lund."

There it was. The hole in his heart had a cork. But the hole did not feel filled. It felt bigger.

"Lund."

"Yes. L-u-n-d."

"You mean like the radio preacher?"

"His son," said Clara.

"Whose son?"

"Warren Lund. His son. Son of a preacher man."

Oh, Christ. This is awful. Son of a son of a preacher man. Son of a bitch.

Was Sonny's father in the Brotherhood of Pruners gathered at the Devil's Tea Table? Was he one of those in a blue robe helping the guy in the gold gown down from the rock? A son helps his father. Even if his father is an asshole. Doesn't he?

"My name could have been Lund."

"Well, I guess, so. But not really."

What came into Sonny Tolliver's mind was that he would have been in the middle of the alphabet. He had found that most things were done alphabetically. Tolliver was always near the end of the line. There were only Rex Wolf and Sandy Young after him at school. If he were Sonny Lund, he would have about the same number of names on each side of him. He would be the middle of a sandwich. He wasn't sure he liked the idea of being in the middle of anything. He was in the middle of a load of crap right now and he was sure he did not like it at all. And he wasn't sure why the alphabet was the first thing he thought about.

"Did you love him?"

"At the time," said Clara Miller.

"And he loved you?"

"You'll have to ask him."

What was going on? He was talking about love with his mother. He could not remember ever talking about love with anyone. Or even thinking

261

about it. This was getting much too mushy. What did he really want to know? He wanted to know why his father was not with his mother and he wanted to know where this Bob Lund lived. That's all, wasn't it? And about Judith Ellen. Yes. Can't forget about poor Judith Ellen. Was she flushed down the toilet?

"You thought he was dead?" asked Sonny.

"He was in the Navy. They told me he was dead."

"Who told you?"

"Evelyn told me. She heard it from his sister."

"And you believed her? Jesus, Mom, she hates you. Why would you believe anything Aunt Evelyn said?"

"It was the war. Lots of boys got killed. They had a service for him in the church. Warren Lund cried on the radio. He never wrote to me. I never heard. And then one day he just showed up."

"Showed up? Where?"

"At the cemetery."

"Where the picture was taken?"

"I was putting flowers on Judith Ellen's grave. And there he was."

"Judith Ellen was my sister?"

"She was. In a way."

"What way?"

"Ronnie was her father."

"Ron? Ron Miller?"

"I thought he was dead. That's what I told him. He just showed up. I thought he was dead."

"Where was I?"

"Ronnie took you for a ride. I didn't want you there. Ronnie dropped me at the grave and took you for a ride."

"So, this Bob Lund never saw me?"

"Yes, he did. He took a picture of you. He took a picture of both of us."

"What did Ron do?"

"He waited."

"Can't you just tell it to me? Just tell me the whole thing? And then if I have any more questions, I'll ask."

Clara Tolliver lit another Camel. The previous one still burned in the ashtray.

"I used to smoke Luckies," she said.

Bob Lund was a preacher's son. His father Warren held Sunday services on WLOG, "for shut-ins and friends at home." His sign off signature was "God loves you and so do I." And then he gave the address for contributions.

Warren Lund was based at the New Church of the Nazarene as the deputy pastor to the founder, Norton Hickman. Norton did not preach much any more. Norton sat in a large wicker chair behind the pulpit in a white suit and white shoes. He always wore red socks, "to remind me that the devil is in all of us." When the music got loud and the congregation felt the Lord inside them, Norton would tap his cane to the rhythms of the moment.

Warren Lund was the figure in the gold robe, the leader of some bunch of assholes who chanted about prunes. Knowing all of this was much worse than not knowing any of it.

Bob Lund grew up in Loganville. He had his own car when he was 16. Clara was 18 when they met.

"You were older?" Sonny asked.

"I thought so," said Clara.

"But you don't go to church," said Sonny.

"I went with Evelyn. It was a tent revival meeting in Perry. Down by the town hall. She liked this boy."

"Let me guess who."

"He liked me. Right away."

Bob Lund brought the collection plate around at the revival meeting. While his father screamed from the pulpit about the salvation that comes with giving, Bob passed among the flock, holding out a tray that looked like a tambourine. Coins clinked and slid over each other and it sounded like a tambourine. Bob Lund shook it to the rhythm of his father's shouts.

"Give for Jesus! Give for Jesus!" Warren Lund's voice boomed from the pulpit.

Bob Lund paused when he reached the two girls sitting on folding chairs in the middle of the eighth row, the pretty small one with dark hair and the larger one who stared at him with her mouth open. He grinned, showing his straight white teeth. His hair was greased and combed straight back. It shone under the light of the bare bulbs that were strung along the spine of the tent. He reached out to touch Clara's hand when she fumbled in her purse for change.

"This one's on me," he said, and moved the tray over to Evelyn. He shook the tray until she dropped in two nickels, never taking his eyes off Clara. "I've got the spirit in me!" yelled Evelyn.

Bob Lund leaned in and spoke into Clara Tolliver's ear. "Let me walk you home,"

"Okay," said Clara.

"I've got the spirit! The Holy Spirit! It's in me!" Evelyn grabbed Bob Lund's wrist. "In me!"

Bob tried to pull away from Evelyn's grip and the tambourine tray went flying. Coins and a few bills scattered over the congregation. The tray cracked Marge Norris in the side of the head, causing a slight cut that bled more than it needed to.

"The blood of Christ! The blood of Christ!" Wayne Lund chanted from the pulpit.

Clara knelt down to help pick up the coins and Evelyn knocked over her chair trying to do the same. Clara's hand touched Bob's when they tried to pick up the same 50-cent piece. "Wait for me," said Bob Lund. "By the statue."

Oh, shit, thought Sonny. He's a holy roller. Why couldn't he be Duck's dad? Duck's mom is a holy roller. If he was Duck's dad that would solve both their problems. Unless Charlie was Sonny's dad. Why did boys have to have dads?

265

Evelyn's animosity to Sonny now made sense. His mother had stolen her boy friend, though Sonny doubted if he ever was her boyfriend.

"Evelyn didn't always look like she does," said Clara. "She was always big, but not, you know, fat. That wasn't until after..."

"After what?"

"After I was pregnant with you."

His mom had stolen Aunt Evelyn's boyfriend and she was responsible for her getting fat. Jesus, did Sonny need to know all of this? Sonny could not picture either his mother or his Aunt Evelyn as girls, silly flirty girls.

"She thought I was getting fat," said Clara. "She couldn't have been happier. She was over the moon when she learned why I was getting fat. She raised hell with Dad and he threw me out. I was always his favorite."

Sonny thought he should have been taking notes. Preacher's son. Holy rollers. Stolen boyfriend. Fat aunt. Kicked out.

"He took me behind the doughboy and kissed me."

Oh, shit, thought Sonny. Not the doughboy. Don't involve the doughboy.

"And then you came along. It's an old story."

Clara gathered her Camels and the Ronson lighter and stuck them into her apron pocket. She rose and left the room. Sonny sat there. That's it? He kissed me and you came along? Sonny didn't know a lot about the way these things worked but he knew enough to know a few steps had been omitted.

Clara returned and handed Sonny a piece of paper. In her fine cursive hand she had written: "Bob Lund, 153 Washington St., Loganville."

"That's where he lives. Let him tell you the rest."

"What about Judith Ellen?" Sonny asked.

"That has nothing to do with you."

"You're not going to tell me?"

"When you're old enough."

Chapter 23

Clara's New Story

The story that Clara told to Sonny was not the same story Sonny told to Duck and Ink Ear.

"You know the octopus?" Sonny asked.

"The squishy thing with 10 legs?" asked Ink Ear.

"Eight legs," said Sonny. "But, no. Not that one. The octopus at the fair."

"The ride?" asked Duck.

"Yeah, that one. My father saved my mother from certain death on the octopus. That's how they met."

Sonny was sorry but Clara's story would not do. It was not good enough. It had kisses in it and his Aunt Evelyn. And holy rollers. It was not a story he wanted to tell to Duck and Ink Ear. His father seemed a bit of an asshole, too. A preacher asshole. He didn't want an asshole for a father. He wanted a hero. Duck and Ink Ear wanted a hero, too.

"And then he saved 16 men from drowning in the war after his ship was torpedoed. He pulled them out of the water and put them in a boat and then he pulled the boat to an island. He had to swim through sharks to an island."

"Wow," said Duck.

"He kept them alive with coconuts and berries and stuff until they were rescued. He was the only one with a gun and he shot a wild pig and roasted it over the fire. He started the fire with the glasses of one of the men. He learned that in the Boy Scouts. He was an Eagle Scout and he had merit badges in swimming and wilderness survival. That's how he could do it."

"Boy Scouts. I want to be a Boy Scout," said Ink Ear.

"The admiral of the Navy gave him a medal," said Sonny. "It was gold with three silver stars on it."

"You saw it?" asked Duck.

"No, but I will."

Sonny did not lie as a rule. He did not exaggerate. He had no need to lie. Not with Duck and Ink Ear. One of the great things about being smarter than everyone else is that whatever you say tends to be believed. Sonny lied to his mother sometimes. Sure, but this was not the same. This was a big lie; it was the biggest lie Sonny had ever told. But it was a lie he had to tell.

"Clara told you all of this?" Duck asked.

"Well, not at first, but I made her."

"How did you do that?"

"I just told her I was old enough and showed her the picture and told her about the grave."

"Who's in the grave? Is that your sister?" asked Duck.

"Yes. She died of a terrible disease that caused her toes to fall off."

"All of them?" asked Ink Ear.

"Well, seven or eight of them."

"Little piggies," said Ink Ear.

"What piggies?" asked Duck.

"These little piggies went to market but none of them came home."

Duck laughed. And Sonny laughed, too. Ink Ear was not sure what he had said to make them laugh, but he wasn't going to waste whatever it was. Ink Ear laughed, too. He felt like he was on a roll.

"Your dad saved your mom from a giant octopus?" asked Ink Ear. "When he was swimming through sharks with a torpedo?"

Duck flicked Ink Ear on the top of the head. "Idiot."

Sonny had never imagined his father being a hero or being an asshole or being anything at all. When he did not know who his father was he did not make up fantasies about him. Now that he knew who he was, he could not stop making up stuff.

"It was at the fair," said Sonny. "My dad ran the octopus."

270

Both Duck and Ink Ear sighed. They could not imagine anything better than running the octopus at the fair. The county fair in Loganville was the high spot of any summer. Clara always took Sonny and she had more fun at the fair than any place else Sonny could think of. Clara refused to ride the octopus. Too scary. But Sonny rode it and loved it. It was much better than the Ferris wheel because all the Ferris wheel did was go around in a circle. They went higher up the Perry water tower than on the Ferris wheel. The octopus went around and up and down and jerked and bucked. It was a great ride. All of the boys, if they ever had the chance, would run the octopus. And then they could ride it all they wanted to.

"She was on the ride with Aunt Evelyn," Sonny said. "Remember they were just girls. They weren't much older than us. They were at the very top of it, you know, when the seat is tilting and spinning and you are looking straight down at the ground."

"I like that part," said Duck.

"Me, too," said Ink Ear. But he did not sound convincing. If either Sonny or Duck had thought about it, they would not have remembered any time Ink Ear was on the octopus.

"And then it broke," said Sonny. "It just cracked and fell off the octopus' arm. The seat was just hanging there. It was held by just a skinny little cable. And it would fall at any second."

"It broke," said Duck, imagining himself hanging in midair.

"They were 100 feet up in the air," said Sonny. "Well, maybe not 100 but pretty high. They could die. Aunt Evelyn was crying and Mom was screaming for help."

"Didn't anyone see them?" asked Ink Ear.

"Yes, my dad did. He shut off the ride so it wouldn't start again. He was careful and always thought of everything."

"Be prepared, like a Boy Scout," said Ink Ear.

"Yes, exactly. And then he climbed up the leg of the octopus to get my mom."

"I bet she was scared," said Ink Ear.

"Of course she was scared. She could die at any second. And then she saw my dad climbing up and she wasn't scared. My dad was very strong. He carried her down with one arm."

"What about your aunt?"

"Who?"

"Your aunt Evelyn."

"I guess he left her there."

"You've got a great dad," said Duck. "I knew you would."

"I guess so."

"He was a war hero and he ran the octopus. Who has a dad like that?"

"I didn't get all the details," said Sonny, "so I had to imagine some of them."

"You mean there weren't any sharks?" asked Duck.

272

"No, no. There were sharks. Plenty of sharks. He hit one on the nose when he was swimming."

"And pulling a boat full of wounded sailors," said Duck.

"With his teeth," said Sonny.

"Maybe he lied," said Duck. "Maybe he didn't do anything like that."

"It's in the report," said Sonny. "When he got his medal they wrote it all down. My mother has it. It's in her trunk."

"The medal? I'd like to see that medal," said Duck.

"I mean the report is in her trunk. It's just paper and stuff but it has the official seal of the official United States Navy on it. He said for her to show it to me when I was old enough."

"I didn't see it in the trunk," said Duck.

"Oh, it was there," said Sonny. "It was in one of those envelopes we didn't open."

"I'd like to see that paper," said Duck.

"I promised her if she told me everything, I wouldn't get in her trunk any more. A promise is a promise."

"My pa promises not to drink," said Ink Ear. "He promises every week."

"Well, I'm keeping my promise."

"What about the little girl with no toes?" asked Ink Ear.

"A tragic story," said Sonny. "My mom cried when she told me."

"Poor, kid," said Duck.

"She was born when my dad was in the Navy," said Sonny. "My dad never saw her. When my mom wrote to him and told him her toes were falling off, my dad called the Navy doctors and told them to come to Perry. The best doctors are in the Navy."

"I know that," said Ink Ear.

"They came. Six of them. Six of the best Navy doctors. But it was too late. They took my poor sister to the Navy hospital and the head doctor just shook his head. They said nobody could do anything and it didn't matter when they saw her, it was a rare disease and she was doomed from the start."

"What disease? What is it called?"

"It is so rare it doesn't have a real name, not like measles or chicken pox. They were going to name it after her but Mom wouldn't let them."

"Tolliverosis, maybe," said Duck. "Tolliveritis. You would be famous."

"I think they wanted to use her first name. Judith. Judy. Maybe they would call it Junice or Judoculous, something like that."

"But your dad never saw her."

"Only pictures. Little baby pictures. They covered up her feet so he couldn't see them."

"I'd like to see," said Ink Ear. "No toes. I bet she looked like a little piggy, with little piggy feet."

Sonny did not laugh, nor did Duck.

"The picture of him in the graveyard was the only time he saw her, just her headstone," said

274

Sonny. "When the admiral learned how his little girl had such a rare disease and because my dad was a Navy hero, they let him come home for a while."

"While the war was still on?"

"Just for a while. He had to come and go in a hurry. They needed him back on the ship."

"The ship that was torpedoed?" asked Duck.

"No, it was a new one. A bigger one. A better one. An aircraft carrier. He learned to fly a plane and was a pilot on an air craft carrier."

"When did he learn to fly?" asked Duck.

"They train all Navy heroes to fly. Don't you know that?"

"What happened to him? Why isn't he here?"

"He died in the sea. His plane crashed because he ran out of gas fighting and protecting the carrier. They gave him another medal."

"You're dad's dead, then?" asked Duck.

"I'm afraid so," said Sonny.

"And why didn't he marry your mom?" Ink Ear asked.

Sonny had an answer ready for the question. He knew one of them would ask. He thought it would be Duck.

"For the good of mankind," Sonny said.

"Bullshit," said Duck.

"Really. For the good of mankind. My mom and dad decided that if they had any more children with rare diseases it might spread and infect everybody. We could have a whole planet of people without toes."

"You have toes," said Duck. "I've seen your toes. They look like good toes."

"My toes are fine," said Sonny, "but it doesn't mean the next child would be fine. Maybe it would be worse. Maybe the next child would be the one that changed everybody's toes. That's what they thought, anyhow. Pretty noble if you ask me."

"I don't believe you," said Duck. "Your mother told you that? For the good of mankind? People without toes? Jesus, Sonny, do you think we're that stupid?"

"I believe you, Sonny," said Ink Ear.

"Does your father have a name?" Duck asked. "Bob, wasn't it? Bob Something."

"Batson. Bob Batson."

"That's Captain Marvel's name. Are you telling me that your dad is Captain Marvel?"

"Captain Marvel is Billy Batson, but where do you think they got his name?"

Duck Stadler considered all the information he had been given. Octopus operator. Navy hero. Toeless baby. Dead at sea. Captain Marvel. Up until Captain Marvel, Duck could accept the rest. He wanted to accept all of it. But this whole story might be from a Captain Marvel comic book. Except for the toeless baby. No toeless baby had ever been in any Captain Marvel comic book Duck had read.

"Did he yell, 'Shazam!' before he rescued your mom on the octopus?" Duck asked.

Sonny realized he might have gone just a little bit too far. He had no real life hero to work from, only comic book ones. Captain Marvel was his favorite, smarter and stronger and faster and braver than anyone else. Better than Superman because he was a real boy when he wasn't Captain Marvel.

Wouldn't that be great? To be 12 years old when you wanted to be and a grown up hero when you needed to be? If Sonny could be anybody, he would be Captain Marvel.

"Okay. I made up some of it," said Sonny.

"Which parts?"

"Almost all of it."

"The octopus, too?" asked Ink Ear.

"The octopus, too."

"Then what is the real story?" asked Duck.

Sonny looked at Duck, a boy who so wanted a father to be a hero, and at Ink Ear, a boy whose hero had just lied to him. Once again Sonny felt the weight of being more than he was, more than he needed to be.

"He's an asshole," said Sonny. "He's nothing special. He just went to the war and came back. He lives in Loganville. They didn't get married because he's an asshole. And the little girl baby had all her toes as far as I know. She just died like babies do."

"Ah, Jesus, Sonny," said Duck. "I'm sorry. It was a good story. I wish it was a true story."

"If it was true, it wouldn't be a story," said Sonny. "It would be the truth."

"Do you know his name? Bob…"

"…Lund."

"Like the radio preacher?"

"The same."

"Your dad is the radio preacher?"

"No, he's the son of the radio preacher."

"That guy's an asshole," said Ink Ear.

"And you are going to go see him?" asked Duck.

"I guess I have to, don't I?"

Chapter 24

Wrong Side of the Window

"Now that you know who he is and where he is, you have to go see him," Duck said to Sonny.

"I don't want to," said Sonny.

"But you have to."

"I know," said Sonny.

"I'll go, too. If you want," said Duck.

"I don't give a shit," said Ink Ear. "He's not a hero so I don't care."

"You're my hero," said Sonny and punched Ink Ear on the arm.

Duck was sitting on the cement railing of the Perry town bridge, spitting into the Jericho River every so often. Duck could spit further than either Sonny or Ink Ear. Duck would hack up a ball of saliva, spew it into the water and watch it float away, a white bubble on an orange sea.

Sonny leaned against the railing with his back to the river. He noticed that the marquee of The Glob was missing several more bulbs. Things had gone to crap since Sonny stopped working there. Ink Ear teetered on the curb, worming his feet out from the edge, keeping his balance until he lost it.

Obligation is some heavy shit, thought Sonny. And why is it on me? Why am I obligated to see this through? What do I want to know about this asshole? The longer the search for his father had gone on, the more the man had become an asshole to Sonny. There was probably a better word for it but none occurred to Sonny. The resentment that Sonny now felt did not used to be there. The less he knew the less anger he had. The more he knew the more pissed he got. Sonny was pissed at Clara, and he was pissed at Bob Lund, the preacher's son. He was pissed at the knowledge that one of his grandfathers was an asshole in a crazy clown robe. Sonny was pissed in general, about all of it. Growing up was a chicken shit thing, as Duck might say.

Duck couldn't wait to grow up. He could not wait to get big enough and strong enough to be a Perry Potter. Sonny was happy where he was, happier where he used to be. If he could be 12 years old forever, that would be just fine with him. Hell, 11 years old would be even better.

If he did not know what he now knew it would be better. Now he had not just his own life to deal with but also all the crap that his mother caused and all the crap his father might cause and all the crap ahead. Crap, crap, crap.

Sonny had stopped looking forward to the Doerr Prize. That was to be the big moment of his life. So far. He was going to be acknowledged as the most special student in his school. And where was all of that now? Was it going to be nothing if some strange asshole from some place before he was even born was not there to approve of him?

Jesus, thought Sonny, they pile it on. Like one of those gob piles at the Brighter Day. Brighter Day, my ass.

"Let's hop the train to Jericho," Sonny said.

"What for?" asked Duck.

"For the hell of it. Because we can. Because we should. Because I need some air. Because...why do we need a reason? Jesus, lately all we need are reasons. There's no reason. We like it. That's reason enough."

"I don't know," said Duck. "I want to go watch football practice. Loganville is this week."

"Those stinking assholes? They can't play football. They're gonna get killed."

"Maybe I can help," said Duck.

"Me, too," said Ink Ear. "I got to be some place."

"You?" asked Sonny. "You never have some place to be. What place do you have to be?"

"Just some place," said Ink Ear.

"What's happening?" asked Sonny. "What in hell is happening?"

"Tomorrow," said Duck and started towards Perry High to help the football team if he could, which he couldn't.

"I'll see you, too," said Ink Ear and started to some place he had to be.

Sonny caught the train by himself. He jumped on when it slowed for Trestle Two, grabbing on to the ladder of a coal hopper. He swung around between cars and stuck his head above the rim of one of them and let the wind rush past him. He wanted to smell the fresh air of the countryside but the stench from the slag pile was particularly bitter and coal dust blew back into this face. Sonny climbed down the ladder as the train rattled on and squatted between the cars. Shit, he thought, I should have stayed in Perry. Why do things have to change? Why aren't Duck and Ink Ear with him? Instead of riding on to Jericho, Sonny jumped off the train, skinning his forearm when he broke his fall.

Sonny got back to Perry in time to get to the Matterhorn. He was supposed to set pins for the Tuesday night open lanes, never much of a night. He'd be lucky to get a half dozen sets. Only one of the eight lanes had any activity. Cuss Mauller, Perry's best bowler, was practicing picking up splits. Cuss carried an average of 237 and he had his Dairy Freeze team in first place. Cuss had one of the few mustaches in Perry, a droopy mess under his tuber of a nose that was nearly always full of whatever he had eaten last. His large stomach did not seem to hinder his bowling actions, a long, fluid stroke that sent the ball seven boards out and always brought it back to the pocket. His given name was Cecil, but he was called Cuss because…

"Criss cross crappy. Poopy poo."

…because he did not know how to cuss. He tried very hard to be profane but it just wasn't in him. "Poopy poo," was about as raw as it got for Cuss. And "poopy poo" is what he shouted in frustration at missing a 5-7 split. He threw a perfect ball, sending the five pin just to the right of the seven pin. The breeze from the five should have knocked it over.

Sonny walked down the track between lanes four and five to the pin setting pits. Marion Legard was setting pins for Cuss, giving him splits to solve.

"You're late, Sonny," Marion said. "I gotta twirl."

Marion was a senior at Perry High and the drum major of the marching band. Perry had never had a drum major before Marion, making do with three majorettes. Not one of the girls could twirl a baton like Marion could. He could throw it high into the air and catch it behind his back. There was nothing sissy about Marion; he just loved to twirl. Marion practiced the baton almost as much as Cuss practiced picking up splits.

"Get back," said Marion. "He's trying the 7-10." Marion slipped two pins into the setter and shoved it down.

The only way to pick up the 7-10 is to whack one of the pins so hard that it caroms off the back wall or the side plate and flies into the other pin. Most bowlers just take out one of the pins and go on to the next frame. Cuss had made the 7-10 in league play and he was determined to do it again.

"Look out! Here it comes!" Marion jumped out of the pit and ducked behind the wall. Sonny moved to the next pit. Cuss heaved the bowling ball at the 10 pin as if he was trying to throw the ball through the back of the pit, which he was. Cuss' ball clipped the side of 10 and sent the pin into the sidewall. It crashed back across the lane, spinning like a propeller, taking out the seven.

"Ching, chong, chonky!" yelled Cuss. "Pee, pus, peepee! I'm quitting on that one!"

"I offset the 10 pin," said Marion, lifting up Cuss' ball to send it back down the return rail. "He'd never get that split otherwise. Watch this."

Marion put just a little bit of backspin on Cuss' bowling ball. It rolled down the return rail and up to the rack to where Cuss was waiting to grab it and put it into his bag. But just as it climbed up to the rack, it stopped and started back down the rail towards the pit.

Cuss took off after the ball, sliding in his socks since he had already taken off his shoes. "Mama doo doo, chicken licking, donkey dingle!" Cuss screamed, directing his anger at both the ball and at Marion, who had already ducked out the back door, laughing as he pulled it shut.

"Sorry, Cuss," Sonny yelled. "I'm not warmed up yet."

"It's okay, Sonny. I didn't know it was you." Cuss retrieved his ball from where it had come to rest on the return rail and carried it back to his bag. "I thought it was that diddly pee pee, Marion."

Silence in a bowling alley is eerie and unnatural, like a pinball machine with the lights off. Sonny soaked in the stillness, waiting for a customer to arrive and to get shoes from Dan Weller. Dan would then flick on the lane lights, push a buzzer alerting Sonny to slam down the pinsetter and the crash and clatter would resume.

At least 15 minutes had passed since Cuss Mauller had left the bowling alley. Dan was behind his counter, reading a magazine, sipping a Coke. Someone was in one of the snack booths next to the shoe rental counter, but Sonny could see only a pair of hands from the distance and from his angle. No, it wasn't a pair of hands; it was two hands but one was holding the other, the fingers of one hand laced into the fingers of the other. Sonny could see a soft drink, maybe a cherry Coke, with two straws.

"That's sappy," said Sonny to himself. "Young love."

Sonny supposed that's how it had been with Clara. It's how it would be for him some day. He imagined Margarite Szabo standing on the ledge at the Clay Hole. Sonny sighed, with more volume than he had intended. His sigh echoed loudly enough to cause Dan Weller to look up from his magazine. One of the hands in the booth left the other hand. Peeking around the edge of booth was Ink Ear Ryan. Raising her head up above the back of the booth to look was Darla Hamilton.

Sonny could not be seen at the end of the lane, merely his legs dangling down behind the pins. All anyone could see was a pair of Wrangler jeans rolled up at the bottom one turn and a pair of blue sneakers, scuffed and dirty, with the white rubber coming off the side of the left shoe.

"Oh, shit," Sonny heard Ink Ear say. "I got to go. I got to go."

Ink Ear slipped around the edge of the booth and raced past Dan and the shoe rental counter and was out the door of the Matterhorn before Darla Hamilton could stop him.

Sonny said nothing to Ink Ear the next day or for many days after that. He felt a little like Clara must have felt; better not to stir things up. He didn't even tell Duck about Ink Ear and Darla because Duck would have been relentless and Ink Ear did not deserve that.

The invitations to Passing Through the Gate had been given to the children, six per child. Embossed on cream-colored linen paper was the date and place and a line left blank for the holder of the invitation to fill in. "Request the honor of (fill in the blank) presence," but Sonny was not sure where the honor was. His honor? Their honor? Honor seemed the wrong word, whose ever honor it was.

The invitation finally nudged Sonny into action. He could mail it, of course, since he had his father's address. Or he could take it and place it in the man's hand. That seemed to be best. Not the coward's way. That's how Captain Marvel would do it.

Sonny made certain his jeans were washed and he made sure to wear the other pair of shoes he owned, his "dress shoes," as Clara called them, brown brogans that came up to his ankles. His feet had grown since he had worn the shoes last and they pinched his toes and crushed the arches of his feet. He would leave the shoes untied until he needed to tie them. He wore a shirt that needed to be tucked in, but he didn't tuck it in. He wore a light, poplin jacket with two huge pockets on the front. He buttoned the invitation into the right pocket. Sonny looked at himself in the full length mirror that Clara had hung on the back of her bedroom door. This was the package he would present to Robert Lund, the asshole, and the asshole could take it or leave it.

Days were shorter and the leaves had already left the trees on Washington Street in Loganville, Ohio. A whiff of wood smoke was in the air from fireplaces in the homes along the street. Streetlights spaced properly allowed a boy to see his way clearly.

Sonny climbed the stoop of a square, two-story house covered with slate gray asphalt siding made to look like shingles. A porch ran from one side of the house to other across the front. Large windows with white lace curtains were on each side of the front door. A swing with wooden slats hung from the ceiling of the porch and moved slightly from the breeze. Lights from inside the house made a golden blush and cast soft shadows. A painted jardinière on a pedestal had been planted with autumn mums, which still bloomed. It seemed to Sonny a welcoming place. The straw doormat said that very thing, "Welcome."

Sonny sat down on the swing and tied his shoes. He spit onto his hand and smoothed his cowlick. He unbuttoned his jacket pocket and pulled out the invitation. He walked to the door and reached for the doorbell button beside it. A small advisory above the button read, "No peddlers or solicitors."

Which was he? Was Sonny either of those? Was he both of those? Under his feet it said, "Welcome." At the end of his finger it said, "Get lost."

Sonny could smell something cooking inside, red meat of some sort, beef most likely, a roast. He never had roast beef at home. Clara fixed chicken, always chicken. How much more satisfying was the aroma of a roast. His tongue tingled in anticipation of an unfamiliar supper.

"Wow, roast beef," Sonny thought. "And probably mashed potatoes, too."

Clara made mashed potatoes some times, but not often. Usually she just sliced the potatoes and fried them in Crisco. Sonny wondered if they were having pie for dessert. Sonny loved pie.

Sonny heard someone laughing. He moved away from the door and looked through one of the windows. A man lay on the floor, his body pointed away from Sonny so he could not see the man's face. He was holding a boy, several years younger than Sonny, straight above him, his arms extended. He would lower the boy and kiss the end of his nose, then push the boy up, lower him again, kiss his nose again. The boy giggled and squealed.

"Do me, daddy, do me, daddy." A girl a year or so younger than the boy, came running into the room. She grabbed her father's arms and the three of them collapsed, all laughing.

"Dinner!" A woman in an apron, with black hair and large brown eyes, appeared in the doorway from the kitchen. She held a stirring spoon in her left hand. She smiled, and Sonny noticed that one of her front teeth was crooked, almost overlapping another tooth. "Dinner, now."

The man got to his feet, his back still to Sonny, and followed the children out of the room. Sonny moved back to the door. He looked down at the mat that said "Welcome."

"That does not mean me," Sonny told himself. The sharp scent of the roast taunted him. Sonny dropped the invitation onto the mat that said, "Welcome," and walked off the porch.

Hitching back to Perry, Sonny could not catch a ride. He walked all the way home and his feet hurt. He had a lot time to think about what he had seen and smelled. Mostly what he thought about was the woman with the crooked tooth and how neat and tidy everything in her house was.

Sonny dropped his second shoe onto the floor of his bedroom. He was sitting on the edge of his bed rubbing his feet when he heard the siren from the Brighter Day mine.

Chapter 25

The Brighter Day

The tipple of the Brighter Day coal mine was a cluttered eyesore even to those who made a living from its organized bedlam. What should have been obvious to anyone is that none it belonged there along the banks of the Jericho River. Maybe the tipple had to be so ramshackle because nature did not provide a convenient place for it. Before the mine was opened, first as the Sunset and now as the Brighter Day, the rolling mound that was Jericho Hill seemed as soft as a pillow. Sonny could see it as a place where a giant might lay his head. The sumac and paw-paw that quilted its sides were now gone, gouged out to make room for progress.

The mine buildings were stacked into the side of the hill and on top of other buildings without giving any sense that they belonged where they were. Sonny told Ink Ear that the surface structures of the mine were the discarded toys of a giant.

"He was playing with an erector set and with some building blocks," said Sonny. "He got pissed about the way it all fit together, and the giant just jammed it all into the side of Jericho hill and went away."

"He doesn't still live there, does he, Sonny?" asked Ink Ear.

"No, he doesn't," said Sonny, "but that doesn't mean he won't come back."

"If he does," said Duck, "I'll kick him in the balls."

Not a bit of civilizing softness was anywhere. The main tower of the tipple climbed higher than the crest of the hill. A long conveyor belt ran from the mine opening in the side of Jericho hill out to the coal washing room. More belts carried the coal to the hoppers and another took away the gob. Gravity and graduated holes in the sorting belt separated the coal by size. The tipple's rambling chutes and sheds, its inclines and angles, its long chimneys and erratically connected pieces were evidence that the real treasure was not what could be seen but what could not.

Naked lights on poorly spaced poles that were strung together by sagging electrical lines created sharp shadows. These were fine places for young boys to keep out of sight. Mine vapors drifted through the pockets of illumination like bad breath on a cold night. The steady thump, thump of ventilation pumps provided the heartbeat of the giant. The mine opening that swallowed the miners twice a day was its mouth.

"What are we doing here again?" asked Ink Ear.

"You'll see," said Duck.

Ink Ear would have had more faith in "You'll see," if Sonny had been there with them. The "You'll see's" from Duck Stadler always seemed to end with Ink Ear running from something or someone.

The two of them had caught the night train to Jericho, jumping onto a ladder of a coal car as the train slowed to a slow crawl for Trestle Two. All three of the boys had done this many times for no other reason than to feel the wind in their faces as the train grumbled and growled its way to Jericho. They would cling to the ladders between the cars, allowing their faces to pop up over the rim of the car and catch the wind.

Ink Ear called it "Riding to the Temple," and it did no good to tell him it was "tipple," not "temple." The hoist tower of the tipple did resemble the bell tower of a church. And it was a temple, sort of, in a lot of ways. It did require prayer and sacrifice. Sometimes Sonny thought Ink Ear was not as dumb as he was.

The boys would ride up to Jericho and sometimes walk back, sometimes hike over the hill to the Clay Hole and then catch the return train later in the day. They might go to the Szabos' store for drinks or candy, but they never felt welcome or comfortable there. And though they always looked for her, they never saw Margarite Szabo.

"Don't touch nothing," Ferko Szabo always warned them from behind his fierce black beard.

They played among the scattered pieces of the Brighter Day, preferring it these days to Fort Corsage. They had not returned to the Devil's Tea Table since their one visit there. They thought of themselves as cowboys most of the time, ducking and shooting behind the corners of the crude buildings. They defended the Brighter Day mine from savages with just as much enthusiasm as they had defended Perry from the mongrel whores.

This was the first time any of them had come to the mine at night.

"I wish Sonny had come," said Ink Ear Ryan.

"He had something to do," said Duck. "He wouldn't say what. I think he went to find his dad."

"I wish we didn't come at night," said Ink Ear Ryan.

"I wish you would shut up," said Duck.

Duck's "you'll see," was his plan to rob his father. Duck still wore a bandage from the beating Charlie Stadler had given him when he caught Duck stealing his whiskey a few weeks earlier. To be exact, Duck had taken two bottles of Early Times. Duck was not going to drink the whiskey. He planned to sell it to the Perry Potters football team. The Potters were holding a bash to celebrate their only victory of the football season, a one-touchdown win over Rehoboth High in the last game of the season. Rehoboth was a team traditionally as sorry as the Perry Potters.

The quarterback, Ken Hunter, had pulled Duck aside as Duck was whooping and cheering the Potters on their long walk back to the swimming pool dressing room from the stadium.

"I knew it, I knew we could do it," Duck shouted. "Wait 'til next year. We'll win 'em all next year. We ain't Piss Pots. We can do it. They are all chicken shit. All of them." Duck slapped the quarterback on the rear end.

"Kid," Ken Hunter said, "listen, if you really want to do something for us, get us some hooch. We'll pay you. We're going to celebrate tonight."

Where the quarterback expected someone as young as Duck to get hooch did not occur to Duck. He only knew that he had been given a job to do by the quarterback of the Potters and he had to do what he could do until he became the quarterback of the Potters in three or four years.

Charlie Stadler kept his liquor in a locked cabinet in what would have been the guest bedroom if the Stadlers ever had any guests. As it was, the room was generally used for storage. A gray metal cabinet held Charlie's booze and Charlie's booze was mostly bourbon. He was partial to Early Times but he had some Jim Beam and Wild Turkey for the guests he never entertained. The whiskey took up each of the six shelves in the cabinet, front to back, much too much for one man. It was no problem for Duck to open the door to the spare bedroom with a skeleton key and to jimmy the flimsy lock until the door of the cabinet opened.

Since Early Times made up most of the collection, Duck decided to take a bottle of it. No, two bottles. The Potters had won, after all. He took the bottles and then moved the remaining bottles forward to make it appear as if nothing had been disturbed. Charlie would never know.

When Duck got to the party at Ken Hunter's house, most of the team had already left. A few empty bottles of Weideman's Bohemian Beer were lying on the lawn but there was no great evidence that the Perry Potters had over celebrated. They had been drinking 3.2 beer and Duck had hard whiskey. Ken Hunter was trying to unhook Susan Martin's brassiere with one hand while he stroked her leg with the other. Duck rushed up to the pair of them.

"I got it," said Duck. Ken Hunter took his tongue out of Susan Martin's mouth.

"Get lost, kid," he said.

"No, I got it. I got the hooch," said Duck.

"Party's over. Get lost."

Susan Martin turned Ken Hunter's face back to hers and, it looked to Duck as if she were trying to swallow Ken's mouth. Ken waved one hand at Duck, and Duck backed away, one bottle of Early Times in each hand.

"Chicken shit," said Duck. "You're all chicken shit." Only the offensive line still remained at the party, sitting in a group on folding chairs on the back patio of Ken Hunter's house, waiting for their quarterback to tell them what to do.

"Especially you," said Duck pointing at left guard Ronald "Blood" Walker. He was called "Blood" because at some point in every game, football or basketball, he would have to leave the game with a bleeding nose. The nose bleed was a congenital defect in "Blood" and not anything done to him by the other team.

Duck Stadler came to the realization that the Perry Potters' commitment to personal excess was no greater than their commitment to winning. On his way back home, Duck Stadler threw the two bottles of Early Times off the Perry town bridge into the Jericho River.

"Wait until I get there," he said. "Wait until I get to high school."

Charlie Stadler recognized right away that some of his whiskey was missing. First of all, Duck had not closed the spare room door or the cabinet door securely, and, secondly, although the bottles were missing from the back of the shelf, the ones in front were not aligned the way Charlie liked, the labels precisely forward so that both words could be read. Some bottles said "Early," and some said "Times," and Charlie knew exactly who had been there.

"Donald! Donald!" Charlie Stadler yelled, heading to Duck's room, slapping the belt he used to teach lessons on the side of his leg. Duck was on his bed, nearly asleep when he heard what was coming. As usual, Duck waited to take it and this time he felt he might even have it coming.

"Did you drink it? Did you drink it?" Charlie Stadler asked the same question with each blow of his belt. Usually he whacked Duck below the waist but this time he aimed for Duck's head and face. The edge of the belt caught Duck below his left eye and opened the skin. Duck threw up his arms to protect himself and the belt bit into his forearms and wrists. By the time Sarah Stadler got to Duck's room, she was a prayer too late. Duck was curled in the corner but he was not crying.

"Please, Lord, save this man. Save this boy." Sarah moaned. "I ask in the name of Jesus."

"Christ," said Sonny when Duck told him what had happened.

"I'm going to get that chicken shit," said Duck.

Charlie Stadler conducted his life in cash, as did most of the town of Perry. Cash or personal credit, rarely checks. The men who made the money doled out what they believed the women who managed the money needed to run a house and to raise a family. Most of the arguments in Perry were over money.

Duck watched his father lay out piles of cash onto the kitchen table. Duck's wounds had mostly healed but the cut on his cheek still seeped. It had taken 11 stitches, sewn in by Sarah. Duck had cried while his mother sewed. The salt from his tears made the wound feel worse so he stopped crying.

Charlie made more money than most miners because he took more risks than most miners. The pile of cash he left for himself was thicker than all the other piles combined, the money that would go for food and utilities and Sarah's contribution to the New Church of the Nazarene. Charlie folded his pile into the left pocket of his Red Kap work shirt and buttoned the button.

"Humph," Charlie grunted and picked up his miner's hat and black lunch bucket. He did not look at Duck. He did not kiss Sarah. He turned and left to work the swing shift at the Brighter Day mine.

Duck knew that the men at the mine changed into coveralls in a changing room next to the coal washer. They locked their regular clothes in lockers and after their shift they put their coveralls back inside the locker and put their other clothes back onto their unwashed bodies. The Brighter Day had no showers, not than many of the men would use them in any case. They wore the coal dust like soldiers wore medals. The miners came home covered in black dust; only where the goggles covered their eyes was there any place that resembled the color of human skin.

Duck knew that Charlie's money would be in his Red Kap shirt, just where he had put it, and

Duck had a key to the lock that hung from the handle of Charlie's locker. That was the "you'll see," part he had not told Ink Ear.

Duck had wanted Sonny to come to the mine. It wasn't because Duck was going to rob his father that kept Sonny away. It was something he had to do in Loganville, so Duck collected Ink Ear and they caught the night train to Jericho, not certain how or when they would get back.

Duck and Ink Ear made their way to the mine changing room. They dodged from shadow to shadow and imagined they were frontier scouts. This added to the fun and kept Ink Ear from asking what they were doing at the Brighter Day. Front loaders and backhoes that shoved the slag and waste rock around sat idle. The second shift of the mine was less noisy than the day activity when the loud clatter of mining discouraged both conversation and a will to be there.

Steam and bitter aromas puffed from hidden openings. Coal cars clanked under the loading chutes as the engines rested, hissing and impatient, waiting to move another work slot up the track. The graded lumps of the shiny black rock that had conveniently changed from layers of living plants into the holy carbon that fueled homes and industry completed their journey through crushing and sorting and washing and tumbled off the conveyor belts to be carried away by the waiting hoppers.

Down and inside Jericho hill, where King Coal had taken away the sky, hidden from sight and with no hint that any living soul might be down there, the daily rattle and removal of black fuel from unwilling earth could gain a careless monotony.

"It's in here," said Duck, creeping up to the slightly opened door of the changing room. Duck looked through the opening and could see no one. He pushed the door a little and still no one came into his line of sight. With one quick move sideways, Duck imagined he was avoiding a tackler from the Loganville Miners and slipped into the men's changing room of the Brighter Day mine.

"Come on," he whispered to Ink Ear. Ink Ear crept around the edge of the half-opened door without nearly as much style as Duck had shown. The room was empty. Low benches were at all angles, moved and not repositioned. Some clothing was draped over a few of the benches. The walls were lined with metal lockers, not unlike the lockers Sonny and Duck and Ink Ear would be assigned when they Passed Through the Gate and moved on to junior high school. Elementary school had no lockers, only desks which opened slightly from the top, leaving just enough room for small hands to reach in for pencils or paper or whatever else a boy or a girl might want to put inside.

"What are we doing?" whispered Ink Ear.

"You'll see," said Duck.

All the lockers looked the same, like so many slices of bread from the same loaf. Which one was Charlie's? Duck walked around the room, examining the padlocks that would match the key he had in his hand. Charlie's lock was a Yale lock but so were most of the ones hanging from the handles of the lockers.

"What are you going to do?" asked Ink Ear.

"I'm going to get even with that chicken shit," said Duck. "I'm going to steal his money."

"Won't he know who did it?" asked Ink Ear. "He knew who took his whiskey."

"He'll think the Szabos did it," said Duck. "They're always stealing shit."

Duck did not know how much time they had, how soon someone might come into the changing room. The swing shift of the mine had just started and Duck figured he had time. There was only one thing to do. He had to try every lock.

"Here's your dad's locker," said Ink Ear.

"What? Where? How do you know?"

"It's got his name on it," said Ink Ear.

And so it did. Scrawled below the wire screen at the top of the locker door was the name "Stadler."

"I could kiss you," said Duck.

"If you do I'll scream," said Ink Ear.

Duck had no idea how much money was in there, buttoned inside the left front pocket of Charlie Stadler's Red Kap work shirt, but he figured it was in the hundreds. Maybe a thousand? Duck was going to buy himself a new football, a

Wilson maybe or a Rawlings, one that didn't have the laces taped down, one he could get a good grip on.

Duck slipped the key into the lock and turned. The lock clicked. Hanging in the locker was the Red Kap work shirt, placed on the same hook and over the same kind of cowl and blue robe Duck had seen at the Devil's Tea Table. As Duck reached for the Red Kap shirt there came a sound so piercing it caused Ink Ear to cover his ears and Duck to spin around to see if the law had caught him. He expected to see Sheriff John Brown standing there pointing his pistol and dangling a pair of handcuffs.

"Ooooooweeeee! Oooooooweeeeee! Oooooooweeeee." The blare of the siren echoed off Jericho hill, off the tipple, off the crusher and the washroom and off the coal hoppers waiting to take King Coal away.

Ferko Szabo knew what that sound was. So did the miners. So did the people in the town of Perry, who did not mistake it for the noon siren. The only souls who could not hear the declaration of disaster were trapped somewhere below Jericho Hill, down inside the earth. One of them was Charlie Stadler.

Chapter 26

The Ashes of Time

Sonny, Duck and Ink Ear were not sure what to make of what they had seen at The Devil's Tea Table. They had seen something that scared them and the fright they felt had nothing to do with tea or with demon furniture.

Sonny was bothered because he had since learned that the fool in the gold gown was his own grandfather. And Sonny would swear he had seen Dan Weller, kindly, reasonable, helpful Dan Weller, among the men in robes.

"Maybe it was him," said Duck. "Maybe it was somebody else. What difference does it make? They're all assholes."

"I know what I saw," said Sonny, even though he was not at all certain what he had seen.

"I don't want to talk about this," said Ink Ear. "I'm sorry we ever went. I want to forget about it."

"You can't forget what you already know," said Sonny.

"Sure I can," said Ink Ear. "I do it all the time."

The Fraternal Order of Eden had been intending to prune its garden ever since Lena Szabo had tricked Robert Lund into marrying her.

"Tricked" was Warren Lund's characterization. And if bending over the watermelons at the Loganville IGA just as Robert Lund was turning from the cereal aisle was a trick, then a trick it was. From that point, whatever happened was Robert's fault and as yet he had found no reason to regret any choice he had made.

"She wasn't even pregnant like the other one," Warren Lund told his wife Martha. Martha Lund had been dead for eight years but that did not keep Warren from talking to her.

Martha had an honored place in an alcove in the rectory of the New Church of the Nazarene. Her urn was a clear crystal hourglass supported by three wooden spindles attached to marble caps. Warren often placed Martha on his pulpit as he preached. He explained to his congregation that the urn was an allegory for the cycle of life.

"It symbolizes the sands of time," preached Warren Lund. "Our Martha is a reminder of life's beginning and its inevitable ending."

Warren might have believed some of that. He could get carried away with his own images. But he had found the purpose of putting Martha Lund into an hourglass was as practical as it was metaphorical. Warren could use Martha to time his sermons. In the church, on the radio or at the Devil's Tea Table, Warren would take exactly 27 minutes to deliver his message. That was the time it took Martha to shift from the top of the glass to the bottom. She was not inside an hourglass at all, not even a half-hourglass.

Even those clerics who scorned the New Church of the Nazarene as a pit of squirming, howling idiots admired Warren for the conciseness of his sermons. If a particular service became infused with the Holy Spirit and got too rowdy, if the congregation was particularly energetic, Warren would just turn Martha over and go with the flow.

In death Martha was serving her husband as she had in life, except in blessed silence. Warren Lund much preferred the soundless Martha to the one who had barked at him incessantly.

"We tried our best with the boy," Warren said to Martha. "But he had the devil in him. He laid with harlots and he still is. First that Tolliver girl and now a Szabo. A Szabo, Martha. We should have pruned the Szabos long ago. It may be too late for our boy, but we cannot allow more seeds to corrupt our earthly garden."

Out of habit, Warren would preach to Martha. And her silence was a confirmation of every daft idea that came into his head.

The Fraternal Order of Eden, the F.O.E., grew out of one of Warren's conversations with

306

Martha. In this case, he imagined he heard her response.

"A flock of gardeners sounds like a very good idea, my love." It was Martha's voice in his head although the trickling ashes in the glass were as hushed as usual. Warren shifted on the stool he sat upon when visiting with Martha in her alcove as he watched her sift from up there to down there. Gravity gave her movement and seemed to give her life.

Warren was certain that it was Martha's voice because she always called him "my love," even when she was being a bitch. This voice was soothing and agreeable, just as he had always hoped hers would have been.

"They can do the pruning and you will not get your hands dirty."

It was Martha through Warren who decided that the workers should dress like monks, wearing the hooded frocks that Sonny, Duck and Ink Ear had seen at The Devil's Tea Table. She chose the colors of the flag to represent America as well as to define the tasks of each group. Those dressed in white were the Weeders, those who wore blue were the Trimmers, and those in red were the Pruners.

The function of all three groups was the same, to rid the Garden of God of unwanted intruders, to restore the Garden of God to its original glory, back to Eden before the Fall, before the arrival of Evil.

In the case of the garden that was greater Perry, Ohio, that would be before the arrival of the Szabos.

Warren Lund would be the Planter, the one who sowed the seeds. He would be dressed in gold, of course, and completely hooded, unseen as is the God of all creation.

"But why not green?" wondered Warren. "Green is color of health in a garden."

Martha, from her vantage point, convinced Warren that she had seen God and that He wore a gold gown and kept His face covered so that His magnificence would not blind those who looked upon Him.

"He is quite approachable," Martha told Warren. "I have touched His sleeve."

The symbol of the cross and the open eye was Warren's own contribution. He reasoned that if Martha had seen God then so had he and so could anyone who looked through an open and untainted eye. Warren himself would determine the degree of taint.

It was Martha who suggested that the F.O.E. gather at The Devil's Tea Table in defiance of Satan himself. The F.O.E. would use the devil's own furniture for their holy cause. They would cut down the devil just as they would remove any of his earthly disciples, any weed that defiled the garden.

"You mean the Szabos," Martha reminded Warren, making sure they were both talking about the same thing.

"Sure. The Szabos. That's understood," said Warren to himself and to the hourglass urn.

What had the Szabos done to anyone but be happy and prosperous, fulfilling the motto of Perry? What had anyone in Perry done to the Szabos, except to blame and resent them? It was a truce that both sides accepted and tolerated until Lena Szabo leaned over the watermelons in the Loganville IGA and overwhelmed the preacher's son.

Ferko Szabo was no happier about the union of his daughter Lena to a *seggfej* outsider than was Warren Lund to have his son pollute the Lunds with heathen blood. Ferko banished his daughter from Jericho and Warren whined to his wife's ashes. But neither was able to keep Robert Lund from marrying Lena Szabo, nor was either father invited to the wedding, a quiet service before a justice of the peace in Dayton.

Ferko's wife Eva, who had attended the wedding ceremony, explained to her husband that this was America and that such things happen.

Peace festered through the birth of two little Lunds, first Walter, known as Wally, and then Dorcas, called Dee Dee by her dad. The gap was forever set with the defection of Robert Lund from the New Church of the Nazarene to his own ministry in the Perry Pentecostal Congregation, a

309

slightly less vigorous flock but still full of the holy spirit.

The purchase of The Glob by the Szabos was supposed to be a private matter between Ferko Szabo and Andy Sloan. But papers had to be filed and word got around that the Szabos were spreading their Szabo-ness from Jericho into the lives of the true and honest citizens of Perry. Andy had to explain the treachery of his doing business with the Szabos to the fellows in the F.O.E. He did what any of his fellows would have done. He lied.

"They threatened to burn it down if I didn't sell to them," Andy told Warren Lund. Not that Andy was against a fire. Since the Skreeno incident, and with more and more television antennas cropping up on Perry rooftops, Andy had considered a little accidental arson himself. But the coincidence of the movie house in Loganville burning down was still too fresh to be accepted by the same company that insured The Glob. When Andy told Warren the price the Szabos were willing to pay, Warren had to admit that there was nothing Andy could do.

"Those devils," said Warren Lund. "They've finally gone too far."

Andy had asked Warren to stop by The Glob. The two of them would consider what had to be done. They stood at the back of the theater at the barrier between the lobby and the seats, a three-quarters wall just tall enough to see over.

"I shudder to think of the kinds of movies they'll show here," said Andy. Both men looked towards the screen of the empty theater, imagining the worst.

"Foreign movies, you can bet," said Warren. "Communist movies. Sinful movies."

"That would be my guess," said Andy.

"The corruption in our garden must be pruned," said Warren.

Andy knew exactly what the Szabos had in mind for The Glob, and it had nothing to do with foreign movies. Ferko Szabo was planning to use the building to house a medical clinic. Neither Perry nor Loganville had a hospital and any serious medical attention was at least an hour away in Lancaster. Ferko's oldest son, Milos, had finished his residency in Cincinnati and would run the infirmary. It would be named after Ferko's late son Gregor, killed in the war. As a gesture of conciliation Ferko planned to add a "y" to the name, canonize his son and make it St. Gregory's Medical Center.

Andy Sloan knew of these plans. Uncharacteristically and enthusiastically, Ferko Szabo had told Andy all about it. But the creation of a badly needed medical center in Perry was not what Andy Sloan told Warren Lund.

"They are planning to turn the place into a synagogue," said Andy.

Warren Lund grabbed his chest. He moaned and shuddered, just as he often did when the Holy Spirit came into him during services.

"Warren?"

"Ack, ack, ack…" Warren Lund collapsed. Andy reached out to catch him, but Warren fell through Andy's arms, his head cracking the paneling on the barrier wall, his body slumping to the soiled carpet, his left ear landing on a spray of popcorn Andy had yet to clean up.

Warren Lund twitched and tried to speak. Andy knelt and lifted Warren's head, brushing away the popcorn from his face, removing all but one whole kernel of corn that had made its way into Warren's ear. Had The Glob been St. Gregory's Medical Center, Warren Lund might have lived, but he did not. He died on the day that Andy was advertising a "Double Creature Feature," with two showings of "The Brain That Wouldn't Die" and the "Attack of the Giant Leeches."

Warren Lund would be cremated with that souvenir kernel of corn from The Glob, an organic piece of God's Garden, still resting against his tympanic membrane. It went unnoticed by the mortician Roy Cannon and it remained unpopped until Warren Lund was heated to 1500 degrees Fahrenheit.

The radio preacher rejoined his wife Martha in a duplicate hourglass and the two of them would be side-by-side for eternity in the alcove of the New Church of the Nazarene. Martha ran smoothly from the top to the bottom of her glass, but Warren would catch every now and then on the puff of corn that did not always pass freely through the connecting tube.

Andy leaned in to hear the last mortal utterances of Warren Lund. He nodded his head and cradled Warren Lund's face to his chest.

Without a vote and without anyone asking him to, Andy Sloan assumed the position as head of the F.O.E. Robert Lund, the natural heir and the only son of the radio preacher, made no objection. Robert had never mentioned their grandfather to his two children and saw no reason to involve them now. On the day of his father's funeral Robert Lund, his wife Lena and his two children were eating *porkolt* and stuffed cabbage at the table of Ferko Szabo, who had forgiven his daughter and who now realized that he loved his grandchildren.

"*Csaladi*," said Ferko Szabo, raising a glass of Zoltan Szabo's wine. "To family."

Andy Sloan donned the gold wardrobe that went with the job as head of the F.O.E. and wore his new cloak of office to the memorial services for Warren Lund. His voice was as formidable as had been the radio preacher's and Andy did not need a microphone to deliver the eulogy.

"This man was a man with a true message," said Andy Sloan to an impressive turn out for Warren's funeral. Some mourners wore the robes of the F.O.E. but with the cowls down. "He preached what he believed and he believed in straight rows and no weeds.

"This man's message was for all of God's true children, for all of God's true brood, for all of the true blooms in God's garden. His voice is still but his message is loud. The last words to me as I held his head in my hands, the dying message to us was 'Prune, prune, prune.'"

Many in the funeral assembly broke into applause. Woody Ryan hooted loudly, the joy in his voice not so much for the message of the departed Warren Lund but because Woody assumed that now his debt was cancelled and he could start running a new tab.

"Prune, prune, prune," the low chant began.

What Warren Lund had actually said to Andy Sloan was not "Prune, prune, prune," but he had said, "The carpet smells like piss." Warren Lund coughed once and died.

"Weeds killed this man." Andy Sloan's voice rose in volume. "We must prune God's garden." Andy lifted his arms, extending them up and out, spreading the gold cloth of Warren Lund's old robe, hoping the effect would be like the wings of a great bird. Andy had seen Warren do this during his F.O.E. sermons and was always impressed by the effect. But Andy Sloan was a bit bigger than Warren Lund and the cloth tended to ride up his arms and stretch across his stomach. A small rip appeared under his right armpit and exposed the pink skin underneath. The hem of the robe rose to

314

just under Andy's knees revealing gartered argyle socks and cordovan wing tips.

Sonny Tolliver attended the service, sneaking into the New Church of the Nazarene, after Andy Sloan had begun his eulogy. Sonny did not know exactly why he was there, but this was the second grandfather he had lost without really knowing either of them. As far as he could determine there would be no more.

Chapter 27

A Sinner's Prayer

Ferko Szabo was the first into the Brighter Day mine. He tied a handkerchief around his black beard, put his forearm over his eyes and plunged into the belching mouth of the Brighter Day.

The alarm siren continued its disjointed screeching, the only noise after the usual jangle and clatter of the mine machinery had stopped.

Ferko followed the shuttle car rail by feel as much as by sight, bent over by the low ceiling of the tunnel, hacking into his handkerchief from the dust and the smothering stench of sulfur.

He had been at the mine entrance in an argument with Jerry Nelson, the night foreman, when the alarm went off. Ferko claimed that Jerry owed him for some yard goods he had taken home for his wife's approval and never brought back.

Ferko Szabo never let anything out of his store unless it was paid for but Jerry Nelson usually

316

treated him with politeness and Ferko bent his rule. Had he known that Jerry was going to have an F.O.E. robe made from the blue cloth, he would have stuck to his motto, the one framed above the cash register: "No touch, no loan, no credit." At Szabo's store, the miners all agreed, the customer was always wrong.

Jerry Nelson saw no reason to pay Ferko Szabo for the cloth because he knew that soon the F.O.E. would prune him and his litter from Jericho. Men were on their way to Jericho to do just that when the mine siren began to wail.

Ferko Szabo felt his way along the damp wall, the lights at the opening fading as he moved down the tunnel. Further on two interior mine lights, strung on a sagging electrical wire, flickered on and then off, their dim glow in the dust like ghostly beacons. Something guided Ferko through two tunnel turns until all light disappeared. The size of the tunnel opening became smaller and smaller. He was on his hands and knees and surrounded in blackness when he bumped into something sharp, hitting his shoulder and then his chin.

"Jezus Krisztus! Shit! Shit! Shit!"

Ferko struck a match to see where he was. Three shuttle cars that carried the coal out of the mine were cocked sideways and off the rails, piled against each other by the collapse of a sidewall and the part of the slab that once was the roof of

317

the tunnel. Ferko pulled at one of the cars, jiggling it sideways, grunting and coughing.

A great groan of sliding rock and shifting metal echoed up the tunnel. Ferko pulled back and covered his head with his hands, expecting the top of the tunnel to come crashing down upon him.

Instead, the rock settled and in the dust a dim slit of light appeared, just enough so Ferko could see the edges of the shuttle cars. A faint glow reflected off the wet sheet of rock above his head.

Ferko Szabo could see through a slice in the stack of dark, jumbled rock a dim light on the other side of the pile. He could barely make out mumbling, recognizing not by the words but by its cadence that someone was saying a prayer, a sinner's prayer.

"God have mercy on me. I am a sinner. I believe in Jesus Christ the Son and in the Holy Spirit. Come into my heart, Lord, and wash away my sins with your blood. Jesus is my personal savior and I will follow him. Thank you, Jesus, for saving my soul, but first would you do me the kindness of saving my body?"

"Okay? Everyone okay?" Ferko shouted through the crack.

"Who's that? Who's that?" A voice from beyond the shuttle cars and rock pile shouted back.

"Ferko. Ferko!"

"Who?"

"Szabo!"

318

"Hell, yes! It don't get no more Szabo that this!"

"Who's hurt? Who's dead?" Ferko yelled.

"Get us the hell out of here!"

As long as the carbide lamps still burned, it meant there was oxygen. As long as voices could be heard, it meant survivors. And just as suddenly as it had appeared, the slit of light vanished. Another groan of moving stone was followed by a human voice, most likely a scream. It was hard for Ferko to hear the indistinct sound from the other side of the rocks.

"Okay? Okay?" Ferko shouted and got no response.

Jerry Nelson had watched Ferko Szabo rush into the mouth of the Brighter Day mine and didn't shout for him to stop. There were rescue teams for things like this and whatever one crazy Hungarian wanted to do was not his problem.

Nelson rushed in the opposite direction, to the shift office that was attached to the men's locker-room. He would run down the list of steps that should be taken, notify the appropriate people and turn off that damned siren. The siren had come on automatically when sensors picked up a disturbance in Tunnel 6.

There had not been a mine death at the Brighter Day since it was renamed from the Sunset Mine. A tally board was kept to announce how many days had passed without a mine-related tragedy, but the tally had been ignored once the

319

number of days grew into four digits. Usual industrial accidents were accepted as the price of doing business, including the loss of Tim Mitchell's left hand, last seen tumbling into a coal car of the Ohio Southern. But according to the tally board, the Brighter Day was a safe mine.

A certain complacency had seeped into the daily routine of the Brighter Day, allowing the miners to be more upset at the prices in Ferko Szabo's store than with the inadequate ventilation and insufficient support beams for the mine.

The rescue team for the Brighter Day Mine consisted of five miners, three of whom were in the mine at the time. That left rescue team leader Floyd North along with Early Lyons to organize and analyze what needed to be done. Floyd, however, was visiting his divorced and dying father in Pennsylvania and Early Lyons had joined the rescue team only for the extra pay that came with it. He had paid very little attention to any of the training, such as it was.

Jerry Nelson clicked the phone, and shouted, rousing Ruth Wilkins from her nap at the telephone exchange. "Ruth, Ruth, get me Early Lyons."

"What's that noise?" asked Ruth.

"The siren. The mine siren. Can't you hear it? Get me Early Lyons."

"You want his house?" asked Ruth.

"Wouldn't he be at his house?"

"Not on Tuesday," said Ruth.

"Well, wherever he is, get him for me."

Ruth pulled one of the phone plugs from its panel and shoved it into the phone slot of the number not for Early Lyons but for Allen Charles. The telephone rang and rang. No one answered.

"I know he's there," Ruth Wilkins told Jerry Nelson.

"Ring again. Ring until he answers."

Ruth reconnected. The phone in Allen Charles' house rang and rang. Ruth was about to pull the connection again when Betty Charles answered.

"Yes," she said cautiously.

"Betty. Ruth Wilkins. Jerry Nelson at the mine wants to talk to Early."

"Early who?"

"Betty. Can't you hear the siren? It's an emergency. Put Early on the phone."

Allen Charles was the local liaison of the United Mine Workers. He took the Greyhound bus to Columbus on Tuesdays, stayed overnight at the Beverly Motel on East Main Street next to the Greyhound station and enjoyed the company of any one of several employees of the Buckeye Escort Service. He told his wife that it was union business and she did not question him. Instead, Betty took advantage of the absence of her husband on Tuesday nights and entertained Early Lyons, who had once taken Betty to the Perry junior prom.

"Damn it, Early, get over here!" Jerry Nelson shouted into the telephone. "Somebody's got to do something."

Early Lyons had no car and he usually pooled to the mine with Floyd North. He asked Betty Charles to drive him. She refused because it would mean that her husband Allen would know she was cheating on him.

"Hell, Betty," said Early, "what do you think he's doing?"

"But he'll know," said Betty. "I know he'll know. I don't want him to know."

"Give me the keys then," said Early.

"You can't drive his car to the mine," said Betty. "How you going to explain that?"

The entire conversation between the two of them was conducted with Early holding the telephone in one hand while both Ruth Wilkins and Jerry Nelson listened. By the time Early reported his transportation difficulty to Jerry Nelson several dozen cars, including two pick up trucks and Andy Sloan's Lincoln were on their way to the Brighter Day. The parking lot at the tipple was beginning to fill and a crowd was beginning to gather outside the mine entrance.

"Early, you asshole!" shouted Jerry Nelson and slammed the phone down.

The speed of the response to the siren was later credited with minimizing the disaster. The truth was that most of the men who showed up so quickly at the Brighter Day were there, not to

322

rescue anyone but to teach a lesson to the Szabos. The F.O.E. had finally decided that the Szabos needed to be pruned from their garden.

The crowbars that would become so handy for prying away rocks from the slide that had trapped the miners had been intended to crack a few doors, break a few windows, maybe a few heads, scare whatever Szabo happened to be around.

Andy Sloan had altered Warren Lund's old gold robe so that it fit him better. He added a wider band of purple on both the sleeves and onto the hem so that when he raised his arms into the golden eagle pose he looked much less like a clown in a gown.

If Andy could convince the F.O.E. members that the Szabos had to be removed, he figured that would be filling not only the legacy of Warren Lund but Andy could keep his movie theater and the money Ferko Szabo had already paid him for it.

"Tonight we prune!" shouted Andy Sloan, and nine members of the F.O.E. who agreed with him pulled up their cowls and set out for Jericho. They fit themselves into two pickup trucks and Andy Sloan's Lincoln. They had just crested the hill that led into the tiny town of Jericho when the siren sounded.

Duck Stadler nearly dropped the wad of money he had pulled from the pocket of his father's Red Kap shirt, but he had managed to slam the locker and stuff the bills into his front pants pocket

323

when Jerry Nelson came barreling into the shift office next to the workers' locker room. Through the glass window that separated the office from the locker room, Duck and Ink Ear could see Jerry on the telephone and but could not hear him shouting at whomever was on the other end.

"Let's get the hell out of here!" Ink Ear shouted, grabbing Duck by the arm.

"Hell, no!" yelled Duck. "You know what that is. There's been a cave in."

"So what?"

"So, Charlie's under there," said Duck.

Jerry Nelson came through the office door and rushed down a side of the room to the mine rescue locker that held the breathing tanks and special gear. The rescue locker was locked. Jerry kicked at the door and looked around for something to break it down. He saw Duck and Ink Ear standing side by side in the other end of the room.

"What are you doing here?" Jerry demanded.

"Uh, uh…" Ink Ear stammered.

"Get the hell out of here. Don't you know what's happened?"

"Sure we do," said Duck. "We want to help."

"No we don't," said Ink Ear.

"Just get out. And stay out of the way," said Jerry Nelson. He pulled the lever on the electrical panel next to the rescue locker and the siren ceased. Except for the scrape of gravel from cars pulling into the parking lot, silence once again swallowed the tipple of the Brighter Day mine.

Andy Sloan had removed his hood but was still in his gold robe when Ferko Szabo stumbled out of the entrance of the Brighter Day mine. Ferko was covered in black dust and with his black beard seemed nothing more than a huge chunk of coal. Or the figure of death itself.

Ferko rushed up to Andy Sloan causing Sloan to shudder and slink back. Ferko grabbled Andy by the sleeve of his gold gown, streaking it with black.

"I know where they are," Ferko shouted. "Come. I know." Ferko picked up the lantern that Andy had set down. He turned and started back to the mine entrance. Andy Sloan did not move.

"You, you, you," Ferko shouted, pointing at several members of the F.O.E. "Come. Come." None of them moved.

Duck Stadler picked up a crowbar that was lying at Andy Sloan's feet and started after Ferko. "I'll go," Duck yelled. "Him too." Duck pointed at Ink Ear, who shrugged and started after Duck. As he turned to go, Ink Ear saw pulling into the tipple parking lot the Black Beast hearse of Cannon's Family Funeral Home.

Sonny Tolliver had no way to get to Jericho. He knew that Duck and Ink Ear were at the Brighter Day and his gut told him that they had done something to set off the siren. Maybe a prank. Not a good prank, but Duck and Ink Ear did not have

Sonny's gift for pranks. Sonny ran from his house carrying his sneakers. His feet were still sore from the walk back from Loganville. Sonny saw the Black Beast of Cannon's Family Funeral Home parked outside Wayne Timmons' house, its motor still running.

He did not see Roy Cannon in the hearse. Sonny checked the back of the hearse and saw no customer in there either. Wayne Timmons had been ill, Black Lung wearing him down. Maybe he was dead. Maybe Roy was just checking to see how soon he would be dead. Sonny opened the door of the Black Beast and leaned on the horn. With the siren still blaring, the noise of the horn was barely noticeable.

Sonny knew a little about driving, very little. He had watched Ron Miller shift through the gears of the Dodge Town Wagon and twice Jim Norton had let him drive the milk truck, but never far enough that he had to make a turn or do anything but stop.

"Ah, shit," said Sonny to himself. "How hard can it be?"

Sonny climbed in behind the wheel of the Black Beast and was happy to find that it had an automatic transmission. He was tall enough to see out over the long hood, but it was still quite a change from the blunt front of the Wiseman Dairy truck.

Sonny pulled the gear lever from "P" to "D" and the Black Beast began to creep forward. The hearse continued down the street at a slow rate, creeping along without any acceleration. Sonny's sneakers were on the front seat where he had tossed them. His bare right foot pushed down on the accelerator.

Whooosh. The Black Beast had lately been tuned by Roy Cannon. It was no longer the oil burning clunker as before. Sonny and the Beast sped down Buckeye Street, through the stop sign at the intersection of Elm, and onto the highway to Jericho. Sonny lifted his foot, pressed down again, lifted it and pressed down. The Black Beast jerked forward, paused and jerked again until Sonny found a rhythm. Within six minutes he could see the lights of the Brighter Day tipple.

Mortician and coroner Roy Cannon had heard the siren and was on his way to Jericho to help however he could. He was certain that he would be picking up some new business. Roy had stopped on the way out of town to relieve his bladder in Wayne Timmons's cherry hedge. Roy returned to the street to find an empty space where he had left his hearse.

Chapter 28

Where's Charlie?

Sonny did not know how to turn off the headlights on the Black Beast, nor did he know how to dim them. The bright lights of Perry's only hearse shone directly at the entrance to the Brighter Day Mine. Sonny saw the figure of a man covered all over in black entering the opening. Behind him was Duck Stadler. And several steps further back, Ink Ear Ryan.

Sonny shifted the gear lever back from "D" to "P," left the motor running and jumped out of the Black Beast. He called to Duck.

"Wait! Wait! Wait for me!" Duck had already entered the mouth of the mine, but Ink Ear heard. He stopped and waited for Sonny to catch up.

"Did you come in that hearse?" Ink Ear asked.

"I drove that hearse," said Sonny. "Nothing to it."

"Hope you can drive it back," said Ink Ear. The two of them followed the light that Ferko was carrying, not needing to crouch as low as he.

"Where are we going?" Sonny asked.

"We're following Duck."

Who's Duck following?"

"Mr. Szabo."

"Which one?"

"The one with the beard."

"Ferko Szabo," said Sonny.

"Bless you," said Ink Ear.

Sonny and Ink Ear hurried to catch up to the faint light carried by Ferko. The shadows of both Ferko and Duck danced along the wet walls.

"Why are we the only ones in here?" asked Sonny.

"They couldn't get the door open," said Ink Ear.

"What door?"

"Where they keep the breathing things and the lights and stuff."

"What?"

"For rescuing."

"How do you know this?"

"Me and Duck saw it. Some asshole didn't have a key."

"What is Ferko Szabo doing in here?"

"Beats me. We only saw him come out."

"You mean Ferko Szabo is trying to save these miners? Why?"

"Beats the hell out of me," said Ink Ear.

Ferko Szabo heard the chatter of the boys behind him. He heard Sonny's question. Why was he trying to save these people who hated him? Because he was a human being and so were they? Maybe so. Because they were his customers and without them he had no income? Maybe that, too. Because two of his brothers, Albos and Tibor, had died in a mine explosion in Oroszlany, back in Hungary? Probably. Had someone gotten to Albos and Tibor in time, they would be alive. Ferko Szabo's instinct was to do what he could but why three boys were following him into the damp and danger of the Brighter Day, Ferko Szabo had no idea.

By the time Jerry Nelson had outfitted five volunteers with breathing packs and coveralls, with all the proper gear for rescue, Ferko Szabo, Duck Stadler, Sonny Tolliver and Ink Ear Ryan had pried and chipped and smashed enough rock to make a hole nearly large enough for the trapped miners to escape.

When Donald Turner peered out the hole that had been made and saw the fierce face of Ferko Szabo lit from below by Andy Sloan's lantern, he screamed and scrambled back from the opening.

Donald had prayed the sinner's prayer and when he saw Ferko's face he was sure the answer was no.

"Come, come," said Ferko Szabo. "You can come. It is all right."

"Ink Ear," said Duck. "You can squeeze through that hole. See what's what and what they need."

Ink Ear climbed onto the rim of one of the shuttle cars and peered into the hole. Duck pushed him from below, his hands cupping Ink Ear's butt cheeks.

"Watch where you're putting your hands," said Ink Ear.

Ink Ear squirmed and squeezed and popped through to the other side. Duck passed Andy Sloan's lantern through to him. A pocket of the tunnel had survived the rockslide. It made a room about the size of Clara Miller's hen house. Seven men were scrunched back against the dark, damp wall. Traces of tears streaked the black of their cheeks. Two of them were moaning. One, Scott Lawrence, made no sound. Gary Adams' lower left leg was at an incorrect angle. Donald Turner was rubbing the side of his head where he had hit it after scrambling back from Ferko's face.

"Are you okay?" Ink Ear asked, meaning it generally.

"I think I'm bleeding," said Donald Turner, speaking in particular.

"They're coming," said Ink Ear, though he had no idea if anyone was coming or not. Duck had told him to try and push one of the rocks through from their side. It would make the hole big enough for a grown man to get through.

"What are you doing here, kid?" asked Gary Adams.

"I was following Duck," said Ink Ear. "He said, 'you'll see,' but I didn't think I'd see this."

Ferko and Duck, working in almost complete darkness, Ferko on his knees and Duck bent over, managed to get one of the shuttle cars back onto the rails. After Donald Turner and Ink Ear Ryan had grunted and shoved and cursed the rock that blocked the hole, it tumbled out into the pile and suddenly there was enough room for Ferko to climb through.

"I thought you was the grim reaper," said Donald to Ferko.

"No, I'm Ferko," said Ferko.

Duck, Ink Ear, Sonny, Turner and Ferko managed to help the miners from one side of the rock pile to the other. The miners were all in the shuttle car and Ferko was pushing it back up the tracks when Jerry Nelson and the rescue crew with their lights and their breathing packs arrived. They looked like the spacemen Sonny had seen in the Saturday serials at the Glob.

"Holy, shit," said Jerry Nelson. "Holy, shit."

Through the breathing mask he wore, the words came out muffled, sounding like "Home it is, home it is."

"That's where I'm going," said Donald Turner.

Jerry Nelson shoved Ferko Szabo aside and he and two others in their rescue space suits continued to push the shuttle car up the tracks

332

and out of the entrance of the Brighter Day, and it was brighter out there. The headlights of the Black Beast still shone, as did dozens of other car lights in the parking lot. The entrance to the mine had been lit with temporary floodlights making it nearly as bright as day. The crowd that had gathered cheered and Jerry Nelson waved.

"We got 'em! We got 'em all!" Jerry Nelson shouted.

"Did you get Charlie?" Gary Adams mumbled. Jerry did not hear, but Duck heard.

"Where's Charlie?" asked Duck. "Charlie's my dad. Where's Charlie?"

"He was pulling pillars in the retreat," said Gary. "I think maybe he caused the cave-in. He's in a thousand foot grave. Poor old Charlie."

To scrape the last bit of coal possible from a seam, columns of coal that are left to hold up the roof of a tunnel are cut away until they collapse. The fallen coal is removed and another pillar is cut as the miner retreats. The last pillar is "the suicide pillar," and it can collapse an entire tunnel. The small, the quick and the foolish are given the job of cutting it. Charlie Stadler had cut many pillars and had always been able to scramble away from the falling roof.

Charlie Stadler was not fearless as much as he was resigned. He had been convinced since the birth of his son, since that horrible day when he was pinned in the space he had dug himself, that he would die one day in just that way. He would be lost and forgotten under earth and rock. He asked himself the same question every morning. Will this be the day? Charlie Stadler had become convinced that any time he spent with his son was time that was charged against the inevitable.

Lately Charlie Stadler had begun to do subtraction in his head, figuring that the average life span of an underground miner was 48 years. Where he came up with that figure he was not sure. But what he knew was now he was 41 and his son, who would soon be 12, had eroded the seven years that should be left to him considerably. He figured he was past due.

Charlie had left the crew behind him while he finished off the retreat of the seam in Tunnel 6. The seam was never much to begin with and should not have been any trouble. The roof seemed solid and the pillars he had already cut had collapsed without difficulty. The crew had cleaned the coal out on Monday and would finish the seam the next night.

When Charlie Stadler cut the final "suicide pillar," and heard the howl of the collapsing tunnel roof, he said simply, "Shit." And what he had always known would be his fate closed in around him.

Duck grabbed Sonny's arm. "He's still in there," Duck said. "I've got to get him."

"Let them do it" Sonny said. "They've got the equipment."

The "they" to whom Sonny was referring were posing for pictures dressed in their rescue equipment. Some had rubbed coal on each other to make it look like they had actually done something. The miners in the shuttle car were grinning and coughing and waving. Scott Lawrence had regained consciousness and stared into the lights. Ferko Szabo remained in the darkness by the side of the entrance, covered by the dark shadow that was created from the concentrated light and the wooden sign that identified the mine as "The Brighter Day." Ferko watched and waited and then walked away, back to his home, leaving the cheers and the lights. He said nothing to Sonny, Duck or Ink Ear. But Ferko Szabo gave them a small wave of his hand.

"They're taking credit," said Ink Ear. "We did it and they're taking credit."

Mark Hunt, a reporter for the Loganville Messenger, was talking to Jerry Nelson, getting details of the prompt action that had saved all the lives. Dr. Paul Tedrow was tending to Gary Adams' leg. The doctor's wife Melissa was bandaging Donald Turner's head. Someone had turned on a car radio and cranked up the volume. The Louvin Brothers wailed "Take the News to Mother," bringing tears to several faces.

"They forgot about Charlie," said Duck. "I'm going to get him. Are you coming or staying here with these chicken shits?"

Sonny, as did Ink Ear, shrugged and started back into the mine, each picking up a crowbar and a lantern. Margarite Szabo, standing in the crowd dressed only in her nightgown, watched the three boys she remembered from the Clay Hole disappear down the track.

"I drove the Black Beast," said Sonny.

"No, shit," said Duck.

"I saw him do it," said Ink Ear, confirming Sonny's story.

The three of them said nothing more as they worked their way back to where the rockslide had trapped the miners. A soft drip, drip, drip of water came from somewhere. One after the other they climbed through the hole they had made earlier with Ferko Szabo. With the additional light they now had, they could see one wall had slid and crumbled, covering what was very likely another small tunnel.

"Charlie's back there, I bet," said Duck. He put his lantern down and began scraping at the crumbled coal with the crowbar. Sonny and Ink Ear joined him.

"Don't get mad," said Ink Ear as he pushed the debris behind him. "I got a question."

"As long as it's not an idiot question," said Duck.

"What do you care about Charlie?"

"What?"

"Jesus, Duck. You came here to rob him. He beat the shit out of you. More than once."

"I've heard you," said Sonny. "I've heard you wish he was dead."

"Well, I don't," said Duck. "And if he is, I want to see it."

"They don't care about him," said Sonny. "His own friends. They left him in here. They don't care if he's found or not."

"I care," said Duck, continuing to dig.

Ink Ear crashed his crowbar down on a piece of shale and pulled, causing a small landside of coal to come tumbling at the boys.

"Look out! Get back!" Duck shoved Sonny and scrambled back but the falling coal caught Duck and slid up his body, covering him from the waist down before it settled.

"Duck, Duck, you okay?" shouted Sonny. "Shit, Duck, you're half buried."

"My foot," said Duck. "My left foot. It feels crushed."

"Shit, Duck, I told you. Charlie's not worth it. Look what you've done."

"Shut up and dig me out," said Duck.

Sonny and Ink Ear pulled the lumps of coal off Duck, throwing them behind themselves. The small room was beginning to fill with the debris from all their digging.

"Here," said Duck. "Pull me. I might be able to wiggle out."

Sonny reached under one arm and Ink Ear grabbed the other. Bracing themselves against a wet wall, they heaved. Duck did not move.

"No, no, no!" Duck screamed. "You're making it worse."

"Shit, Duck. Just stay there. We'll dig you out. Don't move anything."

Just before they started picking up the coal again and tossing it behind them, they heard a cough from the other side of the slide of coal and stone.

"What was that?" Ink Ear asked.

"What?"

"Listen."

Again. A cough. Duck felt something pulling at his right foot. He felt his shoe pop off.

"What the hell? What the hell? There's something in there," yelled Duck. "There's something eating my foot."

"It's me, you little turd." It was Charlie Stadler's voice.

Chapter 29

Last Train to Jericho

"Let's take one more ride," Sonny suggested to Duck and Ink Ear. "Let's catch the last train to Jericho."

"How can I do that?" asked Duck. "I can't run. I can't walk. I can't stand without leaning on something."

"We'll help you," said Ink Ear. "I've been thinking about it. I know how you can do it. The train always slows down at Trestle Two. It almost stops. We can help you up on the side strut, the one where we painted our names. And when the train slows down, you just ease over into one of the cars. We'll hold your crutches. Sonny can get in first and catch you if you need it."

"I don't need anybody catching me," said Duck. "You think of this by yourself?"

"Sure, yeah. Me and Sonny."

"You mean it was Sonny's plan."

"Sonny don't have every plan."

"Yes, he does."

"Okay. He does. But I thought about him catching you."

"I don't need anybody catching me."

"So, let's do it," said Sonny.

"Why should we?" asked Duck.

"Are you chicken shit?" asked Ink Ear.

Duck raised one of his crutches and took a swipe at Ink Ear, who sidestepped away.

"We do it because we'll never be able to do it again," said Sonny. "No one else will be able to do it either. All the kids who come after us, they won't have a train. They can swim in the Clay Hole and they can egg the Doughboy and they can mess with the school bus. They might even be able to find a dead body. But they can't take the last train to Jericho because there won't be any more trains to Jericho. I bet there won't even be a Jericho. You don't always know when you have a last chance to do something, but we know about this. We can take a last ride and we'll know that no one else will ever be able to do what we've done."

"I already done what no one else never did," said Duck. "I saved my dad's life."

"Oh, big deal. Big hero, you. We were there, too, you know. If you have to pull a dad out of his grave to get a dad to like you, to hell with dads. To hell with your dad and to hell with my dad and to hell with Ink Ear's dad."

"My pa ran off with the circus," said Ink Ear.

340

"The carnival," said Duck. "It's not the same as a circus."

"Well, still, he ran off," said Ink Ear.

"So, are you up for a last ride, or what?" asked Sonny.

"Hell, yes. Let's do it," said Duck.

Strictly speaking, Duck did not save his father's life. He did go back into the mine to get him, and if he had not gone back Charlie Stadler would have died under Jericho Hill just as he always imagined he would. What Duck did, half buried himself, was to give Charlie something to hang onto until Ink Ear Ryan got the Mine Rescue Team finally to come back into the mine and get them both.

Charlie clung onto the right foot of his son knowing that he was still connected to the world. Stuck in a pocket of space between shale and slate, his miner's hat resting beyond his reach but with the light still burning, with the cruel knowledge that he had enough air to be aware of his own death as it would slowly come, Charlie Stadler reached out and found his son's foot poking through a fresh slide of coal. He pulled off the shoe and grabbed the foot. He knew the shoe, a high top Converse sneaker with the word "Duck" scrawled on the heel. He knew the shoe because he had yelled at Duck often enough to not leave it lying around. And there it was, the foot of life, so to speak, a leg up from his son, and he took it.

Charlie Stadler thought not just about being rescued but he thought that if he was going out of this life, as long as he held onto his son's foot, Duck would be going out with him. The reassurance of that knowledge may have had as much to do with Charlie's sudden peace of mind as the prospect of being freed.

"No, no, no!" Charlie shouted when Duck's foot pulled out of his grasp, the bond broken. Jerry Nelson and the rescue crew had cleared away enough of the broken rock and coal to free Duck. Replacing the Converse sneaker was a gloved hand and Charlie tapped it to show he was still alive. Duck had already been removed to the Black Beast, which would serve as an ambulance to take both father and son to Lancaster General Hospital. The first thing Charlie Stadler asked after he was laid into the hearse beside Duck was, "How's the boy? How's my boy?" Charlie reached over and clutched Duck's right foot and held it all the way to the hospital. Duck pretended to be unconscious but he wasn't.

The owners of the Brighter Day Coal Company, a subsidiary of the Eagle River Resource Corporation of Parkersburg, West Virginia, had been considering closing the Brighter Day for some time. There was still coal under Jericho Hill but profits had fallen and the demand for coal in general was in decline. Many homes no longer used coal to heat, preferring natural gas or heating oil. There seemed to be plenty of both of those and they were a lot easier and cheaper to get to. Something called renewable energy, whatever that was, had been getting lots of attention. There was a picture in the Loganville Messenger of a new house being built that had what looked like mirrors on the roof, solar energy collectors they were called. Perry's miners could not imagine a countryside full of giant windmills or power that was collected from the sun, but investors could.

Add to the competition from other energy sources all those nagging government regulations, union agitation, safety requirements, and the inevitable investigation into the causes of the Brighter Day cave-in, it seemed not worth the bother to reopen the mine. The centuries old method of digging coal from the inside of a hill was giving way to the newer method of stripping away the hill from the top. The Eagle River Resource Corporation of Parkersburg, West Virginia, was trending to the strip method.

Settlements for the Brighter Day cave-in were modest because no one had died nor was anyone critically injured. Medical bills and disability pensions were agreed to for Charlie Stadler and the rest, but the cost was barely a nip of a day's profits. When the Eagle River Resource Corporation of Parkersburg, West Virginia, announced it would not reopen the Brighter Day mine, the miners promised to disband their association with the United Mine Workers union and not insist on even routine safety maintenance.

"We gave up everything and it didn't matter," said Allen Charles.

The coal already dug at the Brighter Day that was easily available would be hauled away and the tipple left as it stood. The tiny town of Jericho would be no more. Ferko Szabo, who had seen this coming, had several years earlier bought the Loganville IGA under his legally changed name of Fred Osborne. He now owned Andy Sloan's Glob Theater in Perry and had plans for it. Ferko was building a house halfway between Perry and Loganville, a mid-century modern design with solar panels on the roof and enough bedrooms and almost enough bathrooms for his family.

The Szabo relocation meant that his children had the choice of going to Loganville or to Perry schools. Only Margarite Szabo would choose to go to Perry Junior High and when she registered in the fall her name would be Marty Osborne and she would wear her long raven hair in a ponytail.

"Maybe we'll see her," said Sonny. "When we get up to the mine."

"You mean..." said Duck.

"Yes, I do," said Sonny. "I thought I saw her that night, but maybe not. I wouldn't mind seeing her again. I wouldn't mind at all."

Sonny had never mentioned seeing Darla Hamilton holding hands with Ink Ear, and Duck and Ink Ear had never talked to Sonny about the black haired girl from the Clay Hole. They didn't talk about girls to each other but they thought about them sometimes. Sometimes they thought about nothing else.

They could hear the last train to Jericho clicking on the rails somewhere below Winslow's Bend. Duck had pulled himself up onto the struts of Trestle 2 just as Sonny knew he could. His left leg hung out from the girder, stiffen by the cast.

"Twist around," said Sonny, "if you don't want to lose the leg altogether."

Duck squirmed until he was roosting sideways to the tracks, his left leg no longer perpendicular to the girder. He would have to fall backwards into the coal car as the train went by.

"You still want to do this?" asked Sonny. The train was now visible, slowing at the crossing of China Street. The barrier was down and red lights flashed. The train would be crawling by the time it crossed the Jericho River at Trestle 2.

"I can do this, no problem," said Duck.

The engine chuffed past the three boys who were hanging onto the struts of Trestle 2. The engineer waved. They waved back.

"I'll go first," said Sonny. "And then Duck. Ink Ear, go last."

The fifth car on the short train moved under the boys. A coal hopper is slanted on each end, which allows the coal to feed down to a release door. The boys often used the slant as a sliding board. Sonny dropped into the coal hopper, grabbing the top edge of the car to keep from sliding down, holding himself against the side. The

345

car moved on slowly but Duck did not hoist himself off the strut. Sonny turned to look behind him as the next car moved under Duck. It was nearly past him, when Duck threw his crutches into the car and let himself go, falling backwards, his left leg sticking straight up. He landed on the slope of the car and slid on his backside down towards the bottom.

"You okay?" Sonny yelled. Ink Ear jumped off into the next car and scrambled up, his head popping above the car.

"You're right," yelled Duck. "We won't ever be able to do that again. Damn! I want to do that again!"

The last train to Jericho picked up speed and rattled on. Sonny and Ink Ear climbed from their cars into the hopper with Duck. They helped him scoot on his backside up the slant of the hopper until all of their heads stuck up above the rim of the car. The cool air rushing over them helped to blow away some of the coal dust from their faces.

"Now, isn't this great?" asked Sonny.

The Brighter Day tipple already seemed haunted. Several of the windows were shattered in the main building. Chunks of coal lay with the broken glass inside on the floor, the ineffective traces of the miners' resentment about the closing of the mine. A very few workers were about. All the heavy machinery was gone and the usual belchings and rumblings of a working coal mine were absent. The only sounds came from the conveyer belt that carried the last of the coal up to the tipping point and then the clatter of the coal into the same hoppers that the boys had ridden from Perry.

There would be no ceremony for the closing of the Brighter Day coal mine, no final observance, no formal funeral. When the last train left Jericho, that would be it. Somebody would turn out the lights, or maybe not even bother. Eight decades of mining would be no more. What remained of the concealed treasure that had sustained, frustrated and defined generations would be buried once again, the only evidence that it had ever been disturbed just a few holes in the ground and the decaying structure of the tipple.

Sonny, Duck and Ink Ear went to the Szabos' store to wait for the departure of the last train from Jericho. They had not thought about how they would return to Perry. The boys assumed they would just ride on top of the coal or hang on between cars until they got back. How Duck was going to jump off a moving train onto one leg was something they would figure out when the time came. If he couldn't get off, Duck said, he would just go wherever the train went.

Sonny pushed at the entrance door to the Szabos' store, but the door would not open. He cupped his hands around his eyes and pressed his face to the glass of the door. He could see that the shelves were empty. A push broom leaned against the counter where the cash register had been. The

347

sign, "no touch, no loan, no credit," was still there.

"We're gone."

Sonny heard a voice behind him. Duck and Ink Ear, who had been peering into the store through side windows turned. The three of them knew who it was even before they saw Margarite Szabo. She wore a pale yellow cotton dress. A wide brimmed man's hat was cocked back on her head. Her black tresses framed her face. She held the leash of large shorthaired brown dog. She smiled; the dog remained suspicious.

"We moved."

"Moved?" asked Sonny, not knowing what else to say. "Moved?"

"I guess we won't be swimming any more," said Margarite.

"You remember that?" asked Duck.

"We remember that," said Ink Ear.

"Moved where?" asked Sonny.

"I saw you that night, the night of the cave-in," said Margarite, speaking directly to Sonny. "You guys are crazy."

"What about your dad?" asked Sonny. "He's crazier."

"He's my dad," said Margarite.

"Your dad? What's that mean?" asked Duck.

"I don't know," she said, still talking directly to Sonny. "Why are you here? How did you get here? No, I see. You're covered with coal. You rode the train."

348

"We're going to ride it back," said Ink Ear.

"It's filthy, the train," she said.

"We don't mind," said Duck.

"Say your name again," said Sonny.

"It's Marty. Short for Margarite."

She took off her hat and held it to her side. Her hair fell forward and surrounded her face. She smiled and Sonny noticed again the slight angle of one of her teeth. He thought it was charming.

"We could take you back," said Margarite.

"Who is we?" asked Sonny.

"She mean me, the crazy man," said Ferko Szabo. Margarite's father, the man who had led the boys into the mine, appeared from around the corner of the store. He was carrying a wooden crate. Sonny could see the top of one boot and part of a globe of the world sticking out of the box. Ferko Szabo had shaved his full black beard. A slight shadow of stubble darkened his cheeks and neck but the man who had frightened miners and children on sight now looked like a grocer or even a banker.

"I got a truck," Ferko said. "You can ride. You…" He motioned with his head at Sonny. "You ride in the seat. You…" He moved his head again to include Duck and Ink Ear. "You in the back."

"But I got a bad leg," said Duck, looking at Margarite. "I should ride in the seat."

"You in the back," said Ferko Szabo.

Duck slid his crutches up the bed of the V8 Studebaker, hoisted himself up over the tailgate and scooted until his back was against the cab. He grumbled all the while that he should be riding in the front. Ink Ear climbed over the side and sat down beside Duck. Margarite's dog jumped in and bounded up to Duck. He sniffed and nuzzled Duck's crotch. Ferko Szabo pushed his wooden box onto the truck bed, slammed the tailgate, slid the catch and went around to the driver's door.

"He likes you," said Ferko, as he passed Duck. "Dog's name is Kutya."

"Why did the moron climb into the truck?" asked Ink Ear, not waiting for an answer. "To ride home in style."

Margarite slipped in beside her father. Sonny squeezed in next to her. Ferko Szabo did not glance at the building that had housed his store and had given him his start in America. He backed away, turned the steering wheel of the V8 Studebaker and pulled forward onto the road from Jericho.

Sonny and Margarite said nothing the entire way back to Perry. Margarite sat with her hat in her lap. Sonny could feel the side of Margarite's thigh through his jeans. It felt like his leg was on fire.

Chapter 30

Through the Gate

The closing of the Brighter Day coal mine in Jericho meant the end of the Ohio Southern's trunk service through Perry. A new highway was being built along the northern edge of town, taking out the curves, skirting the town itself and removing passing commerce from Perry's streets. Neff's service station was being relocated to where the new highway joined the old one at Three-Mile Turn.

The stoplight across from the Perry Doughboy was now entirely superfluous. Fewer and fewer cars traveled along Main Street. The Perry Pottery had cut back its line of ceramics, making only the signature cookie jar, streamlining its production and its work force. The famous Perry Piss Pot water tank was rusting at the seams, looking a little now like a fat freckled banana.

Perry was going to be parked on the edge of interest to outsiders, a relic of another time, a scrap of yesterday. Perry did not know any of this at the time.

Miners covered in black coal dust and potters coated in white clay no longer mingled at Shorty's Tavern. Shorty did not have to wipe down the barstools as often as he once did, but he continued to do so anyhow. The beer was just as cold and it was just as weak, but the drinkers were now distinguishable only by the labels on the bottles in front of them, Pabst for the former miners and Blatz for the former potters. And soon those two breweries would be merging into one. Beer could be sold in aluminum cans and Shorty Wolfe kept a small inventory of canned beer in case someone asked. Long neck bottles were still the first choice.

Russell Hand, the insurance man, had lost interest in keeping Perry at the top of the list of fewest suicides in Ohio. His disinterest was due in no small part to fact that Russell Hand, the insurance man, hanged himself from a cross beam in his detached garage, dressed only in his hunting vest and galoshes. He left a note that said simply, "Count me out."

Funeral director Roy Cannon was planning to trade the Black Beast for something less sinister, something silver, he thought, with fins. He liked the Cadillac but would buy another Buick.

Sheriff John Brown was proposed for membership in the Law and Order Sheriff's Lodge by Loganville sheriff Harry Raines and was admitted by a majority of two votes. Through determined and meticulous police work, Sheriff Brown had solved the mystery of the Perry Doughboy bullet hole, a bullet hole he had no idea existed until Gus Shiner told him about it.

"I seen it all from the cell," Gus told Sheriff Brown one sober morning. "That Loganville cop shot the doughboy."

"What are you talking about, you old fool?" asked Sheriff John Brown.

"I can show you the hole," said Gus. "For a dollar."

"I'll give you another night in the cell," said Sheriff John Brown. Gus Shiner did not mind being arrested because he would have a warm place to sleep and meals on the town. Sheriff John Brown tried not to keep Gus any longer than was needed.

Gus Shiner showed Sheriff John Brown the bullet hole and told the story of how Sheriff Harry Raines plugged the Perry Doughboy and drove away in the night.

"Get me Sheriff Raines, please," said Sheriff John Brown to Bonnie Carpenter at the telephone exchange. And two weeks later, Sheriff John Brown sewed a new patch for the Law and Order Sheriff's Lodge onto the sleeve of his shirt.

Andy Sloan was unable to keep the Fraternal Order of Eden together. It wasn't that the Weeders and the Trimmers and the Pruners suddenly found intolerance intolerable; it was that

353

Andy was too much of an asshole to be their leader and no one else wanted the job. While Andy was just as loud as Warren Lund had been, he was not as charismatic. It was impossible to imagine the man under the gold hood and inside the gold gown was anyone but goofball Andy Sloan, not a miner, a potter or a preacher.

The Devil's Tea Table was put on the list of Ohio attractions. One visitor from Indiana said, "It's not even one of Ohio's *dis*tractions." A plaque was placed by the rock describing how weather, erosion and time had created the formation. Official recognition had made the Devil's Tea Table ordinary, replacing mystery with geology, never a smart trade. It had become an odd rock and nothing more.

On the evening when the school children of Perry would be Passing Through the Gate, summer was already smiling on Perry, Ohio. The green wallpaper of the trees along the ridges, the soft shadows in the hollows, the glinting sun off creeks no longer fouled by acid tailings from the Brighter Day, the Jericho River now odorless if not entirely clear nor wholly fresh, the early marigolds in the window boxes, all of it hinted at a better world. Perry seemed to be a fine place to be.

"Are you passing?" Ink Ear asked Duck.

"Nothing wrong with my arm," said Duck.

"I mean passing through the gate. Can you walk?"

"I can walk. I'll be able to run before too long."

Duck Stadler's left foot and lower left leg were still in a cast, smaller and less clumsy than the one he had worn on the last train to Jericho. He now wore a brace on his left knee. Dr. Tedrow said he would make a full recovery, said he would be as good as new. Duck believed the doctor most of the time. But some nights, when the ache gripped his ankle and shards of pain stung his leg, he was not so sure.

Duck Stadler was, as he always imagined he would be, the school hero, the town hero. He was the boy who saved his father from death. Duck was written up in the Loganville Messenger, the story calling him the "Fearless Boy of Perry." His exploits at the Brighter Day Mine got seven paragraphs in the Citizen-Journal in Columbus. The Athens Tribune printed the story along with a fourth-grade headshot that made Duck look absolutely goofy. Since that school picture was taken, Duck's face had grown to fit his ears and his jaw had firmed. Duck's smile was no longer crooked. He was now much more mature and handsome than the child in the headshot. None of the news reports called him "Duck," but each one mentioned his goal of one day starting in the backfield of the Ohio State Buckeyes just as Perry's own Wilkie Wilkins had done.

There was no mention of why Duck was at the Brighter Day coal mine. No one, not even Charlie thought to ask. The money Duck had taken from

Charlie's Red Kap shirt must have fallen out of Duck's pocket when he was half covered in coal. Both the money and Duck's right sneaker would be forever buried under Jericho Hill.

Ink Ear Ryan was proud to know Duck, prouder some days to know Duck than he was to know Sonny and Ink Ear Ryan worshiped Sonny.

"Duck is my best friend," Ink Ear told Darla Hamilton. "Sonny, too."

Darla sighed at the reflected wonder of Duck Stadler in Ink Ear Ryan and she was pretty sure she was in love with one of them.

Woody Ryan had left his family in the care of Dean Ryan, his oldest son, who was much better suited for the job. For the promise of $20 when the job was done, Woody had helped disassemble the Ferris wheel of the Magical Midway Fun Company, a traveling carnival show that had spent three days in Perry. After loading the pieces onto a long flat bed truck, Woody climbed aboard himself and he was never seen again. Ink Ear told Sonny and Duck that Woody had run away with the circus.

"You mean that chicken shit carnival that was in town?" asked Duck. "That wasn't any circus. Circuses have elephants. It didn't have any elephants. It didn't even have any animals."

"What about the five-legged calf?" Ink Ear asked.

"Yes," said Sonny. "I saw that calf. It had another leg growing right out of its side."

356

"It couldn't stand on it," said Duck.

"So what? It still counts as a leg," said Sonny.

"It's not a leg unless you can stand on it," said Duck.

"Does yours still count as a leg?" asked Ink Ear. "You can't stand on it."

"If I had an extra leg I'd hit you with it," said Duck.

"Maybe Woody is in charge of the calf with five legs," said Sonny. "That's a big responsibility."

"Then I pity the poor calf," said Ink Ear.

This conversation was the last the three of them would have before Passing Through the Gate. The main entrance to Perry Elementary was decorated with colored crepe paper, green and yellow and red, the colors of spring. The paper was stuck down by Scotch tape and it flapped and rustled in the breeze. Fresh flowers in ceramic pots lined the lane from the school door to an archway trellis covered with sprigs and blooms from Imlay's greenhouse. This was the gate through which the children would pass. Each grade took turns, from kindergarten through sixth, a boy matched with a girl when possible. They walked in pairs from the school door under the arch and posed momentarily for any pictures parents and guests might want to take.

Ink Ear did not mind Darla taking his arm when they passed under the arch of flowers from Imlay's greenhouse. They stepped from childhood to whatever was on the other side of it. As they

357

waited for Duck and Sonny to pass through Ink Ear looked at Darla and Darla looked at Duck. The "Fearless Boy of Perry" was waiting to be motioned through the gate by Mrs. Mears, who was guiding the ceremony.

Mrs. Elsie Mears was wearing a white blouse with lace at the neck. None of her little soldiers could be seen, but the boys knew they were still there on her chest, the red ones and the brown ones, ready for action. Mrs. Mears beamed at Duck as if he were her own son. She would have given him a whole package of Neccos, all licorice, if he wanted.

Principal Worthington wanted Duck to be the last child through the gate. It was not every year the school had a celebrated hero to show off. But protocol won over promotion and Sonny and the Doerr Prize were saved for last.

Duck was next to last, following Ink Ear Ryan and Darla Hamilton. Both Duck and Sonny would Pass Through the Gate without a partner. Duck swung himself with ease on his crutches, looking every bit a hero and not an invalid. Duck practically ran through the gate, not stopping for photos, as he should have. Principal Worthington made Duck go back and pause so the Loganville Messenger could get a good shot for tomorrow's front page. Applause from the parents and guests for Duck was the loudest for any child.

The buzz for Duck still had not died down when Sonny Tolliver prepared to be the last to pass through the gate. One parent, no relation to Duck at all, stepped into the aisle in front of Sonny with her Brownie camera to get a better picture of the "Fearless Boy of Perry."

Sonny was able to recite in order all the presidents of the United States. He could name every state and spell them all correctly. He knew all 88 counties in Ohio. He knew how to spell every word in Merrill's Rational Speller, Book 2. He had committed to memory Mrs. Pitcock's abbreviated sequence of evolution—mites, insects, fish, frogs, snakes, birds, animals, monkeys, people. None of it was as impressive as saving your father from death. Bravery gets more attention than brains. Always has, always will.

Sonny wore the same clothing and the same shoes he had worn the day he had gone to Loganville to find his father. The shoes still hurt his feet.

Clara Miller and Ron Miller sat on wooden folding chairs side by side in the section reserved for guests and parents. Clara Miller cried when Principal Worthington closed the ceremony by handing Sonny the Doerr Prize, a framed certificate, and announced that Sonny was the student of the year.

Ron Miller reached into his pocket and handed her the same tissue he had used to wipe the side view mirror on the Dodge Town Wagon. Ron Miller was part of the workers' cut back at Perry Pottery. He had taken a new job in Newark at the

Rockwell Axel and Gear plant. He now needed to commute to work and the Dodge was showing the wear of the round-trip drive every day.

Sonny accepted his prize and thanked Principal Worthington. He did not know what to do next, but he thought some gesture was required, so Sonny held the framed award in his left hand, cocked his right arm on his hip and assumed the pose of the Perry Doughboy.

Only Duck and Ink Ear knew what Sonny was doing. Duck hooted and Ink Ear whistled. The rest of the audience thought Sonny just looked prissy and wondered about him later.

Sonny thought the Doerr Prize seemed much too ordinary. It was just a piece of paper in a cheap frame, and yet of all the awards and diplomas he would receive later on, the Doerr Prize was the only one he ever hung on his wall. His name was scrawled in full in Old English lettering, Theodore George Tolliver. He noticed right away that "George" was misspelled, "Goerge."

Sonny looked for but he did not see in the audience the man who was in the picture he had taken from Clara Miller's trunk. Robert Lund was not among the parents and guests, nor was he included with the strangers who had been attracted by the celebrity of the "Fearless Boy of Perry."

Had Sonny really expected to see the man he had watched through the window playing with his children that evening in Loganville? Maybe. Maybe not. The invitation Sonny had dropped onto the welcome mat on the porch maybe had blown away. It had been a windy day. Maybe.

Charlie Stadler was likely to be out of his wheel chair before Duck was out of his cast. Charlie would have back pain for the rest of his life. The pain would be a reminder that he was alive and Charlie did not mind it for that reason. He was happy that he could no longer squeeze into crevices to gouge out the last bit of coal. The reality of his physical limitations and the pension that came with it, along with the fact that the Brighter Day mine was now closed, improved Charlie's outlook on life considerably.

His son no longer represented doom to Charlie. Duck and his father spent more time together. The competition between the two was now as harmless and as happy as skipping stones across the Jericho River. Duck told Sonny that he thought he saw a fish jump in the river. But it might have just been the ripples from the stones.

Because Charlie Stadler was the father who was saved by the "Fearless Boy of Perry," Charlie, too, was a bit of a celebrity. How great must be the bond between father and son when one of them would risk his life for the other? Such a bond was absolutely biblical.

The eternal, essential, unbreakable connection between father and son, between the Holy Father and the Holy Son, such was the topic of a sermon

361

by Robert Lund at the Perry Pentecostal Congregation. Robert Lund had his son Wally sitting beside him on a high stool as he preached his sermon. Little Wally fidgeted but he did his duty.

The End